OTTO PENZLER PRESENTS
AMERICAN MYSTE~~~~

BLIND
BLUFF

BAYNARD KENDRICK (1894-1977) was one of the founders of the Mystery Writers of America, later named a Grand Master by the organization. After returning from military service in World War I, Kendrick wrote for pulp magazines such as *Black Mask* and *Dime Detective* under various pseudonyms before creating the Duncan Maclain character for which he is now known. The blind detective appeared in twelve novels, several short stories, and three films.

OTTO PENZLER, the creator of American Mystery Classics, is also the founder of the Mysterious Press (1975); Mysterious-Press.com (2011), an electronic-book publishing company; and New York City's Mysterious Bookshop (1979). He has won a Raven, the Ellery Queen Award, two Edgars (for the *Encyclopedia of Mystery and Detection*, 1977, and *The Lineup*, 2010), and lifetime achievement awards from NoirCon and *The Strand Magazine*. He has edited more than 70 anthologies and written extensively about mystery fiction.

BLIND MAN'S BLUFF

BAYNARD KENDRICK

Introduction by
OTTO PENZLER

AMERICAN MYSTERY CLASSICS

Penzler Publishers
New York

Published in 2023 by Penzler Publishers
58 Warren Street, New York, NY 10007
penzlerpublishers.com

Distributed by W. W. Norton

Cover image: Andy Ross
Cover design: Mauricio Diaz

Paperback ISBN 978-1-61316-419-8
Hardcover ISBN 978-1-61316-418-1

Library of Congress Control Number: 2023902468

Printed in the United States of America

9 8 7 6 5 4 3 2 1

INTRODUCTION

It's NOT giving away too much to let you know that *Blind Man's Bluff* is an impossible-crime novel, much like those of the great John Dickson Carr. Here, the problem is that a person obviously alone in a room defenestrates, though there was neither an expectation of suicide nor a rational explanation for the unexpected act.

What is so colorful and exciting that it happens again in a situation that is equally impossible. Or unlikely.

Before the action in the novel begins, we learn that its roots lie in the Great Depression, specifically in the actions of Blake Hadfield, who had been the president of the Miners Title and Trust Company, a large and very successful business until it wasn't, crashing badly in 1932. It's not what you think. Hadfield appears to have acted honorably, doing all he could to salvage his business but also the savings and property of his clients. The State Insurance Department had investigated him thoroughly and found him blameless.

Nonetheless, James Sprague, one of the ruined customers of the bank, regarded Hadfield as responsible, went to his office and shot him in the head before taking his own life. The bullet did not kill Hadfield, though it left him blind. He and his wife

Jill no longer lived together and she sought a divorce in order to marry the family friend and lawyer but Hadfield refused to grant it. (You can tell this story is not set in the present day!)

Jill had raised their son Seth on her own and, as the weirdness of life dictates, he is engaged to marry the daughter of Sprague, the man who had tried to kill Seth's father, presumably making family dinners a bit on the awkward side.

Hadfield asked his son and several other people to join him at the headquarters of the moribund business, a large, dark, old-fashioned citadel of a structure, resulting in Hadfield plummeting eight stories to his death just as his wife entered the building. No one was near him except his son, utterly drunk, and a night watchman who meticulously recorded his whereabouts in the building every five minutes—adequate proof that he could not have been near Hadfield when he went out the window. The police quickly ascertain that neither he nor Seth could have been responsible. Baffled, they turn to Captain Duncan Maclain in the hope that he can look at the case with "a blind man's eyes."

Hadfield's death is far from the only suspicious accident or suicide and Maclain's investigations become complicated by a super-abundance of oddities, which may be clues or just a collection of curiosities: a stolen highball glass with the fingerprints of two dead men; a misplaced ball of twine, a paperweight that seems to have vanished; a bottle of expensive whiskey tossed down an airshaft; a smashed Braille wristwatch; and more challenges than Maclain needs but, as readers of this outstanding series have come to expect, he prevails.

One of the most beloved character from the Golden Age of detective fiction and beyond, Duncan Maclain is a tall, dark, strikingly handsome, immaculately dressed and groomed former intelligence officer who moves with astonishing ease and self-assurance in spite of his total blindness.

Although injured while serving in World War I, Maclain has been able, through ceaseless effort, to master his handicap by developing his other senses. He turned to the profession of private detective—and found that his resources have been challenged to their utmost but that his tenacity brought him success.

Maclain lives in a penthouse apartment twenty-six stories above 72nd Street and Riverside Drive on Manhattan's Upper West Side. His hobbies are reading (in Braille), listening to music on his phonograph records, and assembling jigsaw puzzles, which he does by fingering a piece and then searching for its companion. He has taught himself to shoot, guided only by sound. He is assisted at the detective agency by his best friend and partner, Spud Savage (who is, alas, largely absent in this adventure), his secretary Rena, who is married to Spud, and his two seeing-eye dogs, the gentle Schnucke and the not so gentle Dreist.

Captain Maclain is the creation of Baynard Kendrick, one of the giants of the American Golden Age of detective fiction. Choosing a blind detective was no mere whim but the nearly inevitable result of his military service.

In World War I, Kendrick was the first American to enlist in the Canadian Army—exactly one hour after that country declared war—and served in the Canadian Expeditionary Forces. When he visited a hospitalized fellow Philadelphian who had been blinded in battle, he met a blind British soldier who had the remarkable ability to tell Kendrick things about himself that exceeded what a sighted person might have known. The experience impressed him and eventually enabled him to create a believable, if somewhat idealized, blind character.

During World War II, Kendrick was a consultant to the staff of the Old Farms Convalescent Hospital for Blinded Veterans (for a dollar a year).

Long interested in the problems of the blind, Kendrick was an acknowledged expert on the subject. He once served as the only sighted advisor to the Blinded Veterans Association and was its organizer and chairman of its board of directors. He held honorary life membership card number one and received a plaque for this work from General Omar Bradley in July 1940.

Kendrick's experiences provided him with the source material for his series hero, Captain Duncan Maclain, and for a non-mystery novel, *Lights Out* (1945), which was filmed as *Bright Victory* (1951), a romantic drama set during World Warr II about a soldier blinded by a German sniper; it was directed by Mark Robson and starred Arthur Kennedy, who was nominated for an Academy Award, and Peggy Dow.

One of the founding members of the Mystery Writers of America, Kendrick carried membership card number one. He served as the organization's first president and was named a Grand Master in 1967.

Born in Philadelphia in 1894 and educated at the Tom School, Port Deposit, Maryland, and the Episcopal Academy, Philadelphia, Kendrick married Edythe Stevens in 1919 and, following her death, married Jean Morris in 1971. He traveled extensively in Europe and the Middle East and lived in almost every part of the United States. A lawyer and certified public accountant, he had several jobs in the business world before becoming a full-time writer in 1932. His first mystery novel, *Blood on Lake Louisa*, was published in 1934 and the majority of his subsequent fiction was in the same genre.

That first novel was a stand-alone mystery that was followed by a couple of novels featuring Kendrick's first series character, Miles Standish Rice, *The Iron Spiders* (1936) and *The Eleven of Diamonds* (1936), who also was the hero of fourteen stories that appeared in *Black Mask*, the most prestigious pulp magazine in the detective fiction world, between 1937 and 1942. Rice, generally known as Stan, worked as a private detective who, uncharacteristically for P.I.s in this era, had a close relationship with the police. Earlier, he had been a deputy sheriff in Florida, where all the stories are set. The third and final novel in which Rice appears is *Death Beyond the Go-Thru* (1938), but by then Kendrick had created Captain Duncan Maclain, who became a more popular crimefighter.

The first novels in which Maclain and his service dogs, Schnucke and Dreist, appear are *The Last Express* (1937), *The Whistling Hangman* (1938), and *The Odor of Violets* (1941). It was reissued several times under the title *Eyes in the Night*, the title of the 1942 film that featured Edward Arnold as Maclain, Ann Harding as Norma Lawry, and Donna Reed as Barbara Lawry. Schnucke was renamed Friday for the film, which was directed by Fred Zinneman.

Intended to be a long-running series of detective movies following the success of *Eyes in the Night*, M-G-M made a sequel, *The Hidden Eye* (1945), also starring Arnold, but it did not do well at the box office and the series idea was abandoned.

The tone of *The Odor of Violets* was darker than most of his work, no doubt due to the fact that the world was at the brink of war and the book combined the pulp-inspired tropes of the hard-boiled private eye story with a spy story, which are seldom light-hearted—and certainly not with the reality of war in the air. Maclain's career as a licensed private investigator make him an ideal choice to work in United States Intelligence when the threat of Nazi spies and their plots of sabotage are suspected.

Although most of Kendrick's novels, especially those involving Maclain, are genuine whodunits, their plotting has its roots in the pulp fiction magazines of the time, with a protagonist who has many of the characteristics of such pulp heroes as Doc Savage. Not only is Maclain highly intelligent, but his other faculties have been so profoundly enriched that they appear other-worldly. Add to that his highly attractive physical appearance and his ability to easily dispatch adversaries in fights, and he becomes as close to a super-hero as the Golden Age detective can be.

In all, Kendrick wrote twelve novels about Duncan Maclain but they have been largely forgotten and out of print for many decades. The television series *Longstreet*, which ran for twenty-four episodes in 1971-1972, was created by Stirling Silliphant and starred James Franciscus as Mike Longstreet (an identical twin to Maclain), and Marlyn Mason as Nikki Bell, his secretary. Kendrick is given acknowledgment for his work as the inspiration for the Longstreet character, but some difficulties in the negotiations did not permit Paramount Television or ABC to use the Maclain name as the title.

—Otto Penzler
New York, April 2023

FOREWORD

THE FIRST short story ever written about my blind detective character, Captain Duncan Maclain, appeared in *Ellery Queen's Mystery Magazine* in January 1953 (there has only been one other, which also appeared in *Ellery Queen's*). That was more than fifteen years after the first full-length mystery, *The Last Express*, about Captain Maclain, who was a fictional U.S. Army officer blinded at Messines in World War I. It was published by the Crime Club in 1937. Following is the introduction to this short story, written by Frederic Dannay, co-writer with his cousin, Manfred B. Lee, under the pseudonym "Ellery Queen," who, like this writer, is one of the Grand Masters of the Mystery Writers of America, Inc.:

> Ernest Bramah is generally credited with having invented the first modern blind detective, Max Carrados, but the most famous exponent in the contemporary field of blind detection is, without doubt, Captain Duncan Maclain, created by Baynard Kendrick. Mr. Kendrick acknowledges that it was the earlier blind detective who started him writing about Maclain—but for curious reasons . . . in Mr. Kendrick's opinion, Max Carrados had very strange powers that went far beyond the limits of credibility. For example, Carrados could run his fingertips

along the surface of a newspaper, feel the infinitesimal height of the printer's ink over the paper itself, and "read" any type larger than long primer. Mr. Kendrick questions that feat, and we must say we are inclined to side with Mr. Kendrick. . . .

Indeed, Mr. Kendrick found it so difficult to swallow Max Carrados's supersensory accomplishments that he determined to create a blind detective of his own—a completely believable sleuth who could deduce by touch, hearing, taste, and smell, with no reliance whatever either on sight or sixth sense. And the simple truth of the matter is that while Baynard Kendrick has spent fifteen years of his life unearthing extraordinary things done by the totally blind, he has never had his blind detective do anything which he, Kendrick, had not actually seen done by a living blind man, or had fully authenticated.

When it came to developing the character of Duncan Maclain, Mr. Kendrick again went to the highest authority—real life. He patterned the character of Maclain on that of a real person—a young blind soldier in St. Dunstan's Home in London, who by touching the emblems on Kendrick's own uniform, accurately traced four years of Kendrick's Army career.

Canada declared war on Germany on August 8, 1914, four days after Great Britain. I was living in a boardinghouse in Windsor, Ontario, across the river from Detroit, and left a lunch table to go downtown to the Armory and enlist. So far as can be ascertained I was the first American to join up with the Canadian forces in World War I. After a few weeks' training at Valcartier, Quebec, I became No. 6468, Private Kendrick, B.H., 1st Battalion, 1st Brigade, No. 1 company in No. 1 Section. Since even then I was six feet two inches, I was the tallest man in my company and became flank man on the line. This was a hair-raising experience inasmuch as I was forced to pace 33,000 men in a review before Sir Sam Hughes, of whom the

Canadians gleefully sang, to the tune of "John Peel": "Do you ken Sam Hughes, the enemy of booze. The first champeen of the dry canteen. And the camp so dead you have to go to bed, but you won't have a head in the morning."

The first expeditionary force sailed from Gaspe Bay on the twenty-first of September and the 1st Battalion of 1,200 men was on board the White Star liner *Laurentic*. Thirty-three ocean liners crossed in that convoy in three rows of eleven each—the largest convoy to that date that the world had ever dreamed of or seen. There was certainly no tinge of patriotic fervor in my enlistment. I was twenty years old and the idea of putting an ocean between me and Detroit, where I had once been arrested for vagrancy for sleeping out in Grand Circuit Park, and drawing $1.10 a day plus food and clothes and medical expenses looked like paradise.

If this autobiographical prologue seems prolix and redundant I will have to plead guilty as I put it here for just one purpose— to make the point that not until 1917 when I was twenty-three and blindness confronted me face to face, had I ever given it a passing thought. By that time I had served in France, Egypt, and Salonica and had spent over two years in army hospitals. Subconsciously, I believe, like ninety-nine percent of the people in the world, I blotted the condition from my mind beyond relegating it to the shadowy realm of the tin cup, pencil, and street-corner school.

In the winter of 1917, when I had been marked "C-3" by a medical board (light duty), I was stationed in London working as a pay sergeant in the Canadian Pay Office at 7 Millbank. There, quite by accident, I learned that a boy with whom I had gone to school in Philadelphia had joined up with the Canadians a year after I did. I'll call him Paul Henderson, which was not his name. He had been blinded at Vimy Ridge several months before and at that moment was in St. Dunstan's Lodge, the hospital for blinded soldiers in London.

I took to visiting St. Dunstan's in Regents Park regularly on Saturday afternoons to have tea and play the piano. Once having overcome my initial ingrained fear of the blind, I continued these visits for many months after Paul Henderson had been invalided back to Canada and resumed his U.S. citizenship—as I did later, in December 1918. It was on one such visit that Captain Duncan Maclain was born, although I had no inkling of it at the moment and it was twenty years later—in 1937—before he came to life in print in *The Last Express*. The conditions at St. Dunstan's for the training and welfare of the blind—while modern for World War I—seemed antiquated when compared to Valley Forge, Dibble, or Avon Old Farms. Mobility was given little thought and the grounds of St. Regents Park were festooned with strings for the blinded veterans to follow, and knots marked the benches. When I was visiting there the lodge was so overcrowded with veterans and personnel that it had been necessary to move the piano out in the hall. There was little amusement since radio and talking books were unheard of—the big moments came when some noted entertainer, such as Sir Harry Lauder, Sir George Robey, or Alfred Lester, dropped in for an evening from one of the music halls.

It was on a blustery, freezing December afternoon in 1917 when I first became conscious of the fact that while a blind man might have lost his sight, he hadn't necessarily lost his mind. I had seated myself at the piano and given my usual introduction by leading off with "Tipperary" and the coterie of blinded British Tommies quickly gathered around me. There was just one straightback chair to the right of the piano next to double doors in the vestibule (always closed since a rear entrance was used) that led out onto the grounds. I had shed my cap and greatcoat and put them on that chair.

The Tommies were packed in almost solidly around me and one British Tommy was standing with his hands lightly on my shoulders while I went through half a dozen pieces. When I had finished and some requests were made, he moved around to the right of the piano, picked up my cap and greatcoat from the chair, sat down and laid them across his knees. I noticed while I was playing that he was giving them a thorough going-over with his fingertips ("brailling," although it turns a noun into a verb, has become the common term today).

A bell rang and I was suddenly deserted by my captive audience as they poured into an adjoining lounge for afternoon tea. Only the Tommy to the right of the piano remained. He stood up, replacing my cap and greatcoat on the chair, and started in with a preamble, as though something had been burned into his brain.

Then he said: "You certainly have been around in the Canadian army, haven't you? You've been in nearly every bleeding outfit in it. You came over here in nineteen fourteen with the First Battalion, went out to France with them, were invalided back here to England and then joined up with the Fourth General Hospital from Toronto and went out to Salonica with them. You were invalided back from Salonica through Egypt and landed back here at Netley Fever Hospital at Southampton— that big pile of bricks with the corridors a quarter of a mile long.

"When you were discharged from Netley you went to 134 Shorncliffe to the C.C.A.C. [Canadian Casualty Assembly Center]. There you faced another medical board which marked you 'C-3' and transferred you to the Canadian Army Service

Corps on light duty instead of sending you back to Canada as you had hoped. When they found out that you couldn't even lift a Ford motor, let alone carry one around on each shoulder, the sergeant in charge of the machine shop kicked to the C.O. that he was tired of being sent walking corpses marked 'C-3.' So they sent you up to this cushy job with the Canadian Army Pay Corps here in London where you will stay for the duration of the war."

I stood with my mouth hanging open, staring at him intently until I was positive that I had never seen him before. Then I blurted out, "I suppose you got all this dope from Paul Henderson who was invalided back to Canada from here a couple of months ago."

"Never heard of him," he said smugly. "He was before my time. I have only been in here just over a couple of weeks. I was blinded in the big tank push at Cambrai."

"Then where the hell did you know me and get all my army history? You sound like you had taken it from a sheet in the Canadian Record Office."

"I don't know you, never saw you, and never will," he grinned delightedly. "Sir Arthur Pearson spoke to us here last week about how much a blind man can really see. I decided to try it out on you. Your army history that I just gave you is written all over your uniform."

I took a closer look at his heavily bandaged eyes and decided that even if he had some vision left, it was obvious that he couldn't see. "Okay," I said. "Start at the beginning and spell it out. I'm certainly listening."

"Well, first," he said, "you have blue shoulder straps sewed on the khaki ones on your tunic."

"Blue?"

"Sure, you're wearing brass C-1's—that is a 'C' with a bar under it and a '1' attached underneath. That was your original unit, the First Battalion of Infantry, and all the infantry in the first contingent in nineteen fourteen wears those blue shoulder straps. The Medical Corps wears red. You were invalided back from France because you have a gold perpendicular wound stripe on your sleeve. Right?"

"Right! Go on."

"Well, the metal bars on each of those blue shoulder straps just read Canada in raised letters so the infantry was your original unit. Now, take your greatcoat. It has just the regular khaki shoulder straps but the bars on each shoulder are cut out CAMC, running from back to front, and easy to feel. Over them you have 'four' with a small bar over a 'G' in brass. That shows you were overseas with the Fourth General Hospital. It came from Toronto and was the only unit from the Canadian Army which was out in Salonica. I'm no wizard but I happened to have had a cousin who was with the same outfit, the Fourth General Hospital, and most of the men from Salonica were invalided back with fever through Egypt. So I took a guess that the same thing happened to you. All the men invalided back to England from anywhere with fevers end up in Netley and then at the C.C.A.C. at Shorncliffe. But the badge on the front of your cap is Canadian Army Service Corps, indicating that was the last unit you were transferred to here in England. My cousin went through that light duty routine, only they sent him out to France again driving a lorry. Now, I know you're stationed up here in London with a permanent pass since you are up here nearly every Saturday afternoon, playing the piano. You have sergeant's stripes on your greatcoat so I imagine you're working as a pay sergeant in the Canadian Pay Office. They have no emblem of their own."

Just then, an orderly stopped in from somewhere to collect him for tea, leaving me too dumbfounded even to inquire his name. He left me with a happy smile and a wave of his hand saying, "I'll be seeing you." He never did, of course, and I never saw him again. It was after New Year's of 1918 the next time I went up to St. Dunstan's and my blind detective had gone.

It was ten years later (1927) before I came in contact with Paul Henderson again.

My father died in Philadelphia in January 1927. Banks had already closed in Florida and our family savings were going fast while I fiddled around without much success at writing. But I had tasted blood because *Field and Stream* had bought my first short story, "The Captain's Lost Lake," in 1926 for $60. I hastened up to Philadelphia from Florida to see what could be salvaged from my father's business and the day after his funeral, Mrs. Henderson, Paul's mother, phoned me to say that she had seen the notice of my father's death in the newspapers. She told me her own husband had died five years before. She and Paul were still living in the old family house on Queen Lane in Germantown, and could I come to dinner. I sensed desperation in her voice and went out to see them the following evening—a filthy snowy night.

The house was a mausoleum, housing a frail invalid already feeling the effects of a cancer which killed her in 1930, and her blind, thirty-one-year-old son, who hadn't been out of the house since his father's death, five years before. The dinner was meager but by the time it was served none of us much cared—the bootlegger had made a delivery earlier and the orange blossom cocktails had flowed freely.

Paul's mother, through ignorance, fear, and too much love, did practically everything for him except take him to the toilet. It helped turn Paul into an alcohol-soaked cabbage with nothing to do but sit and look at the back of his eyes and curse at the fictional Max Carrados and his fictional supernatural powers. Paul was too frightened to move from the house that had become the only world he knew—and his mother, through misdirected love, encouraged his indolence.

I sold out the Trades Publish Company that belonged to my father and went to New York, where I obtained a job as general manager of Bing & Bing Hotels. Within three months after his mother died in 1930, Paul Henderson sold the heavily mortgaged house in Germantown and sobered up long enough to catch a train to New York—purely because I was there. He hoped that I could get him a job—at anything, even making brooms. God knows I tried! But I soon realized that Paul had lost all interest in life, and I dreaded the tenth of every month when his small pension check would arrive. He'd disappear from the room I had gotten for him on Bank Street in Greenwich Village and make the rounds of speakeasies where kindly but misguided customers would buy him drinks when his money ran out. I started to think it might be better for him if he were a troublemaker and created a disturbance so the police could pick him up and tuck him safely away long enough to get off the booze. It took me more than a year to enlist the aid of enough friendly bartenders who would call me as soon as he came in.

The Depression caught me full in 1932 and I was laid off with twenty other administrative office workers a week before Christmas—facing a world that seemed utterly jobless. I determined at that moment that I'd never work for a corporation again and I'd succeed at writing or starve to death trying. I rented an apartment for $25 a month in a basement in Astoria and started my first full-length book—a Florida mystery called *Blood on Lake Louisa*. Paul moved in with me two months later and on and off for a year we existed on what short unsigned pieces I could sell to *The New Yorker* and *Liberty*. I established a moderate credit rating at a nearby friendly Italian grocery and ate so much spaghetti that I finally broke out with a wheat rash. During this time, I sought out a great deal of material regarding famous blind people and read about them to Paul. I hoped that some of their accomplishments would inspire him, but I eventually realized that Paul had slipped into his own private paranoiac world—identifying with Max Carrados, using liquor to bolster confidence that he could duplicate the impossible feats of Ernest Bramah's overdrawn character. Paul would also challenge the accomplishments of blind persons with a negative approach that defied argument, such as claiming that John Milton "was educated at Cambridge, besides being an established poet before he went blind at forty-four."

By 1932 I had reached the point of utter desperation with Paul and made an attempt to convince him that someone with even more severe handicaps than his could do something productive. I finally succeeded, through my agent, in getting in touch with Mr. John A. Macy, whose wife was the famous Anne Mansfield Sullivan who had trained Helen Keller. Mr. Macy was quite ill and died several months later, in August 1932, but the lengthy letter I wrote his wife interested her enough to furnish me with a list of famous blind people—and in reply to my complaints about Max Carrados, she wrote me: "You're a mystery writer . . . so why not draw on the knowledge that you've accumulated and create a blind detective of your own—one who would be the antithesis of Max Carrados, who would never perform any feat in his detection or deduction that couldn't be duplicated by someone totally blind—presuming they had the necessary brains and willpower to train themselves to try it."

Thus the idea of Captain Duncan Maclain was born. It was in 1937 that the Crime Club published the first of the books about him, *The Last Express*. For forty years he has served me well—in serialization, syndication, movies, and foreign editions. He's responsible for the organization of the Mystery Writers of America, Inc., and for the Blinded Veterans Association—formed at Avon Old Farms Army Schools of the Blind at Avon, Connecticut, in 1945, in which I hold honorary life membership Card No. 1. Even today, if you sit up late enough and watch the third repeat of *Longstreet* on ABC, you can see that the series is based on "Characters Created by Baynard Kendrick."

Speaking to the B.V.A. on the occasion of their twenty-first annual convention at the Deauville Hotel, Miami Beach, Florida, on August 20, 1966, I was asked by one of the members if I happened to remember the name of that young blind soldier in St. Dunstan's Home in London who through his perspicacity had quite unwittingly been the progenitor of the B.V.A. I was forced to say no—I hadn't forgotten his name for I never knew it; he was merely one of a number of blinded British Tommies ensconced for the time being in St. Dunstan's.

I intended to call this piece "The Birth of a Blind Detective" because, to me, Captain Duncan Maclain was really born—and I hope will live forever—showing to sighted people that although the blind of the world may have lost their eyes, their brains and their work live on.

—BAYNARD KENDRICK

BLIND MAN'S BLUFF

TO
LEFTY AND NAT

FROM
UNCA' BAY

*All of the characters, situations, institutions, and animals in
this book are products of the author's fevered imagination and
consequently fictional. Any resemblance to anyone or anything
living or dead is pure coincidence, and most unfortunate.*

B. H. K.

CHAPTER I

1

JULIA HADFIELD cleared the dishes away from the drop-leaf table laid for three and stacked her own in the sink against the coming of her part-time maid in the morning. With the two unused sets returned to the china closet, she realized with a qualm that a grown son and his fiancée were undependable company.

Her reactions were not new. Seth had been slipping away into a mannish world of his own since he reached the age of fourteen. Julia, being unselfish and loving him very much, had made no move to stop him. When the army had engulfed him six months ago, she had accepted the inevitable calmly and sent him off with a smile and a word of cheer. The inward turmoil was her own, a private heartache which never dimmed the glint of humor in her wide-set hazel eyes unless she knew that no one could see.

Of late, the opportunities for indulging in such introspection had become increasingly plentiful. Friends were leaving New York for Washington and points west, moved about like puppets on the strings of national emergency. With Seth in camp, Julia had ample time to reflect that a woman of forty, separated from her husband, might still be most attractive and yet live very much alone.

Tonight, apprehension had been added to disappointment and loneliness. Seth, bounding in on leave in the afternoon, had announced his intention of bringing Elise to dinner.

Julia left her unread magazine on a chair and made another trip to the kitchen, a fruitless trip, to stare at her own unwashed dishes and frown at the wreckage of a fallen soufflé. It was easy to make excuses for a Second Lieutenant on his first night home on leave, but thoughtlessness was a trait lacking in both Seth and Elise.

There had been times in the past when too many cocktails or a moment's vital interest in something devastatingly feminine had delayed Seth, yet he had always managed to reach a telephone.

Back in her chair, she abandoned the idea of calling the 310 Club, a favorite of Seth's. No matter what her worry, she had invariably given her son credit for ability to take care of himself. Her policy was to act like a friend, and checking on his whereabouts smacked too much of a military patrol.

Julia went to a window and for a time looked down at the frost-hazed lights of Sheridan Square far below. A few pedestrians hurried along, bent against the bitter cold, but none of them resembled the couple she so anxiously wanted to see. She was still at the window when the buzzer rang.

Philip Courtney, looming large in a rough-cloth overcoat, was standing in the hall. He smiled his slow smile at her ill-concealed disappointment and said, "I dropped in to say hello to Seth and Elise. If you'd rather see someone else, say the word and I'll go."

"Don't be an idiot, Phil," Julia told him with the warmth of real affection, and ushered him in with a touch on his arm. "My precious pair were due here for dinner at seven. It's nine now. I finally ate alone. They haven't even telephoned."

"Young love, Julie," Courtney declared as he hung up his coat.

His casualness helped, but Philip Courtney was always helpful. The lucrative law practice of Courtney, Garfield and Steele had been built largely on his common sense and calm.

Julia watched with contentment as he settled his wiry figure into an armchair. The eight long years since her separation from Blake Hadfield had not been easy. They would have been unendurable without the counsel and support of Phil. For an instant, resentment burned deeply inside her against her husband. Blake had fought a divorce, and won, fought it not because he wanted to hold her, but because he was Blake Hadfield, and deep in his brilliant brain he knew that someday she would desperately want to marry Phil.

"Highball?" Julia suggested.

Phil nodded and took out his cigar case. When she returned from the kitchenette with glasses and soda, he was sitting with his long legs crossed, staring at an unlit cigar.

"I'm not the only one who's upset." Julia put the glasses down and poured his Scotch. "What's bothering you, Phil?"

"Blake." Courtney drank deeply, as though the Scotch might wash the unpleasant word away. "He phoned me half an hour ago."

"What's strange about that?" Julia asked unconvincingly. It took something strange to get a visible reaction from Philip Courtney, and thirteen years of living with Blake Hadfield before their separation had never revealed to her what was going on in Blake's mind.

Phil dropped a bombshell by saying quietly, "There's something up, Jule. He wants me to meet him in his old office on the eighth floor of the Miners Title and Trust Building at ten o'clock."

"But he hasn't been back there—" Julia touched a hand to her breast and paused.

"Not in six years," said Courtney. "Not since the night Sprague shot him and committed suicide."

"What can he want down there?" Julia spoke to herself more than to Phil.

"That's what I'm wondering." Courtney puffed thoughtfully. "It's a funny errand, Jule—a trip downtown on a freezing night to a practically deserted building, a difficult errand for a man who is totally blind."

"Someone must be going with him."

"Of course," Phil agreed. "But still Blake can't see anything. What does he expect to find? He'd tell me nothing over the phone."

"There's nothing down there at night."

"Furniture, a watchman and ghosts of the past." Courtney grinned. "The Receiver's staff of about thirty accountants works on the eighth floor during the day. They're under the direction of the State Insurance Department."

Julia nodded. "Elise is Carl Bentley's secretary, Phil. He gave her the job when he was appointed Comptroller there two years ago."

"I'd forgotten that." Phil finished his drink and stood up. "If I'm to get downtown by ten, I have to go." He stood briefly holding her slim hands in his own. "I wonder if six years of blindness hasn't softened him, Jule. God knows he's paid heavily for giving you and the kid a rotten deal."

"He's a difficult man to fathom, Phil. Blake never considered he might be wrong."

"He never considered anything," said Phil.

Julia watched him from the window until he disappeared from sight across the square, then turned to gaze with critical appraisement at the furnishings of the comfortable room.

The chairs were good, but showing signs of wear. Lamp shades were the same. She badly needed a decent picture to brighten the north wall—all things she had promised herself once Seth was out of school. Well, Seth was out of school, had been for some time, and now there was the war, and always Blake's meager allowance remained the same.

For a few years, she had pieced it out by working as librarian for a private collection of first editions. At no time had it been easy. Every semester had been a period of terror when bills arrived from Seth's school. Deep inside, Julia knew that only stubborn pride had kept her going. Blake was so smugly sure she would fail and have to come cringing to him for help to educate their son.

It had been worse after he was blinded by the bullet from James Sprague's gun. Blake Hadfield, as President of the Miners Title and Trust Company, had guided that ill-fated bank and real estate mortgage company through its most opulent years. When the crash came in 1932, he was still at the helm.

Cleared of any criminal negligence—a charge which the State Insurance Department had tried industriously to prove—tragedy nevertheless struck at Blake Hadfield four years after the M. T. & T. had closed its doors. Sprague, a ruined depositor, had taken matters into his own hands and tried to settle accounts with a gun.

Julia left her chair and began a nervous pacing of the room.

She felt that the curtain was about to rise for the second time on a distasteful, familiar scene. In 1936, Blake, four years out of the bank, had returned to his office to meet Sprague there at night and had been blinded for life. Now, six years later, in 1942, he was returning to that office again.

Blake's movements were none of her concern, except insofar as they affected Seth. For the life of her she could not shake off the feeling that her husband's blind pilgrimage had something to do with their son. Some unexplained purpose had taken him to the M. T. & T. building in 1936. Was the reason the same tonight, or was it something new?

She aroused from her reverie with a start, realizing that she had sat for some seconds reluctant to answer the spaced ringing of the telephone.

"Julia?"

"Yes." She wasn't surprised. Some telepathic spark had warned her that Blake's cultured incisive voice would greet her.

"It's essential that I talk with you tonight." Just as possessive, just as casual as though they had parted an hour before. "I'm in my office at the M. T. & T."

"You don't expect me to come down there tonight alone?"

"At eleven, Julia. It means everything to the future of you and our son."

2

Lieutenant Seth Hadfield placed his gloves down with a great deal of care as though they might break under the shock of a normal landing. A young man in uniform was staring at him through a wall of polished bottles and glasses, a nice-looking duck whose face was hauntingly familiar. It might well have been himself, except that Elise was with him, and he had personal information that his head was twice the size of the other officer leering at him from the mirror back of the bar.

A friendly fellow in a white jacket interposed himself between Seth and his vision.

"Something else for you, sir?"

Seth regarded the newcomer curiously. He had materialized out of nowhere and obviously wanted to talk. Seth was quite willing except that he didn't know the newcomer's name. He pointed a trifle unsteadily to a sign with removable letters hung above the shining bottles on the wall. It announced that Roy Tracy was the attendant on duty, as if that made any difference to anyone with the possible exception of Roy Tracy.

Seth collected his gloves so that Roy Tracy couldn't steal them, and put them safely away in his cap, which he placed on a stool beside him.

"Are you Roy?" he asked.

"Yes, Mr. Hadfield. I still am. Was there something else for you?"

"Am I tight," asked Seth, "or is there another officer hiding back of those bottles?"

"Both," said Roy frankly. "It's a reflection of you."

"Well, I shouldn't be here. What time is it?"

"Seven-fifteen, sir." Roy consulted a large clock on the wall.

"We'll be late for dinner, Elise. Let's go." Seth turned to the empty stool beside him. "Now where the hell did she get to?"

"She went home sir, a couple of hours ago—if you're talking about the young lady who came here with you."

"Who else came here with me?"

"No one, sir."

"Well, where did she go?"

"Home, sir. You had a bit of a quarrel, if you happen to remember. She said she wasn't going to marry you."

"Don't be insulting, Roy." Seth rested his elbows on the bar and found it much more comfortable. "Who's she going to marry? You?"

"No, Mr. Hadfield. I'd have a bite of something to eat, if I were you."

"That's absolutely silly," Seth declared after some reflection. "Where did Elise meet you?"

"I've never met her," Roy explained with professional patience.

"Then why's she throwing me over to marry you?"

"She's not, Mr. Hadfield. I'm just here tending bar."

"Well, tend it, will you, and bring me another zombie."

"You have a dinner engagement." The bartender studied him closely.

"She broke it." Seth's young face was suddenly suffused with sadness. "Threw me over just because her old man shot mine and killed himself. I'm asking you, Roy, isn't that one hell of a thing to do?"

"She'll come back, Mr. Hadfield. I can tell by the way she looks at you."

"How can you tell when she's gone?" Seth demanded suspiciously. "I believe she's going to marry you."

"Your engagement, sir," Roy reminded.

"So I have an engagement . . . . What's it to you?"

"It's late, sir."

"Well, the hell with it!" Seth slid down in dignified disgruntlement from his stool. "If I can't get a drink here I know where I can. I'll go pay a visit to my old man."

Blake Hadfield had never moved from the apartment which in earlier years had been Seth's home. At first, after his parents' separation, Seth had visited his father more or less regularly, although they were visits more of duty than of pleasure. The austere man with his finely chiseled patrician face was cynically critical. Young Seth called him "Father," but never could in his presence escape a tinge of fear. This grew more in the boy after Blake Hadfield was blinded. His visits became fewer as his father retreated behind a bitter invisible wall.

Walking up Park Avenue, Seth found himself confronted with memories. The fire hydrant he had stumbled over while skating, a chink in the ornamentation of a corner building which he had knocked off with a hockey stick years before. The cold stung his eyes and made his head feel more stuffy. Suddenly the old uneasiness of seeing his father once again flooded back in full. It nearly turned him away as he passed Fifty-sixth Street and hesitated in front of the apartment house door.

A new attendant stopped him in the lobby.

"I want to see Mr. Hadfield."

"Is he expecting you, sir?"

"I doubt it." Seth eyed him owlishly. "Tell him it's his son."

"Yes, sir." The man pushed a button and picked up the lobby phone.

The unused furniture of the lobby had remained unchanged— the same settees scrupulously clean and slightly gaudy, the domestic oriental on the white tile floor. Seth remembered how it used to slide when he took it on the run.

"You can go right up, Mr. Hadfield. Six twenty-four."

"Yes," said Seth. "I know."

The elevator door closed silently behind him, and the car moved upward. Shut in with the steel-gray-uniformed operator, he began to wonder what crazy motive had prompted him to come. His father would find no sympathy for a broken romance. He would sit in front of the fire in his overstuffed chair, expressionlessly judicial with flames dancing against the blackness of his glasses, and indulgently laugh. It wouldn't help when Seth started prodding at the causes of a slowly healing sore.

He realized that the elevator had stopped and that the attendant was watching him cautiously.

"Pardon me, this is your floor, sir."

Seth said "Thanks," and with determined steadiness strode off down the hall.

Again he paused, outside of 624. Here the apartment house had been refinished: new runners and skillfully tinted walls lighted by hidden bulbs along the molding. He pushed the button and stepped back in surprise at the sudden opening of the door.

A woman was standing there dressed for the street in a shimmering fur coat. She was sleek and polished, and as composed as the Park Avenue apartment itself. Expert grooming made her age impossible to determine.

She looked him over with pleasant crinkly eyes that were soft with humor and said, "So you're Seth! The last time I saw you, you were a long-legged colt. I'm Sybella Ford."

He felt awkward under her scrutiny. "Oh, yes," he said vaguely and shook her hand, wondering if she knew how hazy she looked.

"I was just on my way out when you called. Your father's waiting for you. I've been reading to him."

She stepped out past him and added, "You should come to see him more often, Seth. He gets lonesome. Good night."

Seth watched her lithe walk toward the elevator. Maybe he

didn't get squiffed often enough. He might visit his father more. Somehow he had never pictured women in his father's life. This one seemed to know him, but he hadn't the vaguest recollection of ever having seen her before. He admitted grudgingly that if she was a sample, his father had good taste, but zombies made them all look good.

Blake Hadfield's carefully modulated voice called from the living room: "Is that you, Seth?"

"Yes, Father."

"For heaven's sake, come in and close the door!"

Seth shed his hat and coat in the hall and went into the living room. He couldn't find his gloves. Roy must have swiped them after all.

As he shook his father's hand, he remembered with embarrassment that his last visit had been more than a year before. The apartment had changed for the better in that time. The furniture had been re-covered. A few modern pieces had been added, and some old monstrosities which Seth remembered were gone. The living room reflected the touch of a woman's ruthless, artistic hand.

Seth stretched his palms to the fire. "Where's Kito?"

"Gone with the war," said his father. "Concentration camp or something. Apparently every decent servant in the country was half servant and half Japanese spy."

"It looks nice in here."

"Yes," said Hadfield. "Although I can't see it, I can feel it. Sybella changed it around. How's your mother?"

"Quite well, thank you." Two minutes with his father and he was growing formal again. There had been an instant of ease, the briefest space of camaraderie, and once more the blind man in the chair had retreated behind his wall.

"And to what great circumstances, Seth, do I owe the honor of this call?"

His tone was level and friendly, but Seth felt the acid behind it.

"I'm home on leave, Father." Seth sparred for time. "I wanted to see you and talk with you."

"I heard you had a commission." Hadfield closed a Braille book open on his knees and put it on the floor beside him. "I've taken up Braille, but it's slow going. It's much more pleasant to be read to. You've had a few drinks, too, haven't you?"

Seth pulled a chair closer to the fire. The logs snapped and crackled. Again he was ten years old and trying to tell this stranger the cause behind some boyish prank.

"I needed them," he said with the candor of intoxication. "If Mother had nursed me on rum I'd probably have been able to tell my troubles to you."

Hadfield's white hands lay motionless on the arms of his chair. "You're very flattering, son."

"No." Seth grew sorry for himself and included his father and mother, too. There must be some human quality in his father to attract a woman like the one he'd met in the hall. "My girl threw me over this afternoon," he blurted out. "Frankly I'm as stewed as an owl."

"You were engaged to James Sprague's daughter, weren't you?" Blake Hadfield's glass-shielded eyes were turned toward the fire. His high forehead under the thinning hair was creased with a frown.

"Yes," Seth declared. He got up and opened a window for a few seconds, welcoming the icy blast against his hands. The room had grown unbearably warm. "I tried to get her to marry me tomorrow."

"And—"

"She decided not to marry me at all. There was another mention in one of the papers today about her father shooting and blinding you."

"That was six years ago," said Hadfield thoughtfully.

"Elise claimed we could never forget it. She said it would be sticking its head up every day, every time we had the slightest quarrel. Who was to blame—her father, or you?"

Hadfield's fingers clenched, and loosened slowly. "Perhaps neither of us was to blame."

"Elise claims that your bank's failure ruined her father, caused his own firm, Sprague and Company, to collapse, caused him to kill himself."

"A blind man has a lot of time to think," said Blake Hadfield.

"Well, what's the truth?" asked Seth, leaning forward hands on knees.

"I wonder." Hadfield pushed himself to his feet. "Let's take a trip together, Seth. Let's go downtown to the scene of the shooting."

"What for? Elise is gone, Father. What the hell's the difference if the fault lies with her father or you?"

"This is the first time you've ever asked me for help," said Hadfield. "Maybe I can give it. Jim Sprague's gone, too, but during the past year I've been wondering about his going. Maybe I can bring his daughter back to you."

3

The inspiring glow of too many zombies was beginning to fade into a depressing drowsiness. Seth decided that the decadent air of the Miners Title and Trust Building had something to do with it. Memories of childhood visits came flooding back to him with sharp distaste as he released his guiding grip on Blake Hadfield's arm and turned on the lights in the office on the eighth floor.

He had called for Elise on the same floor several times during the past couple of years, but both of them had carefully avoided Blake Hadfield's deserted office. Seth had never visited the building at night before. At the first sight of its iron-railed marble stairs and its bird-cage elevators stark in the light of a single large bulb in the downstairs lobby, he earnestly hoped he would never visit it at night again.

Dan O'Hare, the brawny night watchman, had admitted them with marked suspicion. As the creaking elevator crawled upward past one balcony after another, momentary claustrophobia clutched at Seth. The architect who designed the M. T. & T. building might have made a name in the '90s, but Seth had a sneaking suspicion that the plans had been copied from those of a famous jail.

"If it isn't too much trouble, son, would you mind conducting me to my desk?"

Blake Hadfield's measured request brought Seth back with a start to realize that his father was blind and couldn't see even when the lights were on. He led him to the high-backed leather chair in front of the flat-topped desk. Hadfield fingered it briefly and seated himself.

Seth found that he was perspiring. He shed his greatcoat and folded it carefully across the arm of a red leather divan. His father's white hands were moving stumblingly over the desk top, touching the double bronze inkwell, tracing the edge of the blotter, fondling the paperweight, an ornate affair of agate base surmounted with a crystal ball.

A sense of futility gripped at Seth, a sensation of having stepped back through time to brush against the gruesome past. The office was swept and clean, everything in place—preserved for what? The row of buttons at the left of the desk had fascinated him as a boy. A touch on the gray one in those days brought a humorless woman with slicked black hair known shadowly as Miss Fowler. A touch of another, by business alchemy, produced a Mr. Farbisham who got shopping money for Seth's mother by contacting an unseen source of supply known as a Cashier.

Seth wondered what would happen if his father's groping fingers pushed them now. Would Miss Fowler pop in unsurprised from the darkness of the outside hall? Would Mr. Farbisham, now paymaster for an American unit fighting somewhere overseas, salute his Commanding Officer and say, "Sorry, sir. I have to rush home to New York. I've just had a call!"?

Blake Hadfield's hands quit their searching and folded in repose. With their quiet, the office grew disturbingly still. Seth fixed his eyes heavily on a spot on the rug. Had they left that, too, waiting for Blake Hadfield's return? Was that the famous X that marked the spot where Elise's father had fallen dead by his own hand?

"You seem nervous, son," said Hadfield. "The price we pay for the comfort of alcohol is the need for more. Slide up the panel in the corner to my left and you'll find a wall safe. I'll call you the combination; among other things in it there should be a bottle of excellent Scotch whisky. Perhaps if you have another drink you'll stop your fidgeting."

"Yes, sir," said Seth.

The panel opened easily.

"Start at ten," said Hadfield. "Turn twice to the left, past ten, to thirty-two."

Seth followed the directions in a semi-haze. Across the width of the building an iron grille door clanged shut. Machinery hummed to life, and one of the bird-cage elevators started its journey down.

"The Scotch is here," said Seth when the safe was opened.

"And a black tin box?"

"Yes, sir."

"Bring me the box, and then fix a couple of drinks. I'll join you. There should be six glasses on the buffet in a silver holder—unless they're gone."

"They're still there, Father." Seth placed the black tin box on the desk and watched curiously as his father opened it.

"Tell me," said Hadfield, "has the furniture been moved in this room?"

"It's been years since I've been here, sir."

"How is it now, Seth? Start at the right as you come in the door."

"First the long table against the stained-glass partition, a chair at each end and three pushed under along one side. The big leather armchair's still in the corner. Then the divan under the windows along the next wall. Your globe is in the corner—and the small buffet's along the other wall. The door to the foyer behind you is curtained. That's about all."

Blake Hadfield nodded with satisfaction and fingered through several papers until he found one bearing the raised impression of a Notary's seal. He held it for a second, then returned it to the box, and picked up the French-type dial phone.

"The phone is disconnected," he said after an instant of listening. "There's a switchboard just outside of Bentley's office on the other side of the building. See if you can connect it up for me, son. This is Extension One."

Seth poured two generous portions of Scotch and carried them through the curtained door in back of Blake Hadfield's chair. The small foyer behind the curtain served the dual purpose of a private entrance and concealment for a washroom. Seth added water to his father's drink and tossed his own off neat. It steadied him momentarily.

Blake Hadfield was sitting rigid in his chair when Seth returned from the washroom. He spoke as Seth put the drink on the desk.

"Hurry, son. I want to talk to Phil Courtney and ask him to come down."

"Yes, sir."

Seth found himself wavering again and remedied it with a second long drink before trying the unwelcome journey across the eighth floor. Away from the light shed through the stained-glass windows of Hadfield's private office, the vast main filing room was dark. Seth felt his way between rows of metal cabinets which formed a narrow alley.

At the end of the alley, with Bentley's office in sight through the gloom, he stopped. The Scotch had been an error, tautened his nerves to painful vibration. He had a feeling of being followed, and that way lay D.T.s. Rum and Scotch when mixed were poison. In another minute he'd be conjuring up frightful shapeless figures sliding toward him over the file cabinets as they seeped in under the doors from the outside hall.

His jerk on the cord almost pulled it from the socket as he

found a light above the switchboard and turned it on. Its welcome brightness brought the ugly floor into proper perspective and dispelled the threatening shadows.

Seth put a plug into hole Number One and rang his father's office.

"Okay, Father," he said. "You can go on with your call."

For the journey back he decided to leave the light on above the switchboard. Let the watchman find it on his rounds and put it out. Seth had no desire to reanimate those formless shapes in the outside hall.

At Elise's desk he paused and idly opened a drawer. The tiny intimate objects, powder, lipstick and nail polish, rolled up a new surge of unhappiness. Why had his father brought him down to this dreadful place? From cellar to roof it was crawling with shattered hopes and miserable memories.

An overpowering desire to get out of the building seized him. He didn't want to return to his father's office. Nobody could ever bring Elise back to him—she was gone and irreplaceable. He didn't want to see his father seated beside those silent call-buttons, staring blindly back into the past. All of Blake Hadfield's mumbo-jumbo could never return Elise, never piece their broken engagement together again.

Not quite knowing what he was doing, he staggered back to the switchboard and put out the light. He was sorry immediately, for the shapeless ones returned to taunt him.

Well, the shapeless ones could wait. He'd sit down in Elise's chair and stay there forever. Sleep was what he needed, long deep soundless sleep. Only Elise could find him at her desk, waiting there for her forever.

Seth closed his eyes and lowered his head on his arms. The

smell of Elise's lipstick and powder was strong and comforting. Blake Hadfield could wait in his office forever, and the shapeless ones could wait in the hall.

4

It was after ten when Julia Hadfield picked the heaviest of her coats from the closet and slipped it on with a mental note that the lining would scarcely last the winter. She scribbled a note for Seth, left it propped against a table lamp, and opened the door to encounter Elise standing in the hall.

"Is Seth home?" Elise's tall dark beauty was perfection, but her smile was troubled and her question slapped at Julia with the sting of an open palm.

"I thought he was with you. I've heard nothing from him—" Julia made a valiant effort to keep her own voice steady, but Elise, sensitive and alert in her reactions, was quick to sense a note of alarm.

"You've been worrying. Oh, Jule, he's a dog not to have called you. I left him about five."

"Where?"

"In a bar on Fifty-third Street. I was certain he'd phone."

Julia glanced at her tiny wristwatch. Ten fifteen. She could make it downtown in twenty minutes on the subway. "I want to know what happened, Elise. Why didn't you come for dinner as we'd planned?" She opened the door wider. "Come inside and sit down."

"You were going somewhere." Elise followed her in.

"Blake phoned."

"Mr. Hadfield?" Elise widened her dark eyes in astonishment, then covered her feeling of unintentional rudeness by lighting a cigarette as she sat down.

"You're no more surprised than I am," said Julia. "He wants me to meet him at eleven in his office downtown."

"Jule—in that place? Surely you're not going."

"But I am. Blake said it had to do with Seth's future, Elise. That means both yours and mine. He called Phil Courtney, too, to meet him there at ten." Julia opened her heavy coat and leaned against the edge of a table. "What happened between you and Seth this afternoon?"

"We quarreled."

"Oh!" Julia moistened her delicate humorous lips and made a business of putting a glove back on. "Seth's fault?"

"No more than mine." Elise crushed out her cigarette. "I'm miserable, Jule! There was a mention of Dad in the paper today. I got to thinking—"

"That you'd let a tragedy already gone and forgotten ruin your life and Seth's. You have more brains than that, darling."

"I realized it was silly of me, but not until after I'd gone. That's what I came here for—to tell him so."

"Where do you think he is now, Elise?"

The girl was silent for a second or two. "He said he was going to drink himself to death on zombies. Heaven knows where he is, Jule. I'm afraid he's tied one on."

"Drunk?"

Elise nodded. "Otherwise he'd never forget to telephone you."

"Maybe you're right. I feel better anyway." Julia straightened up and closed her coat, then bent over quickly and touched her lips to Elise's soft cheek. "Wait here, if you like. The remnants

of your dinner are in the icebox. Seth will probably come rolling in about one. I don't think I'll be gone long, but right now I
have to hurry."

"You're a dear." Elise's dark eyes were misty as she walked
to the door with Julia. "Maybe I love you even more than I do
Seth."

"Never commit yourself to a mother-in-law," said Julia. "I'll
hold that over your head until my first grandchild reaches the
age of twenty-one." She blew a kiss to Elise from the hall.

The subway station was nearly deserted. Julia caught a downtown train and sat huddled in a corner, mulling over the fact
that drunks were funny only when they didn't happen to in-
clude one's son. Absorbed in disturbing reflections, she almost
passed Chambers Street and only made the platform by squeez-
ing through a closing door.

Up from the tepid warmth of the tunnels, she felt the cold
bite sharply through her coat. When she turned south on
Broadway an ingrained dread returned, the dread of facing
Blake's searing sarcasm about women who were late for ap-
pointments. It hastened her steps until her walk increased to a
spasmodic run.

Rumbling with traffic all day, by nine o'clock at night lower
Broadway becomes as deserted as a back street in some phan-
tom village. Its commercial hum and bustle gives way to an air
of waiting where every movement is a resented intrusion. Even
the vigilant patrolman moves softly as he tries the doors of vacant eateries that were bursting with patrons seven hours before.
At eight o'clock, lower Broadway has become a chaste old maid
ready to retire. By nine she has locked her windows, tucked her
unattractive angular frame into bed, and pulled up the quilts. By

eleven, lulled to sleep by the buried grumble of subway trains, she's begun to snore.

The dirty brownstone bulk of the M. T. & T. building, once considered stately and imposing, had passed its day. Its nine stories lay dwarfed in the slot between two giant neighbors. Julia, eyes streaming from the searing blast sweeping up from the Battery, recognized its ugly masonry and stopped. No medieval fortress could have looked more formidable, or more lonely and impregnable. For a second she doubted that she would ever gain admission through the great bronze doors that had closed forever on a million hopes ten years before.

She groped along one side, found a button and pushed it.

Back of the doors a summons rang on a clattering gong. Huddled down in her coat, Julia waited, then clamped her freezing lips and rang again. Her hands and ears were rapidly growing numb.

A smaller door was set in the big one on the left. More to restore circulation than with any thought of attracting attention, Julia clenched her fists and beat against it desperately. It gave under the attack, swinging open inward. Gratefully she stepped inside, turning sideways like Alice going through the looking-glass into the other room.

Caught by a sweep of wind, the small door slammed shut behind her and she saw that the Yale lock which fastened it was latched back. Her first thought was that the watchman had gone out on some errand and left the door ajar.

Rubbing her ears, which had turned to fire in the warmer air, Julia took a few steps forward and looked about her. In the center of the M. T. & T. building the lobby stretched upward nine full stories toward a glassed-in dome to form a hollow square. Pointed cathedral windows rose nearly to the top, making a blank side over the great bronze doors she had just come through.

Offices opened off from the lobby on the other three sides. Julia surveyed them briefly. By night they were unfamiliar, although she had seen them in daylight many times before. To her left, double doors shut off the skeleton of the once prosperous bank. Beyond the double doors, in a corner, twin bird-cage elevators were set in the well of an iron-railed marble staircase. Julia stared at the staircase through the fretwork of the elevator shaft, half expecting to see the watchman coming down.

Straight ahead of her, glass-paneled swinging doors guarded a desk-studded hall where minor officials of the M. T. & T. had sold a clamoring public gilt-edged guaranteed first-mortgage certificates in a happier day, certificates sealed in blindness and death, not even useful for decorating a wall.

Julia looked upward. She knew that eight iron-railed balconies flanked three sides of the lobby, rising dizzily tier on tier. Spacious offices opened off the balconies, as they did off the ground floor. From the top floor an onlooker could see straight down to the lobby's tiles. She remembered vividly a caning Seth had received from his father for pouring a glass of water over the railing to drench an indignant depositor eight stories below.

A single high-powered bulb, hung not far overhead, blinded her like a malignant star. Once she had stood on the stage of a great theater and stared up toward the gridiron after a show. The make-believe was stripped of its glamor, leaving only stark girders and harsh shadows. The tinsel and beauty were gone, the laughter silent. Like the Miners Title and Trust Company—the comedy was done.

Somewhere in the building a heavy switch made contact and a motor whirred. Julia walked back toward the elevators. The clocklike indicator of one pointed to nine. The other had just left five and was moving slowly down.

Julia stood frozenly watching the creeping pointer. Far above her a wavering scream of a man in mortal terror had struck through the resonant desertion of the cavernous lobby and gone echoing up to the dome.

She didn't want to look, but implacable fear held her head in a moving vise and turned her white face upward to watch the shadow grow above the single light—to stare in hopeless horror as it hurtled closer flapping long arms like the wings of a helpless eagle.

It seemed to take ages for the man to fall.

He moved just once after he struck the tile in a huddled inhuman heap, then lay quite still.

She knew it was Blake, but seconds of blankness passed before she grasped the fact that he was dead, seconds of terrible blankness while her frantic feet moved—carrying her halfway up a flight of the marble stairs, then turning and rushing her down again while her brain stood still.

Wind had swept across the lobby and stopped her at the foot of the stairs to face two men who had entered by the little door. She pointed speechlessly to Blake's broken form. One of the two men left her and knelt down. The other held her hypnotized with eyes of flinty gray.

"Who are you?" Julia forced herself to whisper. "I've seen you before."

"Inspector Larry Davis, Mrs. Hadfield," said the gray-eyed man. "New York Homicide Squad. Perhaps you can tell us what you saw upstairs that frightened you so."

"Upstairs?" she repeated dully. "I haven't been upstairs." She saw that another man was watching her, standing stolidly in the elevator door.

"No?" The Inspector's gray eyes took a journey up the staircase, paused, and came back down. He turned to the man in the elevator door. "Where were you, O'Hare?"

"Making my rounds," the Irishman said stolidly. "I came down to answer the bell."

"We didn't ring," said Davis. His disturbing gaze returned to Julia.

"Somebody did," O'Hare insisted. "And if you didn't ring, then how are you after gettin' in?"

"The door was open—" Julia felt suddenly trapped and encircled. The man beside Blake had risen to his feet and added another pair of eyes to stare.

"Indade, now," said O'Hare, "what the hell goes on?"

"Suppose I do the questioning," Davis suggested softly. "You see, O'Hare, Sergeant Archer and I just dropped over from Headquarters to answer a murder call."

CHAPTER II

1

Captain Duncan Maclain drained a cup of black coffee, pushed back his plate untasted, and with a brief "Excuse me, Rena" left the breakfast table.

Rena Savage, her wide humorous mouth drooped with lines of worry, watched his tall form in its confident progress from dining room to office through the penthouse foyer.

"He ain' et his brekfus' again," Sarah Marsh the cook complained as she took the Captain's plate away. She shook her head dolefully. "Ain' the same, the Cap'n ain't—ain' the same sence yo' husband gone off to de wah!"

"Spud hasn't gone to war, Sarah," Rena corrected. "He was a reserve officer. He's in the Intelligence Corps and was called to Washington."

A glance at Sarah's face showed her the futility of explanation. Mr. Savage was away in uniform; *ergo*, Mr. Savage had gone to war. Yet Rena's worry wasn't for Spud, much as she missed him. The cause of her anxiety was Captain Duncan Maclain.

The Captain was blind, had been for twenty years and more.

He had indefinably changed since the Japs had struck at Pearl Harbor and his partner and closest friend had left New York. His step was just as sprightly and sure, his mind as keen; but Rena, who next to Spud knew him better than anyone, could sense his melancholy. He had already, as an officer, given his sight for his country in 1917. Now he was fretting again, inwardly feeling that he was useless because he couldn't don a uniform to fight in a second war.

"Useless?" Rena muttered into her coffee cup and let her mind wander back through the years.

For more than ten, she had been married to Spud and had served as secretary to Duncan Maclain. Mutely she had watched the struggle, the indomitable will, the incessant practice which had forged the Captain, living in perpetual blackout, into almost perfect efficiency. Fearfully she had seen him pit himself against desperate men with sight; against enemies of country and society; deliberately thrust himself into danger—and invariably win.

Spud had always been at his side—not quite so brilliant, not half so dangerous, but filled with loyalty. No matter what Maclain's dark mood, Spud's strange yellow eyes would glint with merriment and his quick sarcastic words would goad the Captain into a softening grin.

It was Spud who had conceived the wild idea of making a private investigator out of Duncan Maclain. Not for money entirely, for the Captain was wealthy, but merely to prove to Maclain himself that with the aid of Schnucke, his Seeing Eye dog, he was as good as any man who could see.

Rena finished her coffee and set the cup down. With Spud gone, she was faced with a double duty: to carry on for her husband and to find some interest to revive the spark in the Captain.

Her soft chin set in defiance. The world could tear itself to pieces with war—she didn't intend to let it sabotage Duncan Maclain, to pour the emery powder of self-pity into the cogs of such a perfect human machine.

The telephone rang while she was thinking. She picked up the dining room extension.

"There's a Miss Sybella Ford and a Mr. Lawson downstairs," said the desk clerk. "They want to see Captain Maclain."

"I'll talk to her," said Rena.

She listened to the velvet-like voice for several minutes, then said, "Wait just a little, Miss Ford. I'll call you back," and hung up.

In the office she found the Captain sitting rigid in a straight-back chair with Schnucke's smooth head on his knee.

"Miss Sybella Ford and a man named Lawson from the State Insurance Department are downstairs," said Rena quietly.

"I'm interviewing no one, Rena." Maclain got up and took his place behind his flat-topped desk.

"They're not interviewers," Rena persisted. "I talked with Miss Ford on the phone. She says it's most important. It's about the—"

"A woman with a name like Sybella is bound to be an interviewer," the Captain interrupted coldly. "She's fat, uses cheap perfume, and has tendencies toward too much midriff when her girdle's gone. She's vacuous, and will cover her lack of brains by working her jaws offensively on a piece of chewing gum." He gave a noisy demonstration. "There should be a law against chompers. Imagine what it does to those who can see them, too. Human bovines, two-legged ruminants. The world's in tatters, and they solace themselves with a lump of coagulated goo!"

"A man was killed last night," Rena went on patiently. There were moments when Captain Maclain needed skillful handling. "Are you going to deliver a treatise on gum-chewing and jump to a lot of conclusions, or are you going to help?"

"Twenty-five thousand men were killed last night," said Duncan Maclain, "and fifty thousand the night before. We're working to win a war." He rubbed his high forehead. "I can't develop much interest in Sybella Ford and her silly problems, Rena, or in the inefficiency of the State Insurance Department. You'd better ask them to excuse me."

"The world is very much interested in the man who was killed last night, according to the papers. They've given him enough front page to shove off part of the war. He was Blake Hadfield, former president of the M. T. & T."

"Please, Rena!"

She knew the tone and braced herself against the coming sarcasm, then continued doggedly: "The police are holding his son, Seth Hadfield, for investigation, claiming that he must have some knowledge of how his father fell to death from the eighth floor inside the M. T. & T. building. The son's a Second Lieutenant. Davis found him roaming around in a daze short-ly after his father fell. The boy denies all knowledge of it. He says—"

The Captain's sinewy expressive hand which could move with such delicate precision came down on the desk top with an irritated blow.

"How in the name of all that's holy can the death of this chiseling financier be of the slightest concern to anyone, partic-ularly me?"

"He was blind—like you," said Rena brutally.

Maclain's mobile face was as blank as the paneled wall. He

took a cigarette from the cloisonné box on the desk, lit it with his quick mechanical skill of movement, and reached down to scratch Schnucke's soft ear.

"Indeed?"

Rena watched the blue smoke curl up around his crisp black hair and took a chance that he expected an answer. "Perhaps you remember. He was shot and blinded by a man named James Sprague six years ago."

"Indeed?" Maclain repeated with annoying disinterest, then asked unexpectedly, "How old is the boy?"

"Seth Hadfield?"

"Naturally," said Maclain. "Is there any other boy concerned?"

"No," said Rena. "None at all. He's twenty-two according to the papers. His mother, Julia Hadfield, has been separated from her husband for almost ten years."

"Is he a homicidal maniac?" The Captain concentrated more fully on Schnucke's ear.

"The boy?"

"Naturally."

"The papers didn't say. What makes you think that?" Rena was glad he couldn't see her jubilant smile.

"I can't recall that I've said I was thinking anything," said Duncan Maclain. "I'll admit that for a moment I was pondering about the abnormal psychology that could turn a young army officer into a monster."

"Who said he was a monster?" Rena played him carefully along.

"The facts," Captain Maclain stated flatly. "How many years have I worked with Davis and Archer?"

"A dozen or more."

"Exactly. Since you've known them, have you seen any indications that either of them was a fool?"

"Never," Rena admitted.

"Then Davis has more than a casual reason for holding this young man. Therefore, the young man is a monster."

"The Inspector might be mistaken, of course," Rena protested gently. "Blake Hadfield might have—"

"Rather obvious, isn't it?" Maclain interrupted. "Hadfield was blind. The railings in the M. T. & T. building are more than waist-high—I've been in there several times. Can you picture a blind man rushing about so wildly that he'd precipitate himself over such a railing?"

"No," said Rena. "There's suicide, of course."

"I wouldn't have to go downtown to commit it." The Captain deposited ashes neatly in a tray. "I could always find a high enough window in my own neighborhood. I'm interested in the son, Rena. It takes a monster to throw his own blind father over a railing, and from what I know of those railings, Hadfield was thrown. He didn't fall."

"So?" said Rena.

"What's happened to the people who were coming up here?"

"They're waiting downstairs."

"It's not very polite," said Duncan Maclain, "to keep people waiting in that downstairs hall."

2

Friendship with Blake Hadfield had left Sybella Ford with many ingrained impressions of the blind—impressions gleaned from one man and consequently not entirely accurate when applied to the blind as a whole.

Seated in the lobby of the apartment house at Seventy-second and Riverside Drive, waiting for word to admit them upstairs, she discussed her forebodings with Harold Lawson, who was partly the cause of her coming there.

Lawson, an assistant investigator for the State Insurance Department, hid a great deal of common sense and real ability under a jovial devil-may-care air. A heavy muscular man with a cleanshaven face and merry blue eyes, his addiction to tennis had overcome a tendency toward stoutness. Aided by expertly tailored clothes, he carried his two hundred pounds incredibly well.

For the moment he was worried. His testimony against Sprague and Company, where he had served as auditor before that company's failure, had secured him a position with the State Insurance Department. His own ability had pushed him up rapidly until the fate of the depositors and certificate holders in the bankrupt Miners Title and Trust Company had become almost a matter of personal concern.

The M. T. & T. had been a headache from the start. Harold Lawson was a born accountant, and he had an inward hunch that Blake Hadfield had emerged from the M. T. & T. crash with something more than his enormous salary salted away. The courts had held differently.

Then had come Hadfield's blinding and Sprague's suicide to place an even greater stench in the public's nostrils at any mention of the M. T. & T. Now, six years later, Hadfield's violent death had rocketed the defunct Trust Company into unwelcome notoriety again.

Murder, the police had hinted. There was plenty against the M. T. & T. already without a murder to further shake public confidence. In a desperate hope of proving that Blake Hadfield had committed suicide, and because he knew Sybella had reasons of her own, Lawson had persuaded Sybella Ford to accompany him on a visit to another blind man—Captain Duncan Maclain.

"I feel rather silly," Sybella admitted, taking a third cigarette from Lawson and lighting it from her second. "What can this man do that the police can't do better, Harold?"

"He can look at this through a blind man's eyes, paradoxically speaking," Lawson declared. "I know Davis of the Homicide Squad fairly well. He's a tough one to shake loose from an idea."

"So are you," said Sybella drily.

Lawson laughed. "Are you referring to my perfectly natural desire to marry you, my dear?"

"Perhaps." She patted the back of his hand. "Only your infernal persistence got me to come here."

"If it's a matter of the fees, Sybella—"

"It isn't. It's just that I feel silly."

"Well, anyhow, I'm taking care of the fees. I don't dare call in Maclain in behalf of the State, but I do know that the Homicide Squad and the newspapers, too, have faith in what he says. I'm hoping he can put a bee in Davis' ear."

"Then you don't believe his son killed him?"

"Heavens, no," said Lawson. "I don't believe he was killed. Do you?"

A bell boy interrupted before she could answer. They rode up to the twenty-fifth floor in silence and there a smaller private elevator took them up another floor in Maclain's penthouse. Rena

Savage greeted them in the hall and ushered them into the Captain's office without further delay.

Sybella was prepared for anything except normalcy, and normalcy radiated from the impeccable man who greeted them at the door. He shook hands warmly with Lawson, said "Make yourself comfortable," then clasped Sybella's hand and escorted her to a chair.

He was strikingly handsome, she admitted, appraising his breadth of shoulder and slender waistline under the faultless suit of dark gray. His spirited aquiline face was strong and sympathetic, filled with interesting hills and valleys that caught highlights from his smile.

For an instant after he seated himself at his desk and pushed cigarettes forward, she had an illusion that his sightless eyes, perfect in contour, were turning inquiringly from her to Harold Lawson. Unconsciously she snapped open her vanity case, touched powder to her nose, and looked to the set of her soft brown hair.

"I have a confession to make." Sybella paused and glanced at Lawson, who grinned reassuringly. Yet she was confident from his expression that he had felt the Captain's magnetism, too.

"You dreaded coming here." Maclain smiled with a touch of ruefulness. "So many people do. But usually they're in trouble. Sometimes I feel like a dentist."

"Sybella's not exactly in trouble, Captain Maclain," Lawson made haste to explain, "and neither am I. I'm really the cause of our being here. I'm connected with the State Insurance Department, and the defunct M. T. & T. comes very much under my jurisdiction. I've been trying very hard to maintain public confidence that the assets would be liquidated to the best advantage of all concerned."

Maclain's expressive eyebrows moved up in slight inquiry.

"There has been enough scandal connected with the M. T. & T.," Harold Lawson continued. "From the point of view of public welfare, Mr. Hadfield picked a most unfortunate place in which to die."

"Sometimes we can't pick our spots," said Duncan Maclain. "How is the public welfare affected?"

"Carl Bentley, the Comptroller, has been doing a splendid job of selling real estate which the M. T. & T. took over on foreclosed mortgages, despite the fact that most people hesitate to deal with a company that has a black eye. Add a murder—" Lawson shrugged expressively, as though the Captain might see. "Well, to put it mildly, the difficulty of Bentley's job will be doubled and the price of the Trust Company's real estate will go heavily down."

Maclain relaxed in his chair, settling back slightly with the utter limpness of a man who has every muscle under perfect co-ordination and instant control. At first, Sybella thought he hadn't heard Lawson's explanation at all. Then he folded his hands inertly on the desk edge and spoke with the tone of a man whose thoughts are far away.

"I have a confession to make, too, Miss Ford. I pictured you as fat, effusive and slightly obnoxious. Possibly it's your name—Sybella."

She laughed. "A family cross I bear. It does smack of verdant luxury, doesn't it? Sybaritic, opulence in the feminine form. Or perhaps the Sibyl, gaunt and old."

Harold Lawson's forehead creased itself in perplexity at this new turn. He opened his mouth to speak, then closed it again.

"Since I've met you," said Duncan Maclain, "it smacks of neither one. You're very beautiful, aren't you?"

She was wise enough not to reply, realizing that she had received an extraordinary tribute, a compliment that was absolutely sincere. Lawson gave her silence an approving grin. Only a ninny would have asked the Captain, "How do you know?"

Duncan Maclain was quietly pleased and went on to explain. "People form pictures for me when I first meet them—indelible pictures which I label and keep in a permanent frame. The lines of the pictures are handclasps, the texture and warmth of the skin, the length of their stride as they walk beside me. The colors are tone of voice, sincerity, choice of apparel and perfume."

There was an electric quality in his statements which caused her hand to tremble as she put out her cigarette. She said quite simply, "Thank you, Captain Maclain."

Again she thought he hadn't heard, and looked for support to Lawson, who was staring with interest at the Braille books lining one wall of the room.

"Tell me about Blake Hadfield, Mr. Lawson," the Captain said after a time. "Have you known him for long?"

"Professionally only." Lawson twisted in his chair at the Captain's shift of conversation. "I was auditor for James Sprague's brokerage house before it failed. Then I obtained a post with the State Insurance Department. Sprague and Hadfield were close friends. I met—"

"Friends?" asked Duncan Maclain. "I understood Sprague shot and blinded him."

"That was later on. Sprague had lost heavily in the M. T. & T." Lawson hesitated as though uncertain just how much he might ethically reveal. "Mr. Sprague had tried to recover some losses, I'm afraid, by manipulating some of our customers' funds."

"You tell me about Blake Hadfield, Miss Ford. Had you known him for long?"

"Many years." Sybella found it difficult to concentrate, so quickly had the Captain changed. His face was as friendly as ever, his voice the same, but she was talking to a man she had never met before, a lay figure dominated not by emotion, but by the functioning of an uncompromising brain.

"Our conversation is being recorded in my secretary's office," Maclain announced. "It's only fair that both of you know. I have detecto-dictographs set in the walls. They pick up every word said in here and record it on an Ediphone—audible records which I can use at any time. If either of you object, I'll be glad to cut it off."

"Inspector Davis told me of that when he gave me your name," said Lawson. "I have no objection at all."

"Nor I," added Sybella.

"So Larry Davis sent you to see me." The Captain chuckled. "I'm beginning to believe there's a flat side to this ball. I was asking you about Hadfield, Miss Ford. Did you love him?"

"No, Captain Maclain." Her answer was decisive.

"That's one for the record," said Lawson with a pleased laugh. "I've been trying for some time to get an admission from her that she's in love with me—with no success at all."

"Blake's wife is still alive, Captain," Sybella went serenely on. "She stuck with him through the investigation of the bank crash; then they separated in nineteen thirty-three."

Maclain asked, "Why?"

"I could hardly be expected to answer that, could I?"

"Why not?" The Captain's question was pure surprise. "You say you've known the man for years. At least you can give me your opinion from a woman's point of view."

"All right," she said after an instant's pause. "I'll try. Blake was a money-maker, but cold as a fish and resentful of anything that took time from his money-making. Julia took enough of it and finally left, taking the boy. Blake was rather nasty about it and successfully fought her divorce action."

"Yet you liked him."

"He could be perfectly swell," Lawson put in. "It takes that type to reach the top of an outfit like M. T. & T."

"That's quite true." Sybella searched for the proper answer. "After he lost his sight—well, he was alone a lot. He had a brilliant mind, Captain Maclain. Maybe I was in love with his brain. Last night I saw his son, Seth, for the first time in years. He's a good-looking, likable boy—" Sybella paused.

"And both of you think his son killed him," said Duncan Maclain.

"No," said Lawson flatly. "The police think his son killed him. I think he died accidentally. I came here in hopes you could prove it, by putting yourself in his place. Figuratively speaking, of course."

"Of course," chimed in Maclain.

Sybella watched fascinated as he took a fifty-piece jigsaw puzzle from a drawer and dumped it on the flat-topped desk. His marvelous fingers moved swifter than her eyes could follow, sorting and rejecting until three irregular pieces were hooked together.

"He always moved around with the greatest caution, Harold," Sybella reminded Lawson, not softly enough to escape the Captain's ear.

Maclain's agile fingers stilled. "Tell me, Miss Ford, what brought *you* here?"

"Thirty-seven thousand dollars," said Sybella. "I lost that

amount in the crash of the M. T. & T. This morning I learned from Phil Courtney, the Hadfield attorney, that Blake had returned it. Like Harold, I hope you can prove Blake's death was accidental. It isn't very pleasant to be remembered in a murdered man's will."

"No," Maclain admitted. His fingers located another piece of puzzle and once again were still. "Did Inspector Davis say why he thought Seth Hadfield was guilty of his father's murder—assuming it was a murder?"

"He has a theory that there was no one else in the building except the watchman and Seth's mother, and both of them were downstairs when Hadfield fell. The police found the boy wandering about the eighth floor in a dazed condition. He'd been drinking."

"So there were just those three in the building; the watchman, the mother, and the boy." The Captain held a piece of the puzzle poised above the desk. "That looks very bad for the boy, Mr. Lawson."

"Why?" asked Lawson. "There may have been someone else in that building. It's a big place. Davis may have been mistaken."

"Larry Davis is the best man in the New York Homicide Squad, which is full of good men. He doesn't make mistakes," said Duncan Maclain.

3

Julia Hadfield rolled over painfully in bed and stared uncomprehendingly at a window where a watery frozen sun was vainly trying to inject some cheer into the room. Her body felt as though it had been on the wrong end of a terrific beating.

Her head was stuffy and overfull. Usually energetic, even on awakening, this morning she had lost all desire to move. She lay quietly for a while, pondering over a savory smell of coffee and the pop of frying eggs wafted to her from the kitchenette off the living room.

Elise came in carrying a tray. "Up and at 'em," she said with a smile. "It's after ten and we've work to do before noon." She placed the tray on a chair and pulled Julia's pillow up into position.

An avalanche of numbing recollection swept crushingly over her at sight of the girl. There were things beyond the limit of human endurance and she had faced them the night before, keeping herself well in hand when every fiber in her was breaking; talking and acting sensibly . . . .

"Yes, Inspector, the door was open. I knocked on it and came in."

"You saw no one in the lobby, Mrs. Hadfield?"

"No, Inspector."

"And you had no idea of the whereabouts of your son?"

"No, Inspector."

"Your husband phoned you to meet him?"

"Yes, Inspector."

"Don't you think it extraordinary that he said nothing about being accompanied by your son?"

"It was like him, Inspector. He also phoned Mr. Courtney to meet him at ten."

"But Mr. Courtney wasn't here when you arrived?"

"No, Inspector."

"And Mr. Courtney—when he received that telephone call—came to your apartment. Why?"

"He dropped in to see Seth and Elise. They were coming for dinner."

"But they didn't." Gray eyes as noncommittal as spots on a dress. "Yet you had no word from your son."

"He's been drinking, Inspector. He's told you that himself."

"We'll have to hold him, Mrs. Hadfield. For his own good, you understand."

"Seth isn't a murderer. He isn't—he isn't!"

"We're holding him for his own protection, Mrs. Hadfield. Inebriation."

"I'll take him home with me."

"Not tonight, Mrs. Hadfield. When he sobers up—"

As though she were an idiot. Tonight. Tomorrow. The next night. Something worse than murder—parricide. The murder of Blake Hadfield charged against his son.

Julia sat up in bed and said listlessly, "I'd forgotten you spent the night, Elise. Thanks for the tray, but—"

"You'll eat it and like it," Elise told her grimly.

"But, darling—"

"And like it," Elise repeated making motions toward the tray which she had placed on Julia's knees. "Snap out of it, Jule. My besotted Romeo got himself in a jam, and it's largely my fault. But he didn't kill his father and you know it as well as I do."

"Elise, what are we going to do?" Julia decided there were moments in one's life when bullying was most welcome. She nibbled at a piece of toast and found it tasted better than she expected.

"I've already been burning up the phone." Elise lit a cigarette and sat on the foot of the bed. "I told Mr. Bentley I wouldn't be down today. The place is a beehive of curiosity. Most exciting, from what he said on the phone."

"Elise!"

"I'm sorry, Jule." She patted Julia's knee. "But you're making yourself ill over nothing, aren't you? After all—"

"After all, Blake was my husband and Seth's father, and the police are holding Seth in jail."

"And after all, Blake is dead." Elise inhaled soberly. "And about that, mother-in-law o' mine to be, there is nothing anyone can do. You've scarcely seen him in years, so his absence can't have much effect on Seth or you."

"You sound cold-blooded, darling."

Elise grinned impishly. "You're eating your eggs and drinking your coffee. Mr. Courtney will be here shortly. I've shooed two reporters away already—most attractive."

"Elise."

"You're going to fix your hair in its snazziest curl and put on your vamp-'em outfit of oyster-gray. Then we're going downtown with Mr. Courtney and bail young Ten-Nights-in-a-Barroom out of the can."

"Darling, are you sure?"

"Aren't you?"

"Of course, but—"

"Mr. Courtney's preparing a writ of habeas corpus. They have nothing to hold Seth on at all. Mr. Courtney says he'll have him out today."

"Out," said Julia slowly, "but still not in the clear." A buzzer sounded in the kitchenette. "There's Phil now, Elise. See, will you?"

She put the tray aside and got up when Elise had gone. A stinging cold shower almost brought on a chill, but she stood it with clenched teeth and felt repaid when after a brisk rub she found a suit of lounge pajamas and slipped them on. Scarcely stopping to pat her hair into a semblance of order, she headed for the living room, to stop embarrassed in the door. Harold Lawson, occupying the biggest armchair, she knew. The tall self-assured man in faultless dark gray, companioned by the even more self-assured shepherd dog, she had never seen before.

He stood up as she entered and made his own introduction.

"Mrs. Hadfield?"

"Yes." Julia walked forward, puzzled a mite, to take his outstretched hand. Nearer, she saw the blankness of his perfect eyes and realized that he was blind.

"I'm Duncan Maclain."

"I barged in on Captain Maclain this morning before he had finished breakfast," Lawson explained. "He's one of the best private investigators in the country."

Julia said, "Oh, yes, Captain. Do sit down."

Lawson continued, "I understand they're holding your son. That seems utterly ridiculous, Mrs. Hadfield. Due to the fact that Mr. Hadfield was blind, I've been fortunate enough to interest the Captain in helping us to clear things up."

"I'm also blind," said Duncan Maclain.

Julia covered a momentary agitation by sitting down. Tragedy, overwhelming in import, wasn't enough. It had been turned into *opéra bouffe*. Utterly ridiculous, Lawson had said. It was worse than ridiculous, it was almost profane at such a time to bring another blind man into her life, into her very living room.

"I don't quite understand," said Julia formally.

"How I can help, Mrs. Hadfield? That's not to be wondered at." There was a sympathetic understanding in the richness of his voice that quieted Julia's irritation with soothing magic. "Mr. Lawson has talked with your attorney earlier this morning. I understand your son will be released today. That's scarcely enough, is it?"

"It's all I want, Captain Maclain," Elise put in. "I want him back again, to tell him that when I broke our engagement last night I acted like a fool."

"You're not his mother, Miss Sprague. You're his sweetheart," said Duncan Maclain. "Mrs. Hadfield knows her son is innocent and so do you. He can still be executed—and both of you will die with him."

"Executed!" Julia breathed the word through a throat violently constricted.

"By public opinion," said Duncan Maclain. "Your husband was blind, Mrs. Hadfield. I know what goes on in a blind man's mind—how he thinks, reacts, and feels. Has your son said why he went to the office with his father?"

"I saw him only a few minutes last night before they—" Julia paused to get her thoughts in hand. "He said his father had told him he might patch up the quarrel between my boy and Elise. Seth was intoxicated, Captain Maclain. He was in no condition to know."

The buzzer sounded again. The living room was silent as Elise admitted Philip Courtney and introduced him to Captain Maclain.

Julia found herself staring openly at Phil's left arm—bandaged and splinted and hung in a black silk sling.

Elise took his brief case and helped him off with his overcoat. The lawyer shook hands heartily with Lawson and Captain Maclain, then took a chair.

"I've heard much about you, Captain," he announced in his best professional manner. "Your work in Hartford last year was almost miraculous. I'm certainly glad to have your help."

"And I'm very sorry you've had an accident," said Captain Maclain. "Did you break your left arm, or sprain it?"

"I sprained it." Courtney took a cigar from his vest pocket, bit off the end and puffed it to life from Lawson's lighter. "I had a fall on the ice last night on my way downtown to keep my appointment with Blake. I never got there."

Julia said softly, "Oh, Phil!"

Courtney gave her a reassuring glance of affection and suddenly exhaled a heavy cloud of smoke and sat up straight in his chair.

"I don't intend to spend the entire day racking my brains," he said slowly. "How the devil did you know about my arm? I've told no one, and no one else has mentioned it since I came in."

The Captain smiled, and Julia found a comforting knowledge steal through her that this was no *opéra bouffe*—that the man with the quiet beautiful dog beside him saw things that other people missed, that he could really help her son.

"Your injury announced itself in many ways, Mr. Courtney," said Duncan Maclain. "I have no useful eyes, but my other senses have been forced to double duty. You only took one arm out of your overcoat when Miss Sprague assisted you out of it in the foyer. Your step was irregular when you entered the room—an infallible indication of muscular contraction even when the injury's in the shoulder or the arm. You turned far sideways when you shook my hand, an instinctive movement to protect your injured arm. Then there's the matter of odors, Mr. Courtney. Your bandages have a most distinctive smell. For the ear again, the silk of your sling slithers against the wool of your suit whenever you move, and men aren't addicted to blouses of silk. Do you want me to go on?"

"Yes, Captain Maclain," said Julia. "I need your help badly. I beg you to go on."

4

Inspector Larry Davis' office at Headquarters was warm and comfortable for all its businesslike plainness. An aluminum-bronze steam radiator hissed intermittently in one corner giving off a sweet wettish smell. Captain Duncan Maclain became susceptible after a time to its pungency, even though it was blanketed by the overhanging haze of Sergeant Aloysius Archer's favorite brand of cigar. He moved his chair farther away. Schnucke stood up and stretched herself, yawning redly, then found a new place near the Captain's well-shod feet and lay down.

"Hell, Maclain," said Davis, fiddling with a rubber band, "I'm glad to have your help and all that sort of thing, but you're in something screwy this time. It's murder, I tell you—plain unadulterated murder."

"Without any proof," Sergeant Archer put in disgustedly.

"I gather that," said Maclain, "from the way you both keep repeating yourselves and saying nothing. If you're so certain Seth Hadfield pushed his father over a railing, why did you send Lawson up to me? Now don't tell me for the third time it was because Hadfield was blind."

"Lawson was pestering us," said Davis.

"Oh!" The Captain prodded Schnucke off his feet with a

gentle push of his toe. "Anybody who pesters you, you wish onto me."

"Well, you keep the press amused." The Sergeant stared belligerently at Schnucke and shifted uneasily in his chair. The Captain had two dogs, Schnucke and Dreist. Over a period of years, Aloysius Archer despite his record as a most efficient officer had never been quite able to tell one from the other.

This was apt to constitute a serious if not dangerous error, and the Sergeant knew it. Schnucke, trained by the Seeing Eye as a guide, was capable, lovable and gentle. She adored Maclain and clung to him with a loyalty deeper than death, but viciousness wasn't in her.

Dreist was a weapon. His loyalty to his master was as deep as Schnucke's, but it was an active loyalty trained to defend. Dreist looked on the world with a hostile, suspicious canine eye. He was ready to hurl his sinewy tearing strength at any adversary on command, or without command at a threatening gesture, or sight of a drawn gun.

The Sergeant nursed a secret fear that someday he might inadvertently, in a moment of weakness, lean down to pat Schnucke and find his wrist in a rending vise of shining teeth that would leave his hand on the floor.

"I wish you'd quit staring at Schnucke, Sergeant," the Captain remarked idly.

"And I wish you'd go to Washington with Spud and quit pulling things out of the air." The Sergeant mouthed his cigar. "Witchcraft won't get us anywhere."

"She lies on my feet when you stare at her," said Maclain. "She doesn't do it with anyone else. You must have a particularly malevolent glare."

"He's mad," said Davis, "because Courtney sprang the Hadfield kid and took him uptown. Archer was ready to strap him in the chair."

"Go ahead, Inspector, spill it all." The Sergeant spoke with respectful sarcasm that badly covered his belligerency. "Let's tell him that a whipper-snapper not dry in the seat of his pants has made a bunch of ninnies of the Department. Let him write Spud a letter with a laugh in every line: 'Dear Spud, Davis and Archer are sitting around talking to themselves asking, Was he pushed or did he fall?'"

"Okay," said Davis. He took a nice new toothpick and snapped it, then went to work with the longer end. "Listen to this, Maclain, and then tell me Blake Hadfield committed suicide or sleepwalked over a railing last night or something. Hadfield carried a Braille watch. It stopped at eleven ten—smashed to bits. At ten fifteen, this Department received a murder call."

"From whom?" the Captain asked.

"Hadfield, himself." The Inspector took the toothpick from his mouth and returned it again.

"*Hmm!*" The Captain might have been staring at a brownish spot on the office wall.

"*Hmm*, what?" Davis demanded.

"Fifty-five minutes. You're speedier than the Fire Department in answering a call."

"Now wait, Captain," Archer interrupted. "This wasn't any emergency. I took it myself."

"Obviously it wasn't," Maclain agreed with relish. "Hadfield was just dead when you got there, that's all."

"Hell and damnation!" The Inspector swore fervently. "Quit needling Archer, Maclain, and listen. I was out on a case when Archer took the call. Hadfield wanted to talk to me."

"Are you sure it was Hadfield?"

"Wait until I finish, then tell me if anyone else would make such a call. Archer told him I was out, but expected back shortly. Hadfield said there was no hurry, but if I'd come up to his office in the M. T. & T. building sometime around eleven, he and his wife and son would be there and he'd show me a neat method of murder."

"He said he remembered the Inspector and me from the investigation of the Sprague affair," Archer added somberly. "It was Hadfield, all right. Who else knew his wife and son would be there?"

"Somebody who overheard him telephone his wife, and who saw the boy," said Duncan Maclain.

"You've been reading too many Braille mysteries," Davis protested. "Murderers planning to knock off a victim at eleven ten don't give the Homicide Squad an hour to answer a call."

"No," the Captain admitted. "What then?"

"Archer dug out the old Sprague-Hadfield case file and he was looking at it when I came in. Attempted murder and suicide . . . . Closed up six years ago tighter than the bank where it happened."

"All right, go on. I have an idea." Maclain placed an elbow on his knee and used one hand as a rest for his square cleft chin.

"Sure," said Davis shortly. "So have I. We drop back six years to the Sprague-Hadfield shooting and begin. It's not what it seems at all. Two men are in a building at night with a watchman, one Dan O'Hare. They've met by appointment, and nobody but the watchman knows they're there. So somebody who doesn't know they're there drops in by accident, bumps one off and blinds the other and rigs up a case that fools us completely."

"You have been fooled at times," the Captain reminded him gently.

"Yes," said Davis, "but not for long. It might not be so hard to fool us, Maclain, but what about Blake Hadfield? Don't you think he knows who shot and blinded him?"

"I wonder," said Duncan Maclain. "Has it occurred to you, Inspector, that blindness changes a man? That sometimes I discover things even you and Sergeant Archer miss, as good as you are? Suppose Blake Hadfield returned to that office last night because he had discovered something, and when he was sure of it, put in that mysterious murder call."

"All right. Let's suppose it." The Inspector discarded his toothpick. "You're in the corner I want you in—huddled up with Archer and me. Now you can start to admit things. You'll admit, won't you, Captain, that we reached that building a minute or two after Hadfield's fatal fall?"

Maclain smiled and nodded.

"You've already admitted," the Inspector plowed on earnestly, "that the railings are too high for anyone to fall accidentally."

Again the Captain nodded.

"Okay." Larry Davis ran a hand through his graying hair. "Now I'll spike suicide for you. Blake Hadfield started to write a note—"

"A note?" Duncan Maclain sat erect so quickly that Schnucke moved in disgruntled surprise. "What did he say?"

"Nothing." Davis took a single sheet of paper from his desk and read: *"I came down here with my son tonight—"* He paused for the Captain to drink it in. "That's as far as he got, Maclain. It's written in ink, and with all due deference to your writing ability, Hadfield's slants uphill in a bit of a scrawl, but that isn't the point. The point is, would a suicide start a suicide note and quit it after a single line?"

"Scarcely," the Captain muttered, and louder: "Are you sure of his writing?"

"Now really, Maclain." Davis sounded sad. "Archer and I occasionally get around. We found specimens of his writing in his apartment this morning, and had an expert on them right away."

"I thought maybe you checked the ink with that in the inkwells," Maclain remarked.

Sergeant Archer said, "There wasn't any. The inkwells were washed out and dry."

"Oh!" The Captain sighed and patted Schnucke, who was growing restless. "But you found his fountain pen?"

"No," said Davis shortly. "We didn't. And we didn't find something else—forty-five cents in change which the kid said his father got back from the taxi driver on the trip downtown. We found the driver and checked with him, and he bore out the boy. Both of them claim Blake Hadfield put that money in his vest pocket and that he had other change there, too, but not enough to settle the cab fare and tip without breaking a bill."

The Inspector pushed back his chair and came around the desk to stand in front of Maclain. "There you have your picture, Captain. There was no change in Hadfield's pockets. There was no fountain pen. Yet he had change, and he wrote a note with something, and we can prove from several people that he owned a fountain pen."

Davis swallowed noisily and the Captain was still.

"Nobody was in that building when Hadfield fell except Mrs. Hadfield, Dan O'Hare the watchman, and the boy—in case that's what you're thinking," Davis went on meaningly. "Will you admit that Archer and I and twelve men know how to search a building?"

"I admitted that to Lawson this morning," said Maclain.

"Then crawl out of your corner," Davis told him. "There are only two exits from the M. T. & T.—the front to Broadway, and a steel fire exit from the basement. The fire door hasn't been opened in months. Mrs. Hadfield says she saw no one and I believe her. The exits are still being covered, but somebody killed Blake Hadfield and vanished with his change and fountain pen. Who?"

"The murderer of James Sprague," said Duncan Maclain as he stood up and stretched. "The little man who wasn't there!"

CHAPTER III

1

CARL BENTLEY, Comptroller of the Miners Title and Trust Company, was a short nervous fellow addicted to bifocals and carnations. The bifocals, mounted in oversize rims of dark tortoiseshell, were constantly being misplaced, since Bentley, moved by some hidden streak of vanity, removed them automatically whenever a stranger entered his corner office on the eighth floor.

Half of Mr. Bentley's time was taken up with interviewing distrait certificate-holders who still hoped to salvage a sizable part of their shrunken investments. This placed a heavy burden on Elise, who as Bentley's secretary had developed the instincts of an office bloodhound in tracking down Bentley's bifocals to their resting place on various ledges and window sills. Vanity or not, once rid of his precious glasses it was very difficult for Mr. Bentley to see . . . .

"Good morning, Miss . . . ?"

"I'm Mrs. Diffenbaugh, Mr. Bentley," angrily. "Considering the fact that your company robbed my late husband of his entire fortune and that I was in here only yesterday afternoon—"

"Mrs. Diffenbaugh, of course, of course. Do sit down, Mrs. Diffenbaugh."

"You put your glasses in the Morton folder, Mr. Bentley," Elise would put in quickly.

"Morton. Morton. Now let me see."

"It's right under your hand."

"Of course, Elise, of course," and, smiling apologetically at the stewing Mrs. Diffenbaugh, "I'd be lost without Miss Sprague. Now what was it you wished to discuss with me?" . . .

Mr. Bentley scarcely realized what a help his serene dark-haired secretary was until she was gone. He had flutteringly dismissed the last of an unusually long line of complainers at five forty-five and dashed out for a bite of supper, a bit taken aback to find a stolid officer seated in the lobby watching the door. Thank heavens, Elise would be back tomorrow. It had been a trying day.

It proved to be a trying evening, too.

Harold Lawson showed up at seven thirty, full of questions. Lawson was always an ordeal to Mr. Bentley. The State man radiated so damn much energy. There were always so many things he wanted to know. Confusing enough during office hours with Elise and a staff on hand. Rather overwhelming at the close of a tiring day.

"This is a hell of a mess, Bentley, isn't it?"

"I wish you'd been here yourself today, Mr. Lawson."

"I suppose there was plenty of comment about Hadfield's death."

"Too much, Mr. Lawson, far too much. Why did he have to come down here to commit suicide? Why do the papers keep jumping on me all the time? That's what I'd like to know."

"You're the goat, Carl," Lawson told him, laughing.

"I'm an ass," said Bentley, goggling. "You couldn't get another man to take what I do for the money I'm getting."

"We're trying to get things cleared up tonight, Carl." Lawson adroitly evaded the issue of Bentley's salary, which came out of the Receiver's funds, but had to have the State's approval. They had been into the matter before. "I've retained a private detective. Captain Duncan Maclain."

"A detective?" Mr. Bentley removed his white carnation and dropped it in a wastebasket. The cold on his trip out to supper had withered it like a Joe Louis blow. "What's the matter with the police? Can't they tell a suicide when they see one? That's what I want to know."

"Maclain's blind. I thought—"

"Blind? Holy Moses, Mr. Lawson!" Bentley fairly twittered. "The press will treat us like a vaudeville show. I have work to do. What will my staff think if I start leading a blind man around? It's hard enough to get a day's work out of them now. What will the certificate-holders think?"

"He has a dog." Lawson lit a cigarette to hide a grin. "You won't have to lead him, Carl. He'll be here shortly with the Hadfield kid and Courtney, the lawyer. All you have to do is tell him anything he wants to know."

"A dog," said Bentley weakly and sat down. "What kind of a dog?"

"A police dog, of course." The noise of the ascending elevator sounded through the quiet building. "It will take the reporters' minds off of the Company for a while. Don't take on so."

"Assuming the reporters have minds," said Bentley miserably. "Yes, I suppose so."

From then on, to a man who dealt in the smooth reliability of figures, percentages and trial balances, the evening became a bit of a nightmare.

Bentley, never at his best when confronted with anything unusual, found it difficult to keep himself composed in the presence of Duncan Maclain. He had through arduous practice mastered a trick of gazing intently into a listener's eyes to drive home the ineradicable accuracy of his statements, especially if he was a trifle unsure.

It left him dejected to find that such a neat trick of *How to Win Friends and Influence People* was wasted on Captain Maclain. Further discomfiture was in the making.

Seth Hadfield, usually blithe and ebullient, answered Bentley's overhearty greeting with a hangdog air that was far from gay. It depressed the Comptroller still more. He left Seth and began an earnest intent search for his spectacles, which had taken cover, although Mr. Bentley was certain he had worn them into the room.

The blind man pulled the chair out from Blake Hadfield's desk and sat down. "If all of you will be seated," he said with quiet authority, "I'll get up and walk around. I'd like first off to get a picture of this room."

Mr. Bentley continued his fluttering search as Seth flopped down in an easy chair and Courtney and Lawson occupied the divan.

"If you're looking for your glasses, Mr. Bentley, here they are." The Captain held them up. "I heard you place them on the desk here just before I sat down."

Courtney coughed, Lawson chuckled, and Seth said gloomily: "You'd be better off if you got a dog, wouldn't you, Carl?"

"I'm a bit upset," Bentley admitted as he took the glasses and put them on.

"For the love of Pete, sit down!" Lawson told him.

Bentley perched himself birdlike on the edge of another chair and watched in mesmerized fascination as man and dog began a tour of the room. The animal moved with uncanny precision, guiding her master by invisible signals transmitted through the brace on her back to the Captain's gripping left hand.

"Is there anything on this table?" asked Maclain.

"Nothing," Courtney answered, nursing his injured arm.

The Captain's right hand touched the table edge, swept along it, brushing the backs of three pushed-in chairs, and moved to the back of Bentley's chair. The dog turned in until the Captain's hand found the wall and followed it to the inset of a window at the end of the red divan. There, Schnucke circled and guided her master clear of Lawson's and Courtney's protruding feet, then wheeled again until the Captain had touched the second window in back of the large divan.

As the Captain reached the globe in the corner, another man stepped quietly into the office, causing Mr. Bentley to start uncomfortably.

"Take a seat, Inspector Davis. You know everyone but Mr. Bentley, the Comptroller, I believe." The Captain gently twirled the globe.

Davis grinned and removed his pepper-and-salt overcoat. "I just happened to be passing."

"It's a habit you have when anything's going on." Maclain moved on to the small buffet, felt the six highball glasses in the silver holder, flicked each one with his fingernail and passed along to touch the lowered Venetian blind of a third window near the buffet.

"There's a wall safe back of the first panel in the corner on the other wall," said Seth. "Father had me get a tin cashbox out of it for him last night—if that means anything."

"The safe was open, Maclain, and we've been through all the papers in the tin box. Nothing important. Do you agree, Mr. Courtney?" Davis faced the lawyer.

"Yes," said Courtney. "I looked them over late this afternoon. Mr. Hadfield's will is already in my possession, and insurance policies taken from the safe by the police last night. There were only half a dozen personal letters in the box."

The Captain stood by the Venetian blind, idly pulling the cord that opened and closed the slats. "Did your father ask you to pick out any letter from the box, Seth?"

"No, Captain," said young Hadfield. "I fixed us a drink from a bottle of Scotch that was in the safe. Then I went to the switchboard across the building and plugged in this phone. Then I—"

"Everything in this office was Mr. Hadfield's personal property. He bought the furniture himself and had the safe put in. That's why it has never been touched since the bank, er—ceased operations," Carl Bentley put in.

Maclain wasn't interested, Bentley decided aggrievedly, and lapsed into silence.

"Have you any idea what your father wanted with that tin box?" the Captain asked as he opened and closed the slats again.

"I believe he picked out a paper, but I wasn't paying much attention."

The Captain turned in the direction of Inspector Davis. "Did any of the papers in that box have any raised-marking on them, Davis? Embossed or engraved lettering, or perhaps a Notary's Seal?"

"None that I saw." Davis spoke slowly, his keen gray eyes fixed on Maclain. "I'm beginning to get what you mean."

"I'm wondering how Mr. Hadfield knew what he was taking from the box," said Maclain. "Like me, he had to do it by feel." He left the window, picked up the six glasses in the silver holder from the buffet, carried them to the desk and sat down.

With the six glasses placed before him, he began to run his fingernails back and forth across them until Bentley's sensitive teeth were edged and he felt himself threatened with a chill.

"Just what did you do here last night, Seth?" inquired the Captain, executing a double fingernail-trill.

Seth repeated his story. The office was very still.

"That's everything?" the Captain persisted. "There's something vital I can't quite place. I need your tiniest actions to help. What about when you were fixing the drinks?" The Captain took two of the glasses and held them out. "Try it now, will you, please? Go through it all again."

Seth disappeared through the curtains behind Maclain. Water ran from a tap. A brief pause followed, and he returned. "There *was* something I forgot to tell you, but—"

"You opened a drawer of a table in the foyer behind me," said Duncan Maclain.

"That's right," Seth admitted.

"Why?" asked Courtney. "Were you looking for something?"

Seth shook his head. "Curiosity, I guess. I used to come down here when I was a kid. That drawer out there in the table by the washroom is where Father used to keep his gun."

Bentley stood up suddenly. "I can tell you something. Somebody's taken a glass-and-onyx paperweight from this room."

"Did you see that here last night, Seth, or don't you remember?" the Captain asked.

"I remember it perfectly," Seth declared. "It was on the desk right where those glasses are now."

The Captain sucked in his lower lip and slowly released it. "We're dealing with a strange criminal, gentlemen, a murderer who kills for change, fountain pens and paperweights, a lowerer of blinds on the eighth floor of a building who cuts the lowering cord entirely off so that the Venetian blind can never be raised again."

2

Harold Lawson excused himself at eight o'clock, pleading another engagement, and left with Carl Bentley.

Seth Hadfield stuck around for the space of a cigarette before he asked rather wistfully, "Will you need me any more?"

"No," said Maclain. "Run on uptown and meet her, Seth, and don't worry yourself into too many highballs."

"Believe me, Captain, I'm off the stuff for the duration!"

"Of the hangover or the war?" asked Courtney.

"Both, Phil."

Inspector Davis snorted. "I make that statement every time I come out of a bar. Run along, Lieutenant—but get in touch with me before your leave is up."

Seth paused with his greatcoat half on, his young face sobered again with a distress that a moment before had nearly disappeared. "You still believe I killed my father, don't you, Inspector?"

"No, Seth," Maclain declared with sudden sharpness. "Get that idea out of your head. It's wrong. The Inspector doesn't think you're guilty of anything except an over-optimistic attitude on the mixing of Scotch and rum. If your father was murdered, Davis will find out who killed him, and it won't take him long."

"Thanks." Seth spoke more cheerfully and left with a quick salute and a wave of his hand.

"Yes. Thanks, Maclain," muttered Davis.

The Captain heard the creak of leather as the officer sat down. A second soft noise followed as Courtney changed his position on the divan and reached in his pocket for a cigar.

"Smoke, Inspector?" Courtney asked.

"Thanks, no," said Davis.

"You're full of thanks tonight," Maclain remarked, hefting one of the highball glasses in one hand, then passing it to the other. "What were you thanking me for?"

"Telling the kid I'd find out who killed his father," Davis said morosely.

"It seems to me, Inspector, that you've let an idea run away with you." Phil Courtney spoke judicially between puffs on his cigar. "I talked to the District Attorney today. Frankly, to get a true bill, the facts against anyone are so meager that the D.A.'s office isn't interested. The Medical Examiner's autopsy shows that Mr. Hadfield was killed by a fall, and nothing else."

"Go on, Mr. Courtney," Davis urged. "I'm badly in need of legal help. I'm just a cop. The State, represented by Lawson, wants a suicide. The County, represented by the D.A., claims it's a suicide. Who am I to quibble?"

"I'm merely presenting the possibilities involved, Inspector." Courtney de-ashed his cigar. "Shall I say your own efficiency has stymied you? Either you must prove that Seth Hadfield, with intent to kill, pushed or threw his father over a railing— presumably on this floor; or you must admit accident or suicide."

"That sounds quite logical," said Duncan Maclain, and set down the glass he was holding.

"It's airtight." Davis snapped shut his heavy jaw.

"Let me continue," Courtney went on smoothly. "As I understand it, you have proof incontrovertible that Mrs. Hadfield had no time to get up here, push her husband over, and return to the downstairs hall."

"Judge it yourself," said Davis. "The watchman has a clock he carries with him, and the keys that punch it are stationed around the building chained to places on the wall. He punched one on the fifth floor, his last on that floor, less than a minute before the time that Hadfield's Braille watch was smashed in the fall."

"Timepieces occasionally fail to agree," remarked Maclain.

"Brilliant," said Davis. "Yet here's a neat alibi to try and break. The watchman is out, for he has an unshatterable record of his movements punched every five minutes from the time he started his rounds, working up from the ground floor."

"And Mrs. Hadfield?" asked Courtney.

"Interrupted O'Hare's rounds by ringing the doorbell. A minute or so after she entered—the door had been left unlatched—he started down from the fifth floor. O'Hare was down far enough in the elevator to have seen her if she'd come down the stairs by the elevator shaft. She, under separate questioning, is certain that the elevator pointer showed the car at the fifth floor."

"Of course, she might have seen the location of the car as she passed it on the stairs," Courtney objected. "Then there are two sets of fire stairs at the rear."

"If she'd used those," Davis pointed out quickly, "she couldn't have possibly known the location of the elevator. Now let me go further. In our own bungling fashion, we timed Mrs. Hadfield's trip from her apartment in the Village to the door of this building. Miss Sprague was in the apartment when Mrs. Hadfield left." Davis' fist smacked in his palm. "Mrs. Hadfield had no time to push Hadfield over a railing and neither did O'Hare. Do I need to say any more?"

Courtney shook his Apollo-like head and disposed of his cigar. "What about the boy?"

"He was asleep, or at least had his head down on Miss Sprague's desk last night as he claimed—that's a matter of fingerprints and of two strands of his hair. Archer found him last night roaming around in a daze. Heard him calling, 'Father, what's happened?' and pinched the kid as he came out of this office and started for the outside hall."

"Seth can read, I presume," remarked Maclain.

The Inspector demanded, "What are you hinting at now?"

"The note," said Maclain. "Would you kill your father and leave a note on his desk in his handwriting reading *I came down here with my son*? I'm assuming when Archer found the boy that these office lights were on."

"Certainly they were on," said Davis. "Do you think Hadfield wrote the note in the dark?"

"He did," said the Captain with a spiteful grin.

Davis said, "Oh, hell! Well, anyhow the lights were on."

"Which brings us to the loose change, the paperweight and the fountain pen."

"You've mentioned that before, Captain," said Courtney. "Is it something you don't want me in on?"

"It's something none of us are in on, Mr. Courtney. Davis, you might explain."

"That's queer as the devil," the lawyer said frowning when

Davis had told him the facts. "If I saw it, I could identify that pen. Blake had used it for years. It was red with a gold cap and the barrel had a double gold ring. I remember the paperweight, too. Maybe one of the cleaning women dropped it and broke the ball."

"Except that it wasn't here when we arrived," said Davis. "We searched O'Hare and the boy as a matter of routine and went through Mrs. Hadfield's handbag, although she doesn't know it."

The Captain sat silent, listening. For more than two hours he had followed the trail of the birdcage elevator up and down, traced O'Hare's methodical footsteps as they plotted a course on the seventh, eighth, and ninth floors. Gradually, he had translated the watchman's movements into a map of sound.

Courtney looked at his watch. "It's after nine. I think I'll get home and to bed. I'm not as young as I used to be, and I'm having a lot of pain from this arm. Are you coming?"

"If the Inspector doesn't mind," said Maclain, "I'd like him to stay awhile and show me around."

"Glad to," said Davis. He held Courtney's coat and walked to the elevator with him. When he returned, the Captain had the six highball glasses set out clockwise on the desk.

"That lawyer has a good memory," said Davis, eyeing the glasses. "I suppose you have some idea in messing those up with your fingers."

"I supposed you had some idea in leaving them here," the Captain told him blandly. "I'd like to ask a few questions now that we've out-sat everyone."

"I photoed and fingerprinted all of them last night," said Davis. "We got prints of Hadfield and the kid on the two that were used. That was all. I had them returned today thinking the kid or somebody might make off with one of them. It was just an idea."

"I've been listening to the watchman make his rounds. Tell me something, Davis." Maclain started lifting the glasses again, twirling each one slowly around. "Why, when he rides upstairs, does he stop the elevator only on every other floor?"

The Inspector grunted.

"God above, those ears!" he muttered. "I'll bet you could hear a man's pants falling down."

"That's a noisy process." The Captain gave a short laugh, and then frowned. "What about O'Hare?"

"We checked with him about what he did on the fifth floor. You've noticed, Maclain, that the balcony which runs around three sides of the lobby opens into a hall."

"Are there any keys to be punched in the hall?" asked Maclain.

"Two," said Davis. "One at each end, but there aren't any out on the balcony where you get off the elevator."

The Captain nodded and asked, "Are all the floors the same?"

"Practically," said Davis. "Except for the arrangement of desks and filing cabinets. You'll remember when this outfit was at its height, it employed eighteen hundred clerks or more."

"We were talking about the watchman," said Maclain, "and the fifth floor."

"He left the elevator on the fifth," Davis continued, "walked a little way around the balcony and went through the double doors into the hall. At the north end of the hall he punched his key, then went into the main office where all the desks are and punched two more stations. That covered half the fifth floor.

"Then he walked down the north fire stairs at the rear and punched all his stations on the fourth floor, but never went out onto the balcony at all. He went back up to the fifth by way of the south fire stairs, punched the rest of the stations and finished up with the key at the south end of the hall. He came out onto the balcony, crossed it, and took the elevator downstairs to answer Mrs. Hadfield's ring. Normally he'd have gone on up to the seventh floor."

"Sounds as if you were under oath," the Captain declared. "Still it's something I wanted to know. Whoever shoved Hadfield to his death knew that the watchman never crossed the eighth-floor balcony at any time, because he never crosses the balcony on any even-numbered floor."

The Inspector's jaws closed in a rigid line. "What about the highball glasses, Maclain? You've been massaging them for a hell of a time."

"One of them's different," said Duncan Maclain. "Listen."

He flicked them all with a fingernail and picked but one. "The set's been broken, Davis, and one of the glasses replaced."

"It looks like all the others to me." The Inspector tapped it with a pencil and then tried a couple of the others. "It sounds the same."

"It's as different," Maclain declared, "as notes on a musical chime."

"So what?" asked Davis shortly.

The Captain locked his hands behind his neck and leaned back in his chair.

"Larry," he said in a curious tone, "I've known you and worked with you on many cases, and for a long time. Go over there and sit down while I reconstruct a murder."

The Inspector crossed the office without a word and took a chair.

"Six years ago," said Duncan Maclain, "Blake Hadfield

and James Sprague met in this office. Someone knew it, and knew that Hadfield kept his gun in the drawer of the table by the washroom behind me. That man came in through the curtains in back of me after taking the gun from the drawer. He put the gun to Hadfield's head and pulled the trigger. Then he shot Sprague, his only witness, and rigged a murder and suicide which worked, Davis. It took Blake Hadfield six years to make certain of what happened."

"Why?" asked Davis.

"Because in six years a man's hearing grows more acute, if that man is blind. Last night, Hadfield heard his son open that drawer. Things that had been dark to him were suddenly clear and he put in that murder call. But his murderer was in this building last night, too."

Maclain hesitated and went on. "There's no need to keep your gun in your hand, Davis. I've been blind longer than Hadfield. I could hear the slightest footstep in the outside office, even in the hall."

The Inspector came to his feet like a rubber ball. "You're wrong, Maclain! You've got to be wrong!"

"I have to be right," said Maclain. "You have to crack that six-year-old case, Davis, or you'll crack yourself. What the hell's the matter with you?"

"You know as well as I do, Maclain." The Inspector's voice was harsh as shattered glass. "I've waked up in the middle of every policeman's nightmare and found it true. If the truth leaks out, people will start to die like flies, die from falling. Why the hell is that blind down? Why is that change and fountain pen missing? Why is that paperweight gone? You don't know and neither do I, but what you do know is that Hadfield was hurled off of the balcony on this floor, and that nobody in the building did it!" Davis's strong voice rose to a pitch on the point of breaking. "What the hell do you call that, Maclain?"

"Not what you do," said Duncan Maclain. "We have to break it, Davis. There's no such thing as a perfect crime."

3

There was unquestionably some truth in Seth's contention that it wasn't good for a girl to stare all day at an office where her father had committed suicide. Elise began to realize it as she sat at her desk on the fourth day of Seth's leave. Blake Hadfield, according to Phil Courtney, executor of the banker's estate, had left Julia independent and Seth Hadfield a wealthy young man, although Courtney hadn't committed himself on the extent of Hadfield's fortune.

Seth had pointed all this out to her two nights before over a dinner at a quiet Syrian restaurant in the Thirties where for a time they had dodged a couple of persistent newsmen still interested in the Hadfield show.

Of one thing Elise was certain. The irresponsible Seth had matured overnight, a quick violent change from boy to man. It showed in a dozen ways from the deepening of expression in his hazel eyes to the authoritative manner in which he addressed her and held her hand.

It had been difficult to put him off, much more difficult than two days before when her refusal to marry him immediately had terminated in his disastrous visit to his father. Then, there had been financial considerations, for part of Seth's army pay was going to help out Julia. Now, Blake Hadfield's death had smoothed out that important wrinkle. To offer resentment against a dead man as an excuse for not marrying Seth seemed weak and futile, yet the tragedy of six years before still hung over Elise, clouding her future with him in an unhappy pall.

Seth, of course, had taken it wrong.

"I can't blame you, darling. That Inspector's too damn friend-ly to be real. He's confident he'll have me back in jail before very long."

"Seth, you know that's not true. You didn't—"

"I'm beginning to wonder." His face was so forlorn Elise had wanted to cry. "It's easy to pin anything on a drunken fool. Maybe I walked in my sleep when I was sitting at your desk."

"And maybe you didn't," she told him defiantly. "Your father fell accidentally."

"I still could have saved him, if I hadn't been so far gone. I'll never wake up again, Elise, without hearing him scream."

Elise turned to Mr. Bentley's precise dictation and insert-ed a letterhead into her typewriter. Her fingers answered the guidance of her shorthand notes, but a vision of Seth was sitting across the desk from her, leaning forward, a shadowy interrupt-ing figure, his brown hand on her arm.

"You don't think it was an accident, Elise," he had kept say-ing. "And neither do I. You're afraid, darling, afraid because there was no one else in the building when Father screamed and fell, no one but the watchman, Mother and me. You're afraid, Elise, afraid of what people will say—and so am I."

Her fingers took up the cadence of his whispers and after a while the whispers crept into the clacking keys. Elise got up, went through the outside hall to the balcony and stood looking down, not conscious that her slim hands were clutching the top of the rail.

Wintry sun poured narrow yellow streamers through the cathedral windows over the massive doors which were never opened any more, even in the heat of summer. Only one of the outdated elevators was running. As Elise watched, it crept earthward creakingly, and finally succeeded in liberating a crowd of laughing, lunch-bound accountants onto the lobby floor.

She hadn't realized it was after twelve. Still she remained staring downward, held by a half-unrecognized hypsophobia and an interest in the puppet show eight stories below.

An officer was still on duty, guarding the empty stable. Nevertheless, Elise saw that he conscientiously checked each member of the staff against a list before opening the little panel leading out to Broadway. The police must be very certain that someone else had been in the building to keep a man on duty so long. She happened to know that another officer was posted in the basement day and night, guarding the fire door.

She returned to her desk to find that Mr. Bentley had gone out to lunch. With her letters finished, she sat for a time aimlessly pushing the space-bar while she speculated further about the patrolman on the door.

Why had they kept a guard so long? Mr. Hadfield had fallen on Monday night. This was Thursday. Did they think a murderer was trapped in the vast sepulcher of the M. T. & T., was lurking somewhere in its abandoned network of underground vaults right now?

That was idiotic, she knew, but the whole terrible affair was idiotic—trying to blame Seth for something he could never do. Just as idiotic as trying to blame her father for the failure of Sprague and Company, and for blinding Blake Hadfield. Jim Sprague had never harmed anyone in his life, yet the police . . .

Elise's small white teeth closed painfully on one carmine lip. She was Jim Sprague's daughter and twenty thousand policemen could still be wrong. Dash it all, she *knew!*

Mr. Bentley had put a six-inch pile of reports on her desk to be wrapped for delivery to the sacred precincts of some director's office farther downtown. Elise found brown wrapping paper, wound it skillfully about the reports and went into the Comptroller's office to get a ball of twine.

To Carl Bentley, twine, staples, postage stamps, pins and metal punches were assets ranked along with War Bonds, typewriter paper and ten-dollar bills. Mr. Bentley kept such valuables in the bottom left-hand drawer of his desk under constant supervision, never trusting them to the vagaries of a secretary who might use an unneeded staple or six unnecessary inches of precious twine.

Elise's mind was on other things, but the office habits of two years with Mr. Bentley were strong. She went through the deep desk drawer twice before deciding with certainty that the ball of twine was gone. It wasn't necessary to search the other drawers in Mr. Bentley's desk, although she did so. Carl Bentley kept everything in place except his glasses. If the ball of twine wasn't in the left-hand bottom drawer, its loose end held neatly in place with an encircling rubber band, a cataclysm had struck the office.

She went out and searched her own desk, just to make sure, since she had used the twine a few days before. Let's see, it was Monday. She'd wrapped reports for the State Insurance Department, but she'd put that ball back in Mr. Bentley's drawer. Well, she'd take a look in the desk of the Assistant Chief Auditor, Mr. Dickson. He was a nice fellow with brown eyes and an apologetic air, but he had little reverence for Mr. Bentley's assets, and might under pressure embezzle twine, even in a private ball.

Mr. Dickson's desk yielded nothing. Neither did the desks of four other members of the staff whom Elise considered worthy of suspicion. The last desk she searched was across the building from the Comptroller's office.

Elise had given it a thorough going-over and was about to return to her own desk, when farther down the room Carl Bentley stepped in from the hall. She saw with relief that his glasses weren't on, otherwise he'd have noticed the half-wrapped package on her desk and started his own string hunt. The resultant hubbub would have lasted well through the summer and into the fall. It could all be avoided if Elise slipped quietly out to lunch and bought another ball.

With her mind divided between Seth and Mr. Bentley, she glanced around the private office she had ducked into to avoid Mr. Bentley. There was a spot on the crimson carpet which marked a too thorough cleaning. Her breath came quicker as she stared, and her dark eyes filled with pain. Attacked by sudden faintness, she leaned against the wall.

"Dad," she whispered—"Daddy, darling!" But against the years it was little more than a feeble call.

Blake Hadfield had sat in that high-backed leather chair, and her father beside him. Blake Hadfield, scornful of any emotion, disdainful of personal weakness, a man who could build an empire of finance and casually watch it fall. Blake Hadfield who could save himself by sending thousands of poorer people to ruin, but who could not understand weakness in a friend.

"Blake will help me, Lissy. I'm going up to see him tonight. He's the best friend I have, and he knows damn well I wouldn't deliberately take my investors' money. Blake has plenty left, Lissy, and he's the best friend I have. He'll help. If he doesn't—"

The best friend Jim Sprague had . . . . She was twelve then, but she'd drunk it in as kids of that age do. The best friend her father had—like her own whisper of a moment before, it had been a feeble call.

"If he doesn't—" Her father had never finished that sentence, but the world had heard the answer. There before her, with Blake Hadfield laughing his mirthless laugh at Jim Sprague's plea for help to keep him out of jail, the answer had belched from Hadfield's own revolver, struck every pressroom in the country with the double report of the gun.

Yet how could her father have done it? Mesmerized with misery, she tried to picture his actions. Her father was a simple lovable man with rare quick flashes of temper that were gone like a passing storm to leave the sun of his smile. It wasn't like him to hold his anger long or to plot and plan. Yet he must have plotted and planned to take Blake Hadfield's gun from a drawer outside and reach it in through those shielding curtains, to stretch out an arm behind his best friend and pull a trigger.

That wasn't Jim Sprague, her father. But the police had claimed that he got the gun before, brought it with him when he came into the room. "If he doesn't—"

Her black eyes widened slowly. As though her thoughts had conjured to life some evil invisible genii, the curtains behind the chair had moved and partly opened, yet no one had come through the door.

"Who is it?" she forced herself to whisper. Then, looking

beneath the desk, she saw that the solemn dark eyes of a dog were watching her closely. Following the dog's intelligent head, a man stepped into the office.

"Captain Maclain!" It was difficult for her to speak, relief had engulfed her so swiftly. "You frightened me terribly!"

"I'm sorry, Miss Sprague. Am I intruding?"

"Oh, no," she answered quickly. She didn't want him to know how frightful her thoughts had been; no one must ever know. "I came in here looking for something."

"Yes?" he said.

She had to make a move, for lingering terror still held her and the single word of his question had not helped.

"I was hunting for some string." She stepped around Blake Hadfield's desk, and under Schnucke's questioning gaze pulled open the left-hand bottom drawer.

"Did you find it, Miss Sprague?" asked Duncan Maclain.

"Yes," she said. "I found it." The rubber band holding the end in place marked it indelibly for her. It couldn't be so, but she knew it was, just as she knew so many other things were true. The heavy brown twine in the drawer of Hadfield's desk was without a doubt the missing ball from Mr. Bentley's office.

4

Elise watched with interest as the Captain seated himself at Blake Hadfield's desk. Schnucke, after selecting a place that suited her, finally settled down with a satisfied swish of her tail.

"If you'll excuse me, Captain," Elise said with the punctilious slowness of one in a hurry to get away, "I think I'll run along. I haven't had my lunch yet."

"Certainly, Miss Sprague," said Maclain, but he checked her with an uplifted hand. "I'd rather you didn't go out of here carrying that ball of twine."

"The twine?" Elise turned her gaze from the Captain to stare at the ball in her hand. "It belongs in Mr. Bentley's office."

Maclain said, "Oh!" But his expressive face asked a question.

"I've been looking all over the office for it," Elise explained. "Somebody must have taken it from Mr. Bentley's desk drawer."

"What made you think you might find it in here?"

Elise flushed, feeling guilty over nothing at all. "I didn't, Captain Maclain. As a matter of fact—Well, to tell the truth, I ducked in here to dodge Mr. Bentley as he came back from lunch. He makes such a fuss over little things."

"Such as a ball of twine?"

"Yes, or a postage stamp, for that matter. I intended to slip out to lunch and buy another ball."

The Captain located a bronze paper cutter on the desk and began to bend it back and forth between his fingers.

"I want you to understand something, Miss Sprague. I have one idea in mind and that is to help Seth Hadfield."

"I believe that, Captain Maclain."

"Then please don't take offense at my questions. You've impressed me as a quick intelligent young woman. You probably realize that I'm not much influenced by external beauty."

"Thank you," Elise said vaguely, finding it difficult to follow the Captain's trend. He was obviously interested in the ball of twine, for some remote reason she couldn't quite fathom. Beyond that, she had a feeling that he was adroitly conveying a warning; either that, or he was cleverly pinning her down.

"You say you didn't expect to find that twine in here?"

"I had no idea it would be in this office."

"What caused you to look in the drawer?"

"You did—and your dog. I was watching the curtains and Schnucke—that's what you call her, isn't it?"

Maclain nodded and Schnucke's alert ears pricked up.

"Well, she moved the curtains. I couldn't see anyone and it startled me. Then you came in and I got confused, I guess. Anyhow, I opened the drawer and there was the twine."

The paper cutter made an arc between the Captain's fingers. "One ball of twine looks much like another, Miss Sprague. Have you any reason for thinking this is the same ball that was in Mr. Bentley's drawer?"

She nodded, and flushed again, remembering he couldn't see. "Mr. Bentley has a habit of fastening the loose end of string by putting a rubber band around the ball."

"Would you mind?" Maclain put the paper cutter down and stretched out one hand.

Elise handed him the ball.

He put it on the desk, took out a flat gold cigarrette case and offered her one. Elise gave him a light, lit her own and moved a heavy floor ash stand close to the Captain's chair. After a few thoughtful puffs he settled his cigarette accurately in the small niche on the circular edge of the stand. Only the briefest hesitating search of his hand indicated that he had followed the ash stand's location by sound when Elise placed it beside him.

Once more he picked up the twine. While Elise smoked and watched, he rolled it around slowly, fingering it for weight and texture. Finally he pulled the free end loose from the rubber band and stripped a small length off the ball.

It was heavy brown twine. Elise had her first real inkling of the Captain's tremendous flowing strength when she saw him stretch a piece taut between his two hands and snap it like a piece of thread with a smooth steady pull.

"Quite strong," remarked Maclain.

Elise exhaled softly and said, "I'll say you are!"

The Captain's expressive eyebrows moved in a delighted wriggle. He readjusted the rubber band, tucked the broken length in his pocket and returned the ball to the lower left-hand drawer.

"Let's leave it there, young lady," he said lightly, picking up his cigarette again. "We seem to be full of compliments for each other today. My car and chauffeur are waiting outside. Suppose we lunch together, too."

"I'd love it," Elise declared. "But I'm supposed to be out now. Mr. Bentley—"

"I think I can manage Mr. Bentley," said Maclain. "As a matter of fact I've been thinking of asking him to spare you for the afternoon. Seth's leave is growing shorter." He hesitated. "It's not entirely Seth, either. I have a job I'd like you to do."

"There's nothing I'd like better, Captain, if you can square it with Mr. Bentley." Elise's dark eyes watched him speculatively. "Why didn't you want me to take that twine out of here, Captain Maclain?"

He dropped his cigarette into the ash stand. "Suppose I said it might be dangerous for you. Would that frighten you?"

"A little," she admitted, "but I wouldn't understand."

"Neither do I, nor the police," said Duncan Maclain. "I'm afraid of only one type of thing, Elise—that's a thing that I don't understand. When a murder has been committed, small things connected with it become dangerous. The nerves of a killer after his crimes are painful sensitive strings. You, or I, might pluck one and cause him to strike again if we were seen with a clue. Anything missing from this room, and anything in this room which shouldn't be here, is a clue. Two murders have left their mark on this office, Elise."

"Two?" Her slender throat was tight with a kind of pain. "Who, Captain Maclain?"

"Blake Hadfield and your father," said Duncan Maclain.

"In six years, Captain, that's the first kind thing that's been said about my father, the first statement that was true."

"Then you've believed all along that your father was killed?"

"I haven't just believed, Captain. I knew."

"Blake Hadfield learned it Monday night." The Captain made a tent of his fingers.

"You have proof of that?" Elise asked eagerly.

"No," Maclain told her sadly. "That's the task I've set myself."

"Let me help, Captain Maclain." She went to the desk and sat on its edge close beside him. "I haven't been living since Dad died. It's stood in my way like a shadow, ruining everything I've wanted to do—my marriage to Seth—everything."

He turned his head with illusory slowness, giving Elise a startling feeling that he was actually looking about the office, visually drinking in its furnishings and contour.

"So much can happen in six years' time, Elise. It's so far back to begin. If the police were fooled then, what can we hope to do now?" His lean jaw tightened, deepening the cleft of his chin. "It takes proof to convict a man of murder; airtight evidence of guilt, Elise, to make a Grand Jury bring a true bill in."

"I know my father never did the things that were charged against him."

"That's faith, Elise, not proof. If your father was murdered in this office and Blake Hadfield was murdered in this building

Monday night, one man did the killing." The Captain's hands locked tight together. "In one way, I hope it isn't true."

"I hope it is," Elise said firmly.

"You don't know what you're saying," said Duncan Maclain. "I've dealt with many crimes, before my blindness and since. If a murderer is at large, clever enough to have killed your father, blinded Hadfield and then struck at him again successfully, that murderer is so clever that the safety of a city might collapse before he's through. He's left no evidence, Elise, just traces. Traces can only make us think he exists, but they'll never help us prove it."

"You said you had a job for me." She slid off the desk and stood gently touching his arm. "I've a right to try to help clear my father whatever happens. What do you want me to do?"

His fingers sought a lock of his crisp dark hair and twisted it pensively for a second or two. He pointed in the direction of the small buffet.

"Are there six glasses on there in a silver rack?"

"Yes," she told him wonderingly.

"If someone broke one of them would Mr. Bentley be upset?"

"Would he!" Elise left the answer to the Captain's vivid imagination.

"Who would replace it?" asked Maclain. "Would the task fall on you?"

"Perhaps. It's hard to say what Mr. Bentley will do. He feels responsible for everything."

"Bring the glasses over here, please, Elise."

She set them down on the desk before him. Swiftly he picked them up one at a time, weighing and gently tapping each one. He picked up the first one a second time and suddenly it slipped, struck the edge of the desk top and bounced to the carpet's edge to shatter on the floor.

Elise stood silent staring at the pieces. She was almost certain he had let the glass fall deliberately.

"Pick up the pieces carefully," said Maclain with a smile. "I want you to try to replace it—exactly, if you can—with the initials B. H. blown in the side and all. Keep on trying, every place in the city, but get it exact and take nothing until you're positive you've matched it as closely as possible."

"That's what you wanted me to do?" Her heavy lids were half-lowered.

"Yes," said Maclain. "After you have lunch with me you can start. I'll tell Mr. Bentley I broke it and that I want you to match it."

"And when I find the right match, what then?"

"Keep constantly in touch with me while you're searching," Maclain told her gravely. "I can't impress that on you strongly enough. I don't know where the search will lead, but the answer may clear your father. Be cautious, Elise—I don't want his and Hadfield's fate to overtake you."

CHAPTER IV

1

"You know, Elise," Captain Maclain said over their coffee in the Biltmore dining room, "I may be sending you on the champion wild-goose chase of the world."

"I'll take a chance on that." Elise sipped her cordial and leaned back in her chair.

"It's a bigger chance than you think—about a million to one that it will do any good. Even if you find out where that highball glass came from."

"I don't quite see why you want to know," Elise admitted.

Duncan Maclain tasted his coffee and added a little more cream. She had been a shade ill-at-ease when they first sat down, wondering if she should offer to cut his meat, or just what attentions etiquette prescribed. Her feeling of awkwardness had passed after a minute of watching his perfect assurance. Calling the waiter by name, he had ordered French lamb chops, creamed potatoes and green peas.

"The chops are on the right of your plate, Captain Maclain, the potatoes on the left. The peas are in a smaller dish to the left of the plate." The waiter had whispered instructions discreetly.

Maclain nodded and took over on his own. Ten minutes later, Elise had forgotten entirely that her host was blind.

"A new glass was bought for that set in the office," the Captain told her. "First, I want to find out if it was bought before or after your father's death. If it was bought before—well, I've wasted some of your time. If it was bought after your father died—" The Captain's ever-working fingers caressed a heavy goblet, tracing the Biltmore's initial cut in the side of the glass.

"Then what?"

"I want to know when, by whom, and why?"

"I think it might help, Captain Maclain, if I knew a little more of what I'm trying to do."

"So do I, Elise," Maclain agreed. "Unfortunately, I've already told you all I know. Suppose you find that glass was replaced in that set after your father's death. Would it seem strange to you?"

"I don't believe so," Elise said honestly.

"Well, it would to me. Blake Hadfield had been out of the M. T. & T. for several years on the night he met your father in that office. They had a drink together, just as Seth and his father had last Monday night. The police files show that two used glasses were found—one with Hadfield's fingerprints on it, the other with your father's. Police pictures were taken of the office, but they reveal only five glasses; one on the desk by Hadfield, another on the directors' table, and three in the silver rack on the buffet."

"But they're all there now," Elise protested, "except the one you broke."

"That's it, exactly," he agreed with the smile that fascinated her so. "The M. T. & T. was closed up. Mr. Hadfield wasn't using his office at all. Even the meticulous Mr. Bentley wasn't there at that time. Who had such an interest in Blake Hadfield's possessions, Elise, that he'd have another glass made to match a broken set? Surely not Mr. Hadfield, who had lost his sight. Surely not Dan O'Hare, the watchman, who appears to be the only employee still working in the building who was there at that time."

"And you think I can help clear my father by finding out?" Elise asked with a tiny frown.

"Perhaps," said Duncan Maclain, "but don't pin too much hope on it." His face was blank as though his thoughts had dropped back through time. "Suppose a third man had been there that night six years ago, a man who had a drink with your father and Hadfield. He might have—"

"He would have," Elise blurted out. "If he'd shot my father and Mr. Hadfield and was pressed for time when he left, he'd have taken the glass with his fingerprints on it along."

"Then why didn't he wash his fingerprints off and quietly return it?" the Captain asked softly. "Why did he have another glass made?"

"Maybe he'd thrown away the glass he took," she suggested.

The Captain shook his head. "If we're dealing with a man, Elise, and not a lot of hopeful ideas, I find it most difficult to follow the working of his brain. Let's say it is a man. If he's clever enough to do what he's done, he would never discard a glass he intended to return. I greatly fear that some fine day that highball glass with B. H. on it will show up unexpectedly again."

"But why, Captain?"

"Death," said Duncan Maclain, "will be following in its train."

The Captain's car dropped Elise in front of Covington's plate-glass windows shortly after three. She watched it merge into the crawling traffic of Fifth Avenue, then braved the cold long enough to stare at the expensive assortment of novelties on display to passers-by, and mentally picked out a few wedding gifts that would be an addition to any house.

Covington's was a starting-point resulting from a telephone call to Julia, who had told her that the famous gift shop in the past had furnished many things for Blake Hadfield's Park Avenue apartment.

Elise's conversation with the Captain had unconsciously keyed her up to an intensity of purpose scarcely in keeping with the simplicity of her errand. When she pushed her way through the revolving door, the scintillating brightness of Covington's shelves, stocked with glass, china and chrome, struck a chord of businesslike order that immediately let her down. She smiled at the frock-coated, gray-stocked Adonis on guard at the portal and said, "I'd like to match a glass that was broken."

"Miss Arbuckle will be glad to assist you, madam. The glassware is at the rear of the second floor."

He gave her such a look of sheer pleasure that Elise expected him to double up in a bow. She took the elevator wondering what type of greeting Covington's gave you if you dropped in and announced you wanted to furnish a home.

Miss Arbuckle, who had somehow managed to get a forty-two figure into a thirty-eight black silk and still make it look as though it fitted, was interested but skeptical. She spread the broken pieces out on a square of paper and examined a couple in the hollow of her pinkish palm.

"Did you purchase this here recently, madam?"

"The truth is," Elise told her frankly, "I don't know if it was bought here at all."

Some of Miss Arbuckle's maternal fondness for the broken tumbler was dissipated at Elise's statement. She restored the two pieces of shattered crystal to their fellow companions and used a tiny handkerchief to wipe her palm.

"Normally we can match anything, madam—have it blown, you know; but since the war—"

"I'd like to have one made," Elise insisted, "if you can guarantee it would be exactly the same. This set belonged to Mr. Hadfield. That's the reason I came here. He bought most of his glassware in this store."

"I'd better call Mr. Zinke, madam. Mr. Zinke handles most of our larger accounts. He will probably remember Mr. Hadfield. If you wished to get a new set—"

"I'd like to replace this broken glass—exactly. If you'll be kind enough to call Mr. Zinke . . . "

"Certainly, madam." Miss Arbuckle disappeared, after tugging her girdle into place.

Elise found a chrome-pipe chair and sat down. A tremendous mirror walled two sides of the second floor, reflecting a shattered glacier of glass and silver. Far across the floor a small, unobtrusive man was busy talking to another clerk. Elise regarded his reflection with a frown. He didn't look like the type who might be interested in glassware, and she was positive she had seen his unimpressive figure somewhere before during the afternoon.

She forgot him in the arrival of Mr. Zinke, who spoke with an accent and whose long frockcoat made him look lugubrious and frightfully tall.

"I remember Misder Hadfield quide well," Mr. Zinke announced with a funereal scowl. "He is dead, no? Terrible, terrible. Such a nize man to be killed by a fall!"

"Yes," Elise said timidly. "Do you know, by any chance, if Mr. Hadfield bought these glasses here?"

"Certainly, madam." Mr. Zinke deepened his scowl. "I consulded his account before coming oudt. Terrible, terrible."

"He did get them here?" Elise tried to suppress too much eagerness. She took it for granted that Mr. Zinke's second pair of "terribles" still referred to Mr. Hadfield's fall.

"Certainly, madam. Budt we cannot replace them. Mr. Hadfield tried to haf one replaced several years ago. We couldn't replace it then, we cannot replace it now. Those glasses were made in Slovakia, and the pattern was discontinued."

"You say Mr. Hadfield tried to replace one?"

"Yes, madam."

"When was that, exactly, if you happen to remember?" Elise swallowed with an effort. It was too much to expect success on her very first call.

"In nineteen thirty-six, madam." Mr. Zinke regarded her with growing dislike. "I just consuldted Mr. Hadfield's card. We note every such call. We referred Mr. Hadfield to a place uptown which specializes in such work—imitadting originals."

"Could you give me the name?"

"Certainly, madam. It is the Richelieu Novelty and Decorating Company at Fifty-fourth and Madison Avenue. The lady to consuldt is the owner and manager—a Miss Sybella Ford. Will that be all?"

2

The law offices of Courtney, Garfield and Steele occupied the entire seventh floor of the modern Lawyers' Building which sticks its shapely tower skyward from the edge of Battery Park.

Phil Courtney had dismissed his late-working secretary and was engaged in a last look out of the window at the nine o'clock Staten Island ferry putting out from the dock when he realized that he wasn't alone. He swung around with badly-concealed irritation to face a rolypoly round-faced little man who had insinuated himself into the private office and closed the door.

"What do you want?" Courtney asked abruptly. "I left orders I wasn't to be disturbed."

"Too bad, Mr. Courtney. I do that myself all the time, and never have any success. I fear all your staff has gone home."

"I'm going, too."

"Certainly, Mr. Courtney." The visitor placed a card on the desk, stared at the attorney for an instant out of swimming black eyes, and let his dark round face dissolve into a melting butterball smile. "I just got back from Chicago and learned that Blake Hadfield was dead. I felt it necessary to get in immediate touch with you."

Philip Courtney digested the business card:—

T. ALLEN DOXENBY
ATTORNEY AT LAW
164½ WEST 42ND ST.

There were better addresses in New York, and Mr. Doxenby from the tips of his two-toned shoes to the crown of his snap-brim hat was a shade too well dressed to be quite savory, a trifle too smooth to ring quite true. Courtney typed him as "ambulance chaser," but one who might prove troublesome.

"I'm rather tired, Mr. Doxenby. Tell me what I can do for you."

"Certainly, Mr. Courtney." Doxenby placed his snap-brim on the desk. He removed his pleated black overcoat, folded it with affection so that the heavy satin lining was outward, stroked its velvet collar, and hung it tenderly over the back of a chair. He seated himself with beautiful leisure.

"We're both of us lawyers, Mr. Courtney—both of us in the same racket, so to speak. Brothers in crime."

"Let's get to the point, Doxenby, or whatever your name is." Phil Courtney sat down at the desk, favoring his injured arm. "I don't consider the law a racket, and I don't particularly want to claim you as a brother—either in or out of crime."

"No need of getting ratty, Mr. Courtney. No offense, understand. Just my little way of making a joke, a means of passing the time. I agree with you entirely—a serious business, the law. You must know. You're handling Blake Hadfield's estate."

"Yes," said Courtney, "so I am."

"Fine." Mr. Doxenby washed his pudgy hands in gratification. "Glad to confirm it, Mr. Courtney. Glad to find my client's affairs are in the hands of so capable a man."

"Blake Hadfield never retained you in his life," Courtney broke in, cutting at Doxenby with his sharpest tone.

"Quite right, Mr. Courtney. He never did. Great misfortune for Mr. Hadfield. I tried to point it out to him. Wonderful businessman, Mr. Hadfield. Too bad he was blind. That's where you come in."

"This is where you go out, Mr. Doxenby!"

"Now, wait a minute. Don't get ratty. Bad for a lawyer to get ratty." Mr. Doxenby hitched forward and lit up his buttery smile. "Nice fee you make handling the Hadfield estate,

Mr. Courtney. If you let me help you, there'd be plenty to go around—you, Garfield, Steele, and Doxenby. Not that I'd want my name on the door. I have plenty of practice on my own—like to handle things myself. But taking me in with you on administering Hadfield's estate would really be worth your while."

Courtney leaned back languorously and stared at the little shyster with a frown. Doxenby was sharp, probably crooked, but he certainly wasn't a fool. He had said just enough to convince Phil Courtney that he had to be made to say more.

"You're bordering dangerously close to blackmail, Doxenby." Courtney's lids dropped half over his dark brown eyes. "Do you really want to go on?"

"*Tsk, tsk*, Mr. Courtney!" Doxenby's rotund belly shook with inward laughter. "That nasty word coming from you! I'm astounded, Mr. Courtney. Blackmail? *Tsk, tsk!* I forgot myself and used it again. But, let us say, any attempt on my part to force myself in on Hadfield's estate would be predicated on the fact that you have something worrying you. Is that true, Mr. Courtney? You couldn't possibly be concerned about a loan you made to Blake Hadfield many years ago, could you? A loan that was never repaid?"

"No, I couldn't," said Courtney frankly. "I don't know where the hell you heard about that, for it was a private matter. But I'm not concerned about it, or anything else." He pushed back his chair. "You've an infernal nerve—"

"A private matter of fifty thousand dollars." Mr. Doxenby shook his round head in sorrow. "Did you ever find out what Mr. Hadfield did with that money, Mr. Courtney?"

"No." Phil Courtney's face was carved in disinterest, except for a tinge of darkening red that touched his greying temples. "Hadfield and I were friends."

"Ah, even more!" Mr. Doxenby declared with enthusiasm. "There is something touching in a relationship that just lets a loan of fifty thousand dollars quietly rock along."

"I still don't see that it's any of your damn business," said Courtney with a sudden flash. "But that's what I did. In the first place, it was a fee I waived, and not a loan. So I just let it rock along—and now it's gone."

"But not forgotten." A dimple showed in Doxenby's plushy chin. "The law, Mr. Courtney, as you so well understand, is such a delicate thing. When is a loan not a loan? Who actually owes the money if a borrower, instead of keeping it, happens to pass it along?" Mr. Doxenby spread his arms, imitating a scale. "Such a delicate thing, Mr. Courtney—this way and that way. What would a jury decide, if they heard that the money you loaned Blake Hadfield had been passed along?" Mr. Doxenby hastened to cover himself. "Assuming, of course, that they considered deliberate waiver of a fee until some future date as a loan. Do you follow me?"

"No," said Courtney. "I'm not in the habit of inquiring what my friends intend to do with their money. Blake Hadfield was momentarily pressed—I waived a fee."

"Admirable," said Doxenby. "Mr. Hadfield was so hard-pressed that he added another fifty thousand to the fee you waived and invested the whole amount—half for himself and half for you."

"Suppose he did?" Courtney inquired.

"It was a most unfortunate investment, Mr. Courtney. I happen to represent a couple of investors who lost money in that bankrupt, looted firm."

"Thousands of people lost money in the M. T. & T." Courtney's right hand gently stroked his injured arm.

"Of course, of course," Mr. Doxenby agreed with maddening blandness. "Except that I'm not referring to the M. T. & T. I'm speaking of another firm."

"What firm?"

"James Sprague and Company." The syllables rolled unctuously from Doxenby's heavy lips. "Whether you know it or not, Mr. Courtney, Blake Hadfield invested fifty thousand dollars of your money in James Sprague and Company which still has some unpaid liabilities of over a million dollars."

"What are you driving at?" Phil Courtney asked the question steadily, but the pallor of his face was revealing.

"It means, as you also well know, Mr. Courtney, that you're a silent partner in that bankrupt brokerage house—and a silent partner, like any other partner, is personally responsible for all the liabilities of a partnership firm."

"To put it baldly," said Courtney, "you're hinting that I can be financially ruined if it can be proved that Blake Hadfield invested my money in Sprague's firm."

"Ah!" Doxenby exclaimed. "It's a pleasure to do business with so intelligent a man."

"A mutual gratification." Courtney's quiet speech was dangerous. "Apparently, since I'm quite ignorant, Blake Hadfield was the only one living who knew about this flyer he took with my money—except you, of course. Isn't it going to be difficult to prove these contentions now that Mr. Hadfield is gone?"

"Oh, come, come, Mr. Courtney! The books of Sprague and Company have been impounded by the State Insurance Department. They are there on call. A court investigation would no doubt be able to trace the source of the one hundred thousand dollars loaned to Sprague by Hadfield."

Courtney laughed. "Doxenby, you're not only a black-mailing crook, you're a fool! You've just admitted those books don't even show that Hadfield paid that money in. Well, Hadfield's gone, and Sprague is gone. Now you're going!" Courtney rose so violently that Doxenby drew back in his chair.

"Is that a threat, Mr. Courtney? I don't like threats."

"And I never threaten," said Courtney. "You can do anything you damn well please. Drag out all the impounded books you want to, and raise any kind of a squall. But get the hell out of this office, you little chiseler, or I'll throw you out!"

Doxenby stood up, unfolded his coat, stroked its collar, and put it on. "It's a pity you hurt your arm, Mr. Courtney. I heard that you might have saved Mr. Hadfield if you, yourself, hadn't had a fall."

"Get out," said Courtney, "or I'll run you out, arm and all."

"Think it over," said Doxenby. "You'll decide it's cheaper to have a good man helping you as administrator. You can never tell which way a jury will fall."

He slid out through the door.

Philip Courtney waited briefly, then eased clumsily into his own coat and took his hat from the clothes tree. Before leaving, he unlocked his desk and locked it again. A .32 Smith and Wesson was resting in his silken sling when he followed T. Allen Doxenby into the hall.

3

T. Allen Doxenby was in a genial mood as he left the Lawyers' Building. He headed for the nearest Eighth Avenue subway entrance and caught an express uptown. Mr. Doxenby liked the better things of life, and business hadn't been so hot since the war.

It was nice to drop in on a big-shot firm like Courtney, Garfield and Steele and catch the senior partner with his pin stripes in a lowered position—neat and profitable. Mr. Doxenby smiled at a young lady of doubtful occupation across the aisle and got an inky brush-off in return. Well, even the cleverest lawyers couldn't be right all the time, and Doxenby measured by the evening's work was about the cleverest of them all.

Courtney would pay. A guy would be nuts to take a chance on saving a few bucks and losing it all. He'd been plenty sore, yes. Mr. Doxenby didn't blame him for that, but any guy who'd lose track of fifty grand had it coming to him. What did he mean, lose track of it? Phil Courtney knew damn well what Hadfield had done with that dough. If he didn't, he'd have claimed it long before now.

Mr. Doxenby felt in a mood for celebration. He left the train at Fiftieth Street and walked back down Eighth Avenue to Forty-eighth, where he turned west.

The desk clerk at the Printemps Hotel gave him a grin of welcome. "Maybe she's in. Maybe she's out. How would I know?"

"You wouldn't," Mr. Doxenby admitted blithely, "unless you rang her on the phone."

"She's out," said the clerk, disconnecting. "What a blow!"

"Not for me." Mr. Doxenby set his snap-brim at a slightly better angle. "If one's not in, there's always another for Doxy."

"Is that a message?" the clerk inquired.

Mr. Doxenby laid a dollar on the desk and said, "Hell, no!"

"I'll tell her when you heard she was out you started to cry."

"Don't lay it on too thick," Mr. Doxenby advised, turning legal. "You can't sometimes tell what a dame will do. I've handled too many breach cases in my time."

"Breach of what?" the clerk demanded.

"Just breach," Mr. Doxenby told him with a fillip of his hand. "By-by!"

He turned at the door and came back.

"What gives now?" The desk clerk hastily pocketed the dollar.

"I decided to leave a note." Mr. Doxenby took a sheet of hotel paper from a rack on the desk and wrote:

BRIGHT EYES:—
Give papa a buzz if you hear anything new. Things are moving fast.

He left it unsigned, but put it in an envelope and addressed it to Miss Sophie Munson in his angular hand. The clerk straightened up from leaning across the desk.

"Is what I wrote okay?" Mr. Doxenby asked.

"Sure." The clerk winked, and put the envelope in box 311. "Quick and to the point, and not too long."

"Thanks," said Doxenby. "Drop into the office sometime and I'll retain you. Ta-ta!"

He walked briskly back to Eighth Avenue, and across from the Garden dropped into a famous restaurant and grill. A glance inside had revealed the familiar streamlined contour of a shapely feminine back decorating a stool at the bar.

"Hello, Bright Eyes," Mr. Doxenby greeted her cheerily. "How's your mother? Now don't tell me you never had one." He opened his overcoat and took a stool beside her.

"Well, well, the great Mouthpiece himself!" Sophie Munson pushed back a few inches and indicated the man on her left. "Do you know Mr. Bentley, Doxy?"

"Carl Bentley? Why, sure. We've met a couple of times before." Mr. Doxenby bridged Miss Munson's censor-challenging bosom with an extended arm. "How are you, Bentley?"

"Quite well, thank you." Mr. Bentley shook hands cautiously, peering at Mr. Doxenby with an air of perplexity. "You say we've met before?"

"A couple of times—or maybe we've just bumped into each other in the State Insurance Department's office downtown. Anyhow, I know who you are, but I didn't know you hung out in this part of town. What are you drinking?"

"I'll have a Scotch-and-soda," said Bentley. He removed his glasses and cleaned them with a paper napkin.

"Same for me," said Sophie fixing Mr. Doxenby with a pair of extremely large and melting blue eyes. "Carl and I lunch in the same place, near the building where I work downtown."

Mr. Doxenby fought an attack of coughing as he placed the order. "That's nice," he said when the drinks were in front of them. "I have a frightful memory. I can't even think where you work."

"In the Lawyers' Building, darling," Miss Munson told him spitefully.

"Certainly." A storm cloud moved swiftly across Mr. Doxenby's ingratiating countenance and was as swiftly gone. "It was silly of me to ask." He gulped the balance of his drink and became hearty. "Well, toodle-oo folks. I didn't come in to break up a party. Glad to have seen you, Bentley. Don't take any necklaces, Bright Eyes—remember Pearl Harbor! I have to run along."

Mr. Bentley watched his departure and remarked to his

companion: "I can't tell half the people I meet. In fact, I can't see much of anything without my glasses on."

"You haven't missed much," said Sophie. "You were telling me about that trouble down at your bank. Go on."

Mr. Doxenby crossed Eighth Avenue and caught a bus which finally managed to buck its way through tight-packed traffic to the easternmost side of town. Reflecting on women, as the bus nosed along, he decided that they all blabbed too much and hadn't a grain of sense anyhow.

"'In the Lawyers' Building, darling,'" he mimicked under his breath. Suppose that sap Bentley remembered that crack and started looking for her there someday. You couldn't tell about accountants. They looked like an awful bunch of dopes to T. Allen Doxenby, but they'd furnished him with a lot of clients consisting of smart guys who thought they had discovered a new system of getting away with the boss's dough.

He got out at First Avenue with a mental note to tone down little Bright Eyes the next time they met. The Lawyers' Building indeed! He was a nitwit for telling such a giddyhead anything. The only place she'd ever worked was the little town of Innerspring.

Mr. Doxenby's earlier elation had become diluted. He bolstered it up with a couple of quick ones in a bar, meanwhile appraising a pair of legs hanging on exhibition from a near-by stool. The legs were good, but a look at the exhibitor's face sent him hurriedly out into the cold again.

At Fifty-third Street, he entered a new apartment building, punched the button of the automatic elevator, and left it at the top floor. His mind was on another young lady, not quite as smart as Sophie, but passable. It was twenty minutes to eleven, but on occasion he had phoned her later than that and found her in.

Mr. Doxenby clucked with annoyance to find a visitor waiting for him in the hall outside of his apartment door.

Abe Stutmeyer, janitor of the apartment house where Mr. Doxenby made his home, stirred uneasily in his warm bed and finally nudged his wife's broad back. Basement apartments weren't all they were cracked up to be. Abe had to be up at five to do things with ashes, and the misnomered air-shafts around his apartment admitted very little air, but plenty of unwelcome sound.

"What is it now?" Mrs. Stutmeyer asked sleepily.

"Those Cooneys are at it again. What should I do?"

"You should go to sleep with fingers in your ears," said Mrs. Stutmeyer.

"I should have a disposition like a cow." Mr. Stutmeyer stuck his underweared legs out from under the heavy quilts and moved his tired feet gingerly around on the icy floor. His toes ceased their journeyings at a pair of slippers which Mr. Stutmeyer estimated as three degrees colder than the floor.

He sat up on the edge of the bed, bent over creakingly and put the slippers on. Mrs. Stutmeyer had gone to another dreamland accompanied by a mighty snore. Mr. Stutmeyer muttered something into the darkness as he put his trousers on, and immediately felt better.

A flaring match served to light his pipe and show him that the hour was eleven forty-five—not late, Mr. Stutmeyer knew, as New York parties go. Very late for a janitor with early morning chores to do.

Mr. Stutmeyer went into the bathroom and raised the small window. It opened onto a narrow shaft. The sounds of the Cooneys' party, doubly loud, came pouring down.

Mr. Stutmeyer stuck out his head, looked upward angrily, and waiting for a lull shouted: "Hey, Mr. Cooney! Please pipe down!"

A window raised somewhere above him and a woman's voice called: "Sorry, Mr. Stutmeyer. We'll be more quiet." The upstairs window closed.

Mr. Stutmeyer withdrew his head just in time to escape a bottle that came whistling down. It crashed at the bottom of the shaft, filling the air with flying glass and a heady smell of wasted Scotch.

"Holy Moses!" said Mr. Stutmeyer. "They're raising hell sure enough when they take to throwing bottles full of whisky down!"

4

"Apparently this search for a missing highball glass has led me nowhere," said Duncan Maclain.

"You are unquestionably one of the most complimentary men it's ever been my misfortune to meet." Sybella Ford glanced at his well-knit figure relaxed in her most comfortable chair. He might have been smiling, or the quirk to his lips might have been caused by the play of firelight on his nose and chin.

"Why?" he asked.

"You ask to talk to me about a glass I ordered for Blake Hadfield six years ago. What do I do? I invite you to dinner. I bury myself in my kitchen producing savory concoctions *à la Sybella.* I produce my rarest wines. I even have a steak for your dog."

"Who goes to sleep in a ball in front of your fire. Shameless creature. That's right, Sybella, rub it in."

"At least she doesn't tell me that her search has led her nowhere."

"I was speaking professionally," the Captain protested.

"Do you ever speak any other way?" Her brown eyes, crinkled from much smiling, were unusually grave.

"I try not to." His lips had set into squareness again. "Why should I begin?"

She went into the small dining room glittering with cutglass and antique silverware and returned with a bottle of green chartreuse.

"Drink this." Sybella put a tiny cordial glass in his outstretched hand. He sipped it with a nod of appreciation. The four-room apartment over the Richelieu Shop was silent except for the swish of tires on Madison Avenue, one floor below. "If I answered your question, Duncan Maclain, you'd never come back again."

"I might not come back unless you answered it."

"So what's the difference? Either way you're gone, as you'd be gone from any woman. Are you happy in your marriage, Captain Maclain?"

"I've never been married, Sybella." He set the cordial glass down beside him with a steady hand.

"You're married to your dog."

"She never hurts me with words," said Duncan Maclain.

"And I do—as all women do." Sybella stared at the fire, speaking desperately. "How can a man so brilliant be so stupid?

You pride yourself you can see better than a man with eyes. Yet you refuse to look at life every day. You, the infallible detective, the man who can shoot at sound to kill—you're afraid, frightened you'll be a burden on some woman who—"

"Who what?" He picked up his glass again.

"Who might think it was heaven to have such a burden."

There was a knock on the apartment door.

"Before you let Lawson in, I want to say thank you," said Duncan Maclain.

Harold Lawson in a black Homburg and dark overcoat loomed large in the doorway. Sybella took his coat and said, "Fancy dress, huh? Why the dinner clothes?"

"A. I. A. dinner at the Roosevelt," Lawson explained as he sat down. "Is there a drink in the house? Accounting dinners are always a bore." He turned to Maclain as Sybella went in search of a highball. "I got your message at my hotel as soon as I got in, and came right over. What's in the wind?"

Sybella spoke from the dining room: "I told Captain Maclain you lived only a couple of blocks away. He's interested in a highball glass I had made for Blake Hadfield about six years ago. I thought you might remember something about it. You asked me about it at the time as near as I can recall."

"That's easy," said Lawson. "There was enough fuss made about it." He took his drink from Sybella and swallowed some gratefully. "A cleaning woman or the janitor, or somebody, broke one of Hadfield's set. I tried to duplicate it at Covington's where the glasses came from, and couldn't. Sybella had one made."

"When was the glass broken?" asked Maclain.

"Search me," Lawson said between sips. "I never even knew

Hadfield had any glasses until after the shooting. Then Davis or somebody mentioned there were only five."

"Mentioned it to you or Hadfield?"

"To me. Hadfield was in the hospital at the time."

"And what was the fuss?" the Captain asked gently. "It seems quite a lot of trouble to go to, replacing a glass for a man who couldn't see." Harold Lawson laughed.

"It's a cinch to tell you've never been mixed up in state politics, Captain Maclain. I was fairly new in the State Insurance Department at the time. We'd been after Hadfield hammer and tongs, wouldn't even let him take his personal possessions from the building. He already had some of the newspapers shouting persecution, and his personal possessions in the M. T. & T. building were in my custody."

Lawson paused to light a cigarette.

"Yes?" the Captain urged him on.

"I don't mean any offense," Lawson continued, "but Hadfield had been shot and blinded, and many blind men arouse a lot of sympathy. Little things became important, and nobody knew any better than Blake Hadfield how to take advantage of them. Everything in that office had been inventoried. I intended to keep that inventory intact and I did."

"Then Mr. Hadfield never really knew about the missing glass," Maclain remarked.

Sybella said, "He never mentioned it to me."

"How did you happen to meet him?"

"Through Covington's. They give me quite a lot of decorating business. Mr. Hadfield called me in when he wanted his apartment redone. I worked on it for several years, taking it a little at a time so he could get used to changes as I went along."

"What did you hope to prove?" asked Lawson.

"I hoped to find out the real reason why that highball glass was gone," said Duncan Maclain. "Did you ever see the pieces of the broken one?"

"Never. I sent one of the remaining glasses up to Sybella. That's what she worked on."

"I returned them both to Harold," Sybella put in. "The old one and the new. As you remarked before, Captain, I'm afraid the trail has led nowhere."

The conversation shifted and continued while Lawson finished two more highballs. Duncan Maclain took out his thin Swiss repeater watch and listened to its tiny tinkling chime.

"Heavens above!" he exclaimed. "It's twelve fifteen. I had no intention of becoming a permanent boarder." His contrite expression changed to one of quick alertness, but his voice never varied a half-note as he said, "You might open the door, Lawson. I believe someone's standing outside it in the hall."

Lawson's well-trained muscles lifted him from the chair silently as a springing animal. Half a dozen strides took him to the door. He turned the knob and jerked it wide, then stepped back in stunned surprise as Inspector Larry Davis stepped inside.

"I suppose you heard me come up the stairs, Maclain. I called your office and Rena told me you were here." The Inspector's clipped words were coated with some of the outside cold which seemed to have followed him into the room.

Sybella said, "I don't believe I've met you, but come in and sit down."

"Inspector Davis of the Homicide Squad," said Lawson.

"Drink, Inspector?" asked Sybella, pointing to the cut-glass decanter.

"No," said Davis. His heavy eyebrows made a straight dark line as he stared at Lawson. "How long have you been here?"

"A little over an hour." Lawson went over by the fireplace and sat down.

"And you, Maclain?"

"Too long for Miss Ford's comfort. All evening, in fact." The Captain stifled an imaginary yawn, knowing the gesture would egg the Inspector on.

Davis moved to a chair as if he were walking on a slippery sidewalk, but leaned his arms on the back instead of sitting down. "Did you ever know a man named T. Allen Doxenby, Lawson?"

"Yes." Lawson turned halfway around.

"When did you see him last?"

"Today," said Lawson.

"What time?"

"This morning."

"Where?"

"In the State Insurance office. He's a shyster, always trying to chisel in on something. We've kicked him out of the office a dozen times, but he still keeps hanging around."

Davis gnawed his trim mustache and jerked his hand from his overcoat pocket. "What do you know about this?" He thrust a sheet torn from a desk calendar in front of Lawson.

"You might read it aloud," suggested Maclain.

"See Lawson about Hadfield estate," the insurance man read with a catch in his voice. "Well, he saw me. He came to the office this morning and asked who was handling Blake Hadfield's estate. I told him Courtney was. Where did you find that memorandum?"

"In his apartment. Have you ever been there?"

"Never," said Lawson.

"It's at Fifty-third and First." The Inspector stuck the memo back in his pocket. "About half an hour ago, Doxenby took a header out of his window on the eleventh floor. There isn't enough left of him to make chowder." The Inspector's usually calm voice began to tremble. "God almighty, Maclain, remember what I told you? They're starting to fall!"

CHAPTER V

1

SUICIDE.

Duncan Maclain lay on the divan in his penthouse office listening to his Capehart flood the room with Shostakovitch's Fifth Symphony. A streak of morning sunlight split by the diamond panes in the terrace doors made a band of brightness across his eyes. Mingled with the satiric strains of the symphony, the pleasing word whirled itself around, forming curlicues in his brain.

Suicide—triple and undiluted, clean-cut and unwearying. First: James Sprague. Second: Blake Hadfield. Third: T. Allen Doxenby. One, two, three and out! All of them dead by their own hands.

Rena stuck her head in the office door and said, "Those men are here again."

The Captain got up and switched off the Capehart as Inspector Davis and Sergeant Archer trooped in like an invading army of two. "From music to the murder men," he greeted them, grinning. "The world is full of pain."

"How about a trip across town?" asked Davis, sliding into a chair.

The Captain took his place behind the desk.

"I'll have to have a chair reupholstered if Archer doesn't shed some weight." His eyebrows raised in disapproval. "The whole house shook when he flopped down."

"There's going to be a shake-up in the Department," Archer stated solemnly.

"I've decided to resign before I get fired," said Davis.

"Splendid." The Captain laughed. "With Spud away I can use a couple of good strong men."

"You think I'm fooling?" Davis took one of the Braille books from the bookcase and opened it on his knee. "The Commissioner has even passed an opinion."

"On you and Archer?"

"It amounts to the same thing." Davis ran a finger over the Braille and scowled. "I'll have to learn to read this stuff. *I'm* going blind now. The chief has decided that Hadfield jumped, and Doxenby, too."

"Logical and easy. Look at the trouble it saves you two."

"Sure," murmured Archer. "So would softening of the brain."

"You mentioned a trip across town," the Captain reminded Davis. "Doxenby's place?"

"Yes."

"What do you want me to do?"

The Inspector left his seat and took a cigarette from the box on the desk. "I want you to check on Archer and me and four other members of the Homicide Squad."

Maclain's fingers rumpled his hair with a quick impatient gesture. "Look here, Davis! I've never questioned your Department or your and Archer's ability. I've needed your help and gotten it on every case I've been mixed up in. There isn't a private operator in this city can work without your co-operation. What do you need a check-up of mine for? I'm willing to back up everything you fellows say or do."

"Speaking as a member of the most cussed-out outfit in fact or fiction, let me say we appreciate that." The Inspector dragged deep on his cigarette and returned to his chair.

"I'll even go further, Captain," said Archer. "It's because we know how you feel about us that we've come to you. You're blind, but you pick up one hell of a lot that others miss. The Inspector feels if you agree with us in this Doxenby death, we'll have to believe what we think is true."

"And what do you think is true?"

"I think it's true that Archer and I are past our prime," the Inspector declared without a trace of humor. "We've decided to leave it up to you." There was an emotion deeper than solicitude in the slow motion of the Captain's forefinger as he drew an invisible circle on the desk top and stabbed at its center with the rubber tip of a pencil. Larry Davis and Aloysius Archer were more than capable officers to Duncan Maclain. They were friends. For years they had argued heatedly with him, but it had been friendly arguing, without rancor or animosity. He had counted on them, as he had counted on Spud, in some of the tightest spots of his life. Invariably they had helped.

Now, a deep anxiety bit into his normally calm consideration. Larry Davis was face to face with some frightening, unfathomable problem. Nothing less would drag from such a man even a partial admission that he considered his long career finished. The Captain hated to believe it, but Davis meant what he said. The Inspector really thought that he and his partner were through.

"Hell's blue blazes!" Maclain burst out. "You two aren't quitters. What's gotten into you?"

"People getting pushed to death with nobody present," said Davis bluntly. "Verdicts from the Medical Examiner that it's suicide. Stick around and the little nut bugs will start in gnawing on you."

The Captain's lips worked quickly for a second and settled in repose. "You mean you think this fellow Doxenby was pushed from his window last night?"

"What do you think about Hadfield?" Sergeant Archer countered before Davis could reply. "The verdict is suicide. I don't believe that kid killed him. Neither does the Inspector. Okay. I'm telling you now, there were only three people in that building. Do you think the kid killed him?"

The Captain thought a while before he said, "Frankly, no. Haven't we been over this before?"

"You're damn right we have," Davis put in savagely. "We're going over it again before we're through. Commissioner or no Commissioner. So we start with the fact that the kid didn't kill him and the other two couldn't. Does that mean that the suicide rings kosher to you?"

"No—again," said Duncan Maclain.

"Swell," said Davis. "Here's another point of view. Doxenby, a chiseling little corpse-suit sniffer who's been putting the bite on everybody from politicians to prostitutes since before the Little Flower was in Congress, fell out of a window last night at eleven forty-seven by the meetinghouse clock—about forty minutes before I busted in on you. He landed in an areaway between two buildings. The witnesses who heard him scream when he took this flyer consist of everybody who lives on First Avenue."

"Wait a minute," Maclain interrupted. "Did anyone actually see him fall?"

"If you mean was he pushed from the roof or another room, the answer is no. That's the same answer you're going to give when I ask you, 'Do you think a slug like that would dive to destruction?'"

Maclain shook his head and said, "No."

"But he did," the Sergeant put in grimly. "The M. E. and the Commissioner say it's so."

"I gather you both are certain there was nobody in his room at the time of his fall?"

"We're not certain of anything any more." The force with which Davis snuffed his cigarette rattled the tray. "We live in a world of googly bugs. A man and his wife who live in the opposite apartment were letting themselves in when they heard the daring young Doxenby scream. They stood outside his door listening until a patrolman came up with Stutmeyer the janitor and went in. There was nobody in the room but an open window."

"There you have it," said Archer, "and even that ain't all."

"Wait," said Davis. "You had an idea about a missing highball glass. Did you ever follow it up, Maclain?"

"Yes."

"Where did it lead you?"

The Captain told him.

"Could you make it clear to us why you were so interested in that glass?"

"I'll give you a demonstration," said Maclain. "Get me half a dozen glasses, Sergeant. You know where they are—in the buffet behind the sliding panel in the wall."

The Sergeant took them out, handling them carefully. "What now?"

"Put them on the table," said Maclain. "We'll make believe they're in a rack, and that this is Hadfield's office. Okay?"

"Sure," said Davis. "I've always liked to play."

"On the night of the Sprague-Hadfield shooting," the Captain began, "someone took one of those glasses away. Will you accept that as a premise?"

"Sure," said Davis. "It was in Doxenby's room with some Scotch in it—and the fingerprints on it were those of Doxenby—and of a fellow named James Sprague. It's been six years since they tucked that bird away."

"And," said Archer, "that ain't all. There was no Scotch whisky in the room at all, at all!"

2

The squad car swished in to the curb in front of the late Mr. Doxenby's domicile and stopped as smoothly as a docking speedboat. Under the push of Sergeant Archer's fullback shoulders, an ogling knot of morbid sightseers opened a passage, staring bulge-eyed at Schnucke and Maclain.

"Fee, fi, fo, fum," Davis quoted as the doors of the automatic elevator slid closed. "They smell the blood of a murdered man!"

The Captain said idly, "I've often wondered where they come from; even in the middle of the night they swarm around an accident."

"Street flies," Archer rumbled. "They like to watch sewer diggers, too."

Maclain scarcely heard him. He had made the crosstown

trip in comparative silence, answering the officers' comments in monosyllables. The appearance of Hadfield's highball glass in Doxenby's room had given an unharmonious twist to normal logic. A saying of the French—*"En toute chose il faut considérer la fin"*—was plaguing him.

"In all things it is necessary to consider the end." Well, death was the irremeable end, but the highball glass signed with the fingerprints of two dead men impressed Duncan Maclain as bordering on the superfluous. It was as unnecessary as putting two periods at the close of a sentence and then further explaining in brackets that the sentence was finished.

In Doxenby's apartment, with the door locked and a man on duty in the hall, the Captain promptly took a chair and went into the matter again. Released from his grip, Schnucke made an inquisitive tour before settling down at the Captain's side.

"I didn't bring you up here to rest," Davis protested. "I wanted you, not Schnucke, to look over this place."

"I haven't dropped the matter of the glass yet, Davis. Where did you find it? In the kitchen or in this room?"

"Did I say there was a kitchen?"

"Schnucke said so—that's the first place she heads for in any strange house."

"Did you ever hear the story about the horse that talked?" asked Archer.

"Yes," said Davis, *"and* the dog, *and* the goldfish. But I've never heard one about the ass that kept quiet. We found the glass in the kitchen, Maclain."

"Whisky in it?"

"Yes."

"Diluted?"

"Yes."

"How much?"

"Half an inch in the bottom."

"Then you believe the glass was used."

"Yes, I do."

"Are you certain the fingerprints were Sprague's and Doxenby's?"

"There was another about a horse that sat on watermelons," Archer muttered sarcastically.

"The Fingerprint Division can't make mistakes." Davis waved the Sergeant into silence.

"How long will fingerprints last?"

"These lasted six years. That's one thing we know."

"Does that mean anything?"

Davis tugged at his clipped mustache with finger and thumb. "The chances are that the glass was protected. In fact, it must have been packed away very carefully. We protect them by putting a small square board on the top and bottom of the tumbler and nailing the boards together with a strip on each corner. Then that's put in a cardboard box and the glass can't touch anything."

"There are plenty of other glasses here, I presume?"

"You presume right," said Davis.

"I don't get it!" The Captain's incisive voice was rough with irritation. "Why would Doxenby nurse a glass for six years, then suddenly take a drink out of it and jump out of the window?"

"The goblins will getcha," Sergeant Archer announced a little more cheerfully. "And where did he get his liquor? There's not a trace of a bottle in here. Maybe you think he had the glass filled in a bar and brought it up with him."

The Captain made a noise with his lips, then got up and

touched Schnucke's brace. Guiding her course with soft-spoken commands, he started exploring the living room. Archer swapped a glance with the Inspector and manicured the end from a cigar.

There wasn't much in the living room. Maclain's sentient fingers recorded a table desk, a divan with two cushions, a couple of lamps, two straight chairs and one easy one. He walked into the bedroom and found little more there—a comfortable single bed, military brushes on the bureau, masculine clothes lining two sides of the closet, and an expensive leather suitcase on the shelf—the usual personal possessions of a well-to-do man who lives alone.

He raised the bedroom window, stood listening to the noisy roar of traffic on First Avenue, and closed it again. Returning, he repeated the test with one of the two windows in the living room. At the kitchen door he turned, came back and raised and lowered the other one.

Davis followed him into the kitchen.

The Captain paused in front of the window and felt the frame from sill to top, then stooped and ran his hand along the ridges of a cold steam-radiator placed under the window close to the wall.

"I suppose this is where he fell."

"It was the only window open when we came in." Davis spied a box of toothpicks in the china cabinet and took several.

"Where's the bathroom?"

"Right across a little hall."

"Was the window closed in there?"

"It opens and shuts like a little door—you wind it with a handle. It was open a crack, that's all. It was cold last night."

The Captain and Schnucke crossed the hall. Maclain located

the window over the bathtub, found the metal crank and turned it to open the window as far as it would go.

"What's outside, Davis?"

"A narrow airshaft." The Inspector tried a toothpick.

"Take a look outside. How far down does it go?"

Davis climbed into the tub and poked out his head. "All the way apparently. Why?" He pulled back in and closed the window.

"I'm trying to find out where the whisky went," said Duncan Maclain.

"Well, it didn't go out this window." The Inspector adjusted the sash until it was open not more than an inch. "Feel for yourself. That's how it was set when we came in. I've photographs to prove it. You couldn't get a half-pint flask out through there."

The Captain touched the opening and said, "*Umm*—no. Not unless somebody closed it again."

Davis stalked out of the room and Maclain heard his crisp voice speaking to Archer. There were sounds of an opening and closing door.

Maclain was back in the kitchen when Davis returned. "I've sent for Abe Stutmeyer, the janitor."

"This window Doxenby fell out of opens on an areaway, you say?" asked Maclain.

"That's right."

"Where's the nearest fire escape?"

"Not near enough." The Inspector snapped his toothpick in disgust and tossed the pieces in the sink. "You gave us a long spiel in your office about our knowing our business. Now this thing's got you asking questions like Dick Tracy trying to figure out how the Mole got away. Nobody got in and out of this apartment, Maclain, without using the door. If anybody was in here when Doxenby fell, he must have followed Doxenby out, for that's the only way."

"What's directly across?" the Captain continued, unruffled.

"A blank wall of a storage warehouse, and the roof is seven stories above this window. Now you want me to get out a warrant for Superman."

"You certainly know your funnies, Davis. I'm scared to inquire about the roof overhead."

"Don't mind me. There's a trapdoor up to it on this floor, locked on the inside. There's a ladder to it. The ladder's down and was last night, and besides that people were in the hall outside this door. If anyone pushed Doxenby and climbed out of the window and shinnied up a rope to the roof, then he's the same guy we have bottled up in the M. T. & T. building. Furthermore, he's up there now, or he jumped six stories down to a five-story private house next door."

"I thought the fire escape led down from the roof."

"Into the areaway where Doxenby landed. People were there almost before he hit—people, Maclain, and cops all around the bottom of the fire escape, and nobody came down."

"What about getting in on another floor?"

"Every entrance is barred inside, and was last night. And you'd agree with me that nobody climbed out of this apartment onto the roof if you could stick your head out of the window or go up on the roof and see."

"All right," said Maclain. "I'll agree. That makes it suicide."

"It makes it more than that, Captain. It makes the north end of a southbound horse out of me!" Archer called from the living room: "Stutmeyer's here!"

Maclain said softly, "Do you mind leaving this to me? You've been at him before."

"I don't care if you put your dog on him," Davis declared with fervor. "He's nothing to me." Mr. Stutmeyer greeted the Captain sullenly. "I have work to do. A man falls out the window. So? Should I lose my job?"

"We won't keep you five minutes," the Captain soothed him. "Do you mind answering a couple of questions?"

"Yes," said Abe. "All the answers are out of me. Name? Abe Stutmeyer. Age? Sixty-three. Married? You've said it, God help me! Occupation? Janitor. What for? Because the army won't take me."

"Aw, shut up," said Archer. "You wear on me."

"I just want to know if you were awake when Mr. Doxenby fell."

"I've told all that."

The Captain's chin set. "We'll be here all day if you won't help me."

"Yes," said Abe. "There was a party on the fourth floor. I yelled up the airshaft to stop it and they threw a bottle of booze down at me."

Davis shot a glance at the Sergeant. "Did he tell you that?"

"He didn't ask me," said Abe. "What's that got to do with Doxenby?"

"A bottle of liquor was missing from this room," the Captain supplied. "Is it possible that's the one that was thrown at you?"

"Anything's possible in this place. The bathroom window's on the shaft right over me."

"You spoke of a bottle of booze," said Maclain. "An empty?"

"Like hell!" said Abe. "It spattered all over me. Smelled like good whisky to me."

"I'd like to find the pieces of that bottle, Mr. Stutmeyer. Can we get into the shaft from your room?"

"You can, but you won't find any pieces. They've gone to sea."

"To sea?"

"On a garbage scow. I cleaned that shaft out early this morning."

"That's too bad." The Captain shook his head regretfully. "Was there anything there besides the bottle?"

"Look, mister. The airshafts in a place like this are wastebaskets to everybody but me. Newspapers, a pair of shoes, somebody's drawers, glass, wrapping paper and twine—"

"Twine?" Maclain put in. "Did you save the twine?"

"Mister," said Abe, "everything is garbage to me."

"Thanks," said Maclain, "that's all."

Stutmeyer left, and closed the door.

"Why the twine?" asked Davis instantly.

"Elise Sprague found a ball of it in Hadfield's desk drawer." Maclain told what had happened.

Sergeant Archer sat up suddenly. "When I was a kid," he said, "I nearly broke my old man's neck by stretching a piece of string across a staircase."

"Did you ever manage to train it?" asked the Captain.

"Train it to do what?" the Sergeant demanded suspiciously.

"Open and close windows?" said Duncan Maclain.

3

The universe was an orderly composition of geometric figures to Captain Duncan Maclain. Certain set rules dominated all planes and solids. Years of finding his way about without visual aid in a world bristling with obstructions had made him an unwitting member of the ancient Pythagorean sect whose members considered numbers the supreme concept of existence.

In the Captain's penthouse, twenty-six stories above the streaming traffic at Seventy-second and Riverside Drive, the furniture was fixed immovably to the floor. He walked around his home with ease and swiftness, confident that the pattern was unchanging and that no barrier would be inadvertently placed to block his path.

Geometry governed his movements outside of his home. Schnucke, trained to uncanny perspicacity by the Seeing Eye, could watch traffic for him, check him at curbs, and even keep him from striking his head on low-hung awnings above the sidewalk. But Schnucke couldn't tell him where he wanted to go, and Maclain refused to be entirely dependent on his chauffeur and car.

Gradually he had built up a sphere of existence devoid of apparent color, but none the less real because its components were planes, solids, and sounds. The sense of smell, a matter of life to ancient man, but degraded until it was tainted with vacuous humor by modern civilization, was the color of living to Duncan Maclain. Numbers were his guideposts, numbers of paces, numbers of chairs and tables, numbers of doors, numbers of steps up and down.

Memorized and rigorously practised angles and curves were his highways and bypaths. He shot with deadly accuracy at sound—a matter of seven years' training in translating the noise of a falling coffee can into an answering reaction with a pistol. He flashed his lighter, telling instantly when it caught by the warmth of flame near his finger, and applied it unhesitatingly to the tip of his cigarette by holding one arm close to his side and following the path of an angle, a path delineated by muscular control.

Life was a map to Duncan Maclain, an accurate, surveyed chart to be followed with meticulous care if disaster was to be avoided. If a town or a railroad crossing or a river showed in a certain place, it had to be there. The map couldn't be wrong. It was Duncan Maclain, the traveler, who was lost on an unmarked detour.

As he sat at his desk on Saturday afternoon waiting for the arrival of Julia Hadfield, he was engaged in a game. The six pieces were three men from his hand-carved chess set—a Bishop, a Knight, and a Queen—and the three glasses Archer had taken from the cabinet earlier in the day.

The Captain had backtracked on a line of reasoning and started all over again in an effort to avoid a detour. The detour led to three suicides—James Sprague, represented by the Bishop; Blake Hadfield, the Knight; and Mr. T. Allen Doxenby, rather overglorified by the Queen.

Maclain had turned his desk blotter into Blake Hadfield's private office and had the Knight (Mr. Hadfield) and the Bishop (Mr. Sprague) in conference, when Rena announced Julia Hadfield and Philip Courtney.

The Captain had not expected the attorney, but his only expression of surprise was a quick pucker of his lips as he said "Show them in."

Julia Hadfield's greeting he found a shade too earnest, and the attorney's a mite too warm. He laid her overplay to dejection, but found Courtney's heartiness more difficult to classify. He felt strongly, however, that something had changed Courtney's attitude since their previous meeting.

"I didn't know you were a chess addict," Courtney remarked when they were seated. "I'm fond of it myself. Sometime I'd like to take you on. Are you working a problem?"

"A living one," said Maclain. He raised his head and turned his face to Julia. "You've been through a lot, Mrs. Hadfield. Can you stand just a little more, if it will insure future happiness for your son?"

"Yes." The catch of her handbag clicked open and shut. "But there's more than that now, Captain Maclain. My own happiness is at stake. Phil's become involved in the death of that lawyer who fell from his window last night. That's why I insisted he come with me this afternoon."

"How involved, Mr. Courtney?" The fingers of the Captain's right hand began moving on the desk blotter beating a silent tattoo.

"This Doxenby came to my office last night on an errand of blackmail, Captain—" Courtney went over Doxenby's proposition, speaking steadily, but his face darkening with anger. He kept no detail to himself, bringing each one out for his listener's consideration with legal accuracy, and the nice precision of a man laying tile.

"Do I understand that you have no knowledge of fifty thousand dollars that Hadfield invested in Sprague's partnership for you?" the Captain asked when Courtney had finished.

"None whatsoever." The faintest of sounds indicated that Courtney had moistened his lips.

"Have you any possible explanation why Blake Hadfield would do such a thing without informing you?"

"To ruin him." Julia's statement was unimaginative and cool. "Blake was a past master at thinking up hellish things to do. He knew that Sprague's company was doomed, that buying in on such a partnership was tantamount to ruin."

Maclain asked, "Why not ruin for him, too?"

"Because while he was alive, he could always deny it," Phil Courtney explained. "He could always swear that he had made a personal loan to Sprague, that he wasn't to receive any of the profits from the partnership. That the money was in no sense an investment making him and me liable for the partnership's liabilities after its failure."

"And why can't you explain your innocent participation, just as well?"

"Because with Sprague dead and Hadfield dead, nobody will believe it," said Courtney. "Not even you."

"It seems rather fortunate for you," said Duncan Maclain, "that T. Allen Doxenby's dead, too. How many others know of this?"

"Nobody that I know of, except Julia and you," Courtney replied.

The Captain's fingers ceased their restless maneuvers. "That's a fiendishly clever form of sabotage, Courtney. Blake Hadfield must have hated you."

"He hated me," said Julia. "He was venomous because I couldn't tolerate his outlook on life, his constant disparagement of anyone or anything that I considered decent. Phil kept him out of jail after the bank crash, yet he constantly claimed that Phil was crooked, because he knew that Phil was fond of me. It was typical of Blake to think up something that would enable him to lie in his grave and grin at us two."

"Have you mentioned this to the police?" asked Maclain.

"No." Courtney showed agitation in the length of time he

spent on his one-handed attempt to light a cigar. "On Julia's advice I came direct to you. Should I tell them?"

"First, tell me," said Maclain. "After Doxenby left your office, what did you do?"

Courtney said, "I got a gun out of my drawer and concealed it in my sling. I can't use my left arm, but my fingers are still free."

"The general impression is that when a man gets a gun, he intends to kill someone," said Duncan Maclain. "Was that what you had in mind?"

"Yes," said Courtney. "If anyone tried to kill me."

"You felt yourself in danger?"

"Let's say I was nervous, Captain Maclain. That man had crept into my office very quietly. Hadfield had met a violent death a few nights ago, just why, nobody seems to know. If some half-crazed depositor, like Sprague, for instance, is on the loose, isn't it possible since I cleared Hadfield from jail that Hadfield's killer might turn his attentions to me?"

"Sprague is dead," said Duncan Maclain.

"Of course," Courtney hastened to agree.

The Captain leaned back in his swivel chair. "I was wondering what brought him to your mind just now."

"Nothing in particular. He just occurred to me."

"It's very strange." The Captain pursed his lips in thought. "Just a couple of hours ago something very vivid happened to recall James Sprague to me."

"Indeed," said Courtney guardedly.

"A glass was found in Doxenby's apartment," Maclain continued reminiscently. "On it were Doxenby's fingerprints and those of James Sprague—dead these six years. It's quite an enigma to both the police and me."

"It's impossible," Julia whispered.

"They're mistaken, of course," Courtney added equally low.

"The police think not," said Maclain. "I was wondering if either of you might have an explanation. Only one has seemed feasible, and that's since you have talked to me."

"Feasible?" Courtney repeated. "But really—"

"Doxenby must have taken that glass from Hadfield's office the night that Sprague was killed. Somebody took a glass, and the one found is part of the set. Isn't it possible, Mr. Courtney, that Doxenby overheard a conversation between Hadfield and Sprague in that office six years ago? He got his information somewhere, and from what you say, Hadfield and Sprague were the only others who knew of Hadfield's investment of your money."

"Would Doxenby have waited six years to use it?" asked Julia.

The Captain smiled. "You heard Mr. Courtney say just now that the information was worthless with your husband alive."

"Look here," said Courtney keenly. "Doxenby spoke last night about Hadfield being his client. Is it possible that's true? Suppose Doxenby was in the office with them that night. He might have had a drink fixed for him by Sprague. Certainly he'd have taken the glass with his fingerprints on it after the tragedy."

"Why didn't he wash and leave it?"

"No time," Courtney succinctly explained. "Great heavens— he might have even killed them!"

"Or seen the real murderer." The Captain sat erect slowly, making a mental note that he would have to oil the springs of his swivel chair.

"What do you mean by that, Captain Maclain?"

"He means me, Julia." Courtney's words came with the slow consideration of an address to a jury. "The three men who could wreck me are dead. Last Monday night Blake phoned me, but I fell and never got there. Last night, I haven't any alibi at all. After Doxenby left me I merely went home. When the police learn of that—"

"Phil, don't be a fool," said Julia sharply.

The Captain picked up the chess Queen and twirled it between his fingers. "About the time that Blake Hadfield fell to his death you were riding to your apartment in a taxicab, Mr. Courtney, after being attended in St. Vincent's Hospital for a badly sprained arm. You underestimate the New York police, Courtney. I'm surprised—as long as you've been a member of the bar."

"They'll be certain I killed those three men when I tell them about Doxenby's visit."

"They'll never be certain of anything," said Duncan Maclain, "until you tell them *how!*"

4

The Captain caressed the three chess pieces on his blotter, arranged them in a triangle, and finally set them out in a remarkably straight row.

"I'm going to be frank, Mr. Courtney. I have certain facts in my possession which I think you and Mrs. Hadfield are entitled to know."

It was part of Courtney's training to regard frankness with suspicion. He touched a finger to his lips for Julia's benefit and said, "So?"

"Perhaps the strangest factor in the death of these three men"—Maclain indicated the chess pieces with a slight movement of his hand—"is the very frankness, the utter lack of reticence, which has surrounded the investigation."

"I'm sure neither Phil nor Seth have anything to hide, Captain Maclain."

"Undoubtedly, that is so. Still, Mrs. Hadfield, incongruous as it may seem, the police are geared to unearth falsehood." He clucked softly. "They find it most disconcerting to be told without restraint everything they want to know. I'm afraid I do, too."

He centered his attention on Courtney. "Have you ever worked very hard to prepare a trap for a hostile witness, only to find the witness was presenting facts in your favor?"

"Yes," said Courtney. "You begin to fear that the witness is smarter than you."

"Ah! There we have it," said Maclain. "I want you both to help me." He picked up the ivory Bishop and held it high for their inspection. "This is James Sprague. The Knight is Blake Hadfield. The blotter is Hadfield's office. The time is a certain night, six years ago."

"What about the Queen?" asked Courtney.

"She's a murderer—sex and identity unknown," said Duncan Maclain. "She might be either of you."

"After all—" Courtney began.

Rena Savage opened the office door, looked in, and gently closed it again.

"A matter of stimulating impressions," the Captain explained. "I want to see if we all agree on what a murderer would do. I'll follow out my idea. Either of you may cross-examine when I'm through."

He placed the Bishop and Knight close together, then reached accurately for the cloisonné cigarette box, which he set beside the two chessmen. "Here we have two victims in a conference. They had been arguing over Sprague's conduct of his own company, according to Hadfield's testimony."

Maclain picked up the Queen and set her near the edge of the blotter in back of the cigarette box. "Let's suppose the murderer is standing in the foyer in back of Hadfield. He has overheard the conversation. It is, for some reason, getting dangerous to his own safety. He determines, before anything more is said, to get both men out of his way."

"Why both?" asked Julia, unwittingly speaking aloud.

"Obviously he can't kill one and let the other live. Using normal precautions against fingerprints, he takes Blake's gun from the drawer of the table in the foyer. He has it in his hand when Sprague leaves his place beside Hadfield and steps out through the curtain on his way to the lavatory. That's a part of the police records, I believe."

Courtney nodded. "I looked them over again the other day."

Maclain moved the Bishop to the edge of the blotter to face the Queen. "Now Hadfield claimed that as Sprague stepped through those curtains, he heard him exclaim in anger. Hadfield asked, 'What's the matter, Jim?'—and didn't remember anything more."

Maclain's hands flashed out to seize the Bishop and the Queen. "I believe that Sprague's exclamation was one of fear. As he stepped through those curtains he was met with the muzzle of a gun."

The Captain placed the Queen behind the Bishop. "The murderer forced Sprague to turn around, and holding the gun to his spine started him back into the office. He reached around Sprague and shot Blake Hadfield in the head. Dumb with horror, Sprague saw the gun turned on him again. The murderer forced him several steps from the desk—where his body was found—placed the gun to Sprague's temple and fired. He put the gun in Sprague's hand—"

"Then what?" Courtney was leaning far forward in his chair.

"Then," Maclain continued in his trance-like tone, "instead of running, the murderer took a moment to look around. Does that convey anything to either of you?"

"Yes," said Courtney. "He must have known the location of the watchman, Dan O'Hare, and approximately how long after hearing the shots it would take him to get upstairs."

"Check!" said the Captain with a satisfied nod. "The murderer looked around and saw that a third glass was there, a glass with whisky in it. Now a third glass was a bad thing if the shooting of the two men was to look like murder and suicide. The literal police would immediately conclude that a third person had been there—a thought which might never enter their heads if only two glasses were found in the office."

"Isn't it possible, Captain, that this murderer had a drink with Blake and Jim Sprague and took the glass because his own prints were on it?"

The Captain's eyebrows drew together. "It's the logical thing to think, Mrs. Hadfield, but I'll tell you why it won't do. Your husband was alive for six years after this shooting. He's never mentioned anyone else being there. If Sprague was killed, he was killed before he gave your husband information dangerous to the murderer. Mr. Hadfield was quite open with the police. If the murderer had sat around and had a drink, then left and returned, I think Blake Hadfield would have mentioned it. Don't you?"

"Yes," said Julia, "I do."

The Captain reached for the three glasses on the desk and stood them in a row. "Sprague fixed all the drinks," he stated abruptly. "That we know. His fingerprints were on all three glasses; the two used ones found in the office, and the one found in Doxenby's apartment last night. Blake Hadfield's and Sprague's were found together on one in the office; on the other were Sprague's alone."

"What about cleaning women?" Courtney inquired.

"The police checked that, too. The woman who cleans Hadfield's office is a conscientious soul. Each night she goes over those glasses with a cloth and returns them to the rack, apparently leaving no fingermarks at all.

"To return to our murderer," Maclain went on. "He took a glass with him, judging from its location that it was neither Sprague's nor Hadfield's. He ducked downstairs as O'Hare came up to investigate the shots. Once home, he began to sense the possibilities of the glass he had taken."

"Isn't it possible that he saw the third man who drank in the office?" asked Courtney.

"No third man drank," said Duncan Maclain. "If Sprague's fingerprints stayed latent on that glass, the third man's prints would have been there, too."

"Unless Doxenby was the man."

"What good would it do you to preserve a glass with your own fingerprints on it?" asked Maclain. "It might be a neat way of seating yourself in the electric chair."

Courtney uttered a puzzled, "That's true."

"Then we must admit that our murderer took the glass, Mr. Courtney. He took it because he didn't want the police to think a third person had been there. He kept it because he didn't know who that third person was, waiting to see if that third person would speak. When that third person never came forward, our murderer still preserved the glass. Sometime he might learn that third person's identity. That glass might be used for a little protective blackmail some fine day."

"But why didn't this third person take a drink?" asked Julia.

"Maybe he didn't want one," the Captain answered with a smile. "People often fix a drink automatically when a visitor drops in. There's another possibility, of course, a chance that Sprague took a fresh glass to fix himself a second drink, but I doubt if that's the case. It was no small effort to fix a drink in the office. Water had to be obtained from the lavatory in the little hall. I'm ready for cross-examination."

"Okay," said Courtney quickly. "I'll begin. You believe that while Sprague and Hadfield were talking in Hadfield's office some third person, not the murderer, but identity still unknown, dropped in?"

"Yes," said Duncan Maclain.

"Sprague fixed this visitor a drink, but the visitor didn't touch the glass?"

"Yes."

"I want to think," said Courtney. "Do you have a pad and pencil?"

The Captain took writing materials from a drawer. Courtney put the pad on his knee and began to jot things down. Maclain listened to the whisper of the pencil for a moment, then turned to Julia.

"This is the most painful thing I have to do," he said, his manner warm with sympathy. "I want to return you to the terrible instant when you saw your husband fall."

"I'll do my best." She spoke so low the Captain had to strain to hear.

"Did you hear anything else at the instant of the fall?"

She groped briefly in her memory. "The elevator door closed upstairs and the car started down."

"Before that, even, Mrs. Hadfield. Did glass break anywhere?"

"I was panicky, Captain. I'm afraid I'm not much help." She stopped, looked at Courtney and drew a deep sighing breath. "I had an illusion—"

The Captain relinquished his hold on the chess Queen and gripped the desk edge with one hand. "Concerning your husband's fall?"

"I could see him above me." Julia drove herself ruthlessly on. "Yet I had a hallucination, from sheer fright, I suppose, that he was falling down the elevator shaft—the empty one with the broken car."

Courtney looked up from his notes. "She told me about that, Captain, and I told her to forget it. She's had enough shock. May I put a few more questions?"

The Captain nodded, and for a split-up second seemed to be lost in a contemplation of the paneled wall.

Courtney consulted his notes. "Your theory presents many puzzles. Let's see where we are. Sprague fixed a drink for the visitor—*umm!* You'll admit that Hadfield must have seen such a visitor, and talked with him."

"Yes," said Maclain.

"Why didn't Hadfield mention such a visitor?"

"He forgot him," said Maclain.

Courtney's brown eyes narrowed. "Will you admit that the watchman knew of such a visitor?"

"Yes."

"Why didn't the watchman mention it in the face of a police investigation?"

"He forgot it," said Maclain.

"I might accept such a thing once," said Courtney, "but twice is scarcely up to your standard."

"The nondrinking visitor who dropped in and casually talked to Sprague and Hadfield was Dan O'Hare," said Duncan Maclain.

CHAPTER VI

1

SOMEWHERE IT must fit in.

An hour had passed since Courtney and Julia Hadfield had left the Captain's office. He was still at the desk, but the chessmen had been replaced by the scattered pieces of a jigsaw puzzle. The border of the puzzle was complete, built into a harmonious frame by the selective nerves of the Captain's diligent fingers.

The center of the puzzle was an opening of irregular design. Twenty times the Captain had traced its complicated curves and curlicues, touching the edge with feathery lightness as a surgeon might probe a wound, intent on avoiding pain.

He held a piece of the puzzle in his left hand. Occasionally he attempted to insert it, only to pick it up quickly. There was a definite analogy between a jigsaw puzzle and a problem in human conduct to Duncan Maclain. Pick two pieces of a puzzle at random, trace their outlines, and the chances were it would seem impossible that they could ever form a part of a single unified pattern. Get enough of the pieces fitted together, and the relation of each piece to the whole became increasingly plain.

Years of mastering such puzzles by the sense of touch had taught him that a strong bond existed between the working of his fingers and the functioning of his brain. A puzzle took shape readily just so long as his thinking was clear. Let his ratiocination become forced or cloudy, and immediately his fingers refused to respond. Often, concentrating with full faculty, he would tear a half-completed puzzle down endless times, and start anew to build it up again.

The one on the desk was about to suffer such a fate when the office door opened and closed. Maclain counted footsteps, and heard the creak of leather on the divan as someone sat down. He made no move, except that his right hand clenched suddenly and opened slowly.

"Tricks," he said, wrinkling his high forehead with a frown. "Is that what they're teaching you in Washington? Have a cigarette, and mix us a highball, Spud—and tell me what kept you so long."

"Damn it all, Dunc!" Spud Savage made the Captain's desk in four long strides. There was an instant of silence as his powerful fingers closed on the Captain's hand. "You're a faker. Either Rena told you I was coming, or you can see as well as I can."

"Better," Maclain declared. "I've told you that for years." He put a hand on Spud's broad shoulder, touched a gold insignia leaf, then grinned with pleasure and sat down. "Major Savage!" He shook his head in mock consternation. "The Army Intelligence must be in a bad way!"

"Pure, unadulterated merit," said Spud modestly. "How did you know that the army's brightest light was coming? Rena said you'd spot me the instant I came in the office—and I, like an idiot, bet us a dinner for tonight that she was wrong. I altered my normal stride when I came in, and didn't even breathe."

"Even your best friends won't tell you!" The Captain raised his nose expressively.

"You go to hell," Spud advised him. "Rena told you, or you wouldn't have asked what kept me so long."

"She told me inadvertently," Maclain admitted. "When the perfect secretary sticks her head in the office door while I have two visitors and does it for the first time in ten years, what must I think? The wandering husband's coming home. Well, I was right, that's all."

"There's still something else." Spud went to the buffet and pushed up the concealing panel. "If I'm going to wine and dine you on my meager officer's pay, you'd better give."

"Of course there's the little habit you have of pausing to adjust the throw rug outside the office door just before you step in from the hall." The Captain's eyebrows wriggled delightedly. "How long's your leave?"

"Forty-eight hours. I have to hop back tomorrow night." He put a drink on the desk for Maclain and glanced at the centerless puzzle. "I bumped into our overweight pal Aloysius Archer pegging the incoming planes at La Guardia Field. Do you think I'll be in town long enough for any more bodies to fall?"

The Captain sampled his drink and settled himself more comfortably in his chair. "I'm glad you're here, Spud. I'm in a hole."

"*You're* in a hole?" Spud took a chair nearer the desk and looked at the puzzle again. "Holy moses, Dunc, you don't hold with that tosh Archer passed out to me, do you? From what I've read in the Washington papers, Hadfield killed himself. And this squirt, Doxenby—well, he seems pretty open-and-shut, after all. That's the picture I get."

"It's the picture you're intended to get," said Duncan Maclain.

"Well, what have you got?" Spud twirled the ice in his glass and drank deeply.

"No picture at all, Spud." The Captain pointed to the unfinished puzzle. "All I have is a beautiful frame. If you're interested, I'll deal you in on the game."

"Deal," said Spud. "Attentive listening is my middle name." He leaned back, crossed his legs, and fixed his strange yellow eyes on the Captain's fingers, watching the destruction of the puzzle.

The Captain talked without interruption for more than fifteen minutes. Piece by piece he snapped the sawed-up bits back into position, making a point with each one. When he finally paused to finish his highball, the outline of the puzzle had been reconstructed.

"Well, what do you think?" Maclain asked. His lips were a straight uncompromising line.

Spud mixed another pair of highballs. "I sort of like that six-year-old murder you've committed," he said as he sat down again. "I see what you mean, though. There are holes in the middle you can drive a taxi through."

"I'd like to have somebody tell me about them for a change," said Maclain. "Maybe it would help me to explain them away."

"Motive," said Spud. "Sprague was murdered, you claim?"

Maclain nodded.

"He was also broke," said Spud, "and under indictment for fraud and misappropriation of investors' funds. He left his daughter nothing. Killing him would seem a little silly, if the object was gain. I don't believe in revenge."

"Neither do I," said Maclain.

"That's what put me off of Sprague's shooting of Hadfield. That's what makes me certain that Sprague was killed to keep him from talking. If Hadfield had been the intended victim, he was left six years to talk in."

"I'll swallow that." Spud pressed a thumb and finger to his eyes and went on thoughtfully. "I'll swallow it, even if you can never prove it. As a matter of fact, you can't prove any of this. Has it occurred to you that a man is innocent until proven guilty, Dunc? I can't see convincing any jury that any man is guilty of murder if the alleged murderer is somewhere else, and can prove it, when his victim falls out of a window or off a balcony."

"You're gouging a greater hole in my picture than ever," protested Maclain. "Nevertheless, I'm glad to have you admit such a thing is possible."

"I've admitted nothing," said Spud. "Don't get yourself all hopeful because I'm home overnight. I'm about to point out lots of things that will give you a pain. I'll admit that O'Hare, the watchman, was the man who stopped in the office and didn't have the drink."

"That I intend to check," said Maclain.

"Good," Spud approved. "Here's a point that has me whirling like a weathervane: How does this spectral Houdini that you and Davis are chasing find out the particular nights that Blake Hadfield chooses to have himself shot and pushed over railings?"

The Captain paused with a piece of the puzzle held in the air. "Say that again!"

"Hadfield and Sprague met in a secret conference, in an office Hadfield hadn't visited for years."

"Hadfield had some papers there he wanted to discuss with Sprague."

"I'm not asking why he went there," said Spud. "I'm asking how the murderer knew he was there on that particular night. I'm asking how, six years later, the murderer found out that Hadfield was there again. Don't tell me the murderer trailed him every night for six years, Dunc."

The Captain pulled the telephone to him and dialed a number. When the connection was made he asked, "Is that Dan O'Hare?"

A voice clicked through the phone.

"Never mind," said Duncan Maclain, and cradled the phone. "He's off this week end," he told Spud. "He'll be back on tomorrow night again."

Spud's yellow eyes narrowed to a squint. "Of course," he said. "The murderer must have gotten that information from O'Hare."

"Unless he got it from Hadfield," said Maclain. "Hadfield phoned Courtney, his lawyer, and also called his wife and the police the night he died. Courtney sprained his arm and never got there."

"Don't try to sidetrack me," Spud told him, choking over a swallow. "I'm not through with you, Duncan Maclain. Why was that highball glass left in Doxenby's apartment? Surely, if a murderer had worked out some system of shoving his stooges to death by remote control, he wouldn't be such an ass as to make the police think somebody was there."

"Holy bedlam!" The Captain groaned. "Why must that come into my life again? The glass was intended to prove that Doxenby was present the night Sprague was killed and Hadfield blinded. *Ergo*, Doxenby did it. Then six years later, he takes out this grisly memento, and, with worms gnawing at his cowardly liver, he has a drink out of the glass.

"Whereupon, he decides to commit suicide, probably because Hadfield, the only person who might possibly cause him trouble, is dead and out of the way forever." The Captain allowed an instant of dramatic hesitation. "So what does he do? He throws the nearly full bottle of Scotch out the bathroom window, nearly beaning one Abe Stutmeyer, a janitor on the basement floor. This upsets him so that he closes the bathroom window, goes into the kitchen, opens another window, and with a whoop of delight that's heard for a block, he takes a header out and ends his career eleven floors below. What does that sound like to you?"

"Suicide," said Spud, lighting a cigarette and inhaling deeply. "Same as Hadfield's death."

"They won't bring that verdict in when I get through with you," the Captain told him with a venomous smile. "What else is disturbing that feeble element you like to call a brain?"

"The open door at the M. T. & T. building," said Spud, exhaling. "Why was it unlatched when Mrs. Hadfield went in?"

"To plant obvious thoughts in unfertile intellects," said Duncan Maclain. "To make people such as you who are attached to the obvious believe that the door was often left open and that consequently it was nothing unusual for anyone to be able to gain access to the building without a key."

"*Umm,*" crooned Spud. "I suppose you've thought to check."

"Yes," Maclain said tartly. "Outside of Courtney, Hadfield, Bentley, Lawson, Elise Sprague, the watchman, and thirty accountants, there are probably no keys out at all." He reached for the telephone.

"What now?" asked Spud.

"I'm about to invite a friend to dinner. A Miss Sybella Ford. She's dining on you."

"Good Lord!" Spud exclaimed with fervor. "That's what happens when I leave town. I scarcely get my back turned when you pick up a dame. You'd better keep away from balconies, windows, and terraces."

"I'm watching those," said Duncan Maclain.

2

Harold Lawson finally succeeded in dismissing a garrulous visitor by leaving his desk and almost forcibly escorting the talker to the door. It was nearly one and he had a five-o'clock date for squash at his club, plus work to do in the afternoon. The pale gray of the weather outside made the Insurance Department's offices unpalatably dingy. He'd still had no lunch, and Saturdays always dragged themselves out unaccountably long.

His secretary laid several letters in a pile to his right.

"I have three more, Mr. Lawson. Will you want them this afternoon?"

Lawson considered the matter by staring out of the window for a couple of seconds. "If it's not too much trouble, Miss Shriver. We might as well get everything out of the way for the week end." He gave her an understanding smile. Few men had more facility than Harold Lawson in getting top work out of people without friction.

Miss Shriver returned to her typewriter and opened up an enfilading fire of popping keys. Lawson signed the completed letters, tossed them in the OUT basket, and took time to glance at an afternoon paper.

Some astute reporter had spread himself on the possibilities of a mystery. A front-page story dug back into Hadfield and Sprague. Had James Sprague returned from the tomb? If not, whose ghostly fingers had pressed the highball glass in T. Allen Doxenby's apartment? A cartoonist had gone to town with a spectral drawing of James Sprague pushing two men to eternity from the roof of the M. T. & T. Building.

Harold Lawson's merry blue eyes hardened as he reached for a telephone and called the newspaper's City Desk. He knew Al Cheney, the City Editor, fairly well.

"Good God, Al," he complained, "can't you soft-pedal some of this Hadfield-Doxenby tripe you're running? Isn't there enough war news to fill a paper without continuously putting the Department on the grill?"

"You lads are so colorful these last few days." Lawson could almost see the editor's grin.

"Unless I'm wrong," said Lawson in a mortician's tone, "your wife owns about six thousand bucks of certificates in the M. T. & T. We're trying our damndest to salvage all we can out of the mess. All this guff in the papers, of course, keeps pushing the property down."

"Hell's fire!" A silence followed, and it was Lawson's turn to grin. "It might at that," Cheney admitted. "I'll see what I can do."

"You might pass the word along to some of your honored contemporaries," Lawson suggested. "A lot of them dove into the same pool for a swim."

"That's carcelage and solatium, to say nothing of blackmail," Cheney declared.

"Cut the double-talk," Lawson told him, "and see what you can do."

He disconnected, took a look at Miss Shriver's back, and decided that her three remaining letters were about half-finished. Idly, on a desk pad, he began to jot things down:—

Sybella—$37,000—($37,000)
Mrs. H.—$175,000 (?)
Seth H.—$100,000 (?)
Court—$30,000 (?) for Administrator's fee (?????)
Elise S.—$275,000 (?) Sooner or later—REVENGE!!!
C. Bentley—??? C.P.A.
Doxenby—??? Atty at Law
H. L.—??? That's me!

Miss Shriver brought the letters. Lawson laid them over the desk pad and signed them, then grabbed his hat and coat and left for lunch. When Miss Shriver collected the letters, she noted his figuring, but thought nothing of it. Mr. Lawson was always figuring. She placed the scratch pad near the back of Lawson's desk and went away.

Lawson spotted Carl Bentley as soon as he entered the lunchroom—Bentley and the girl. The Comptroller was bending over a corner table staring at his companion through the upper half of his bifocals with a kind of stony fascination.

Lawson joined them, not because he felt actually perverse, but more for the reason that he was curious to see how Bentley behaved. He had known Carl Bentley for some years, and couldn't recall ever having seen him lunching with a woman before.

Mr. Bentley was a shade disconcerted. He shifted his glass-es a notch higher and said, "This is my friend Sophie Munson, Harold. Harold Lawson, Sophie. Harold's the State Insurance man in charge of the M. T. & T."

Sophie batted her oversize blue eyes at Lawson as though his intrusion might be welcome, and purred, "Won't you sit down?"

Lawson pulled out a chair. "If you're picking them for the Atlantic City beauty contest, Carl, your candidate ought to win." He dared a glance of admiration at Miss Munson's opu-lent charm.

"I tried that once." Sophie showed her sharp even teeth. "The judges picked a babe with thirty-two pounds pressure in her brassière. She used to have to check it at a free air station every morning after a tough night's dancing." Miss Munson eyed her-self in a tiny oval hand mirror. "I'll bet she'll thin out in places with this rubber shortage on. Did Carl say you were in charge of the M. T. & T.?"

"The State end of it." Lawson gave his order to a waitress. "Carl's really the one who keeps things rolling along."

"Funny thing," Sophie remarked, dealing a delicate pat to her hair. "That fellow Doxenby who hopped out his window last night was a friend of ours."

"Now, wait a minute, Sophie." Mr. Bentley set his coffee cup down. "I never saw the man before last night when—"

"When—" Lawson prompted pleasantly.

"We met him in a bar," said Sophie. "I thought he said he knew you, Carl."

"He said he might have seen me somewhere downtown." Bentley's face was puckered with the force of his snappish de-nial. "If I'm any judge, he knew you far better than he did me."

"Maybe." Sophie made her red lips into a brand-new Cupid's bow.

"Well, settle it one way or another," Lawson pleaded with a smile. "Not that it makes much difference, but I do think the fact that you met him in a bar, and the time, are things the police would want to know."

Mr. Bentley said, "Great heavens, Mr. Lawson! I never even—"

Sophie's well-manicured fingers closed on Carl Bentley's wrist, but she was staring at Lawson from under long lashes. At last she asked quite coldly, "Why?"

"I thought you'd seen the papers." Lawson turned to his lunch. "The police are making an investigation."

"You mean the papers are making an investigation," said Sophie. "The police have said that Doxenby committed suicide. Why should we stick our necks out? I'm certainly not going to have a lot of flatfeet beating me with a hose." She stood up. "Come on, Carl. I have to get back to my office for an hour. It's been nice meeting you, Mr. Lawson. G'by."

"I hope you don't think—" Carl Bentley began.

"Skip it," said Lawson. "I'll be seeing you, Carl." He turned back to coffee and pie.

When he returned to the office and the elevator in the modern Receivers' Building shot him up to the sixth floor, it was nearly half past two. Lawson wound his way through a multitude of desks to his own small cubicle and was scarcely seated when a junior clerk stuck his head in the door.

"Nearly everyone's gone, Mr. Lawson, and I'm on my way. Shall I shut the record vault, or leave it open for you?"

"Leave it open," said Lawson. "I have some work on the

Long Island Depositors' Fund to finish. I still have the papers. I'll close up when I put them away."

The clerk waved a hand and said, "Okay."

Lawson heard the clerk's retreating footsteps finally cut off by the closing of a door. Some of the figures in the Long Island case were in a mess. He sorted out the papers, pulled his scratch pad toward him, and sat staring vacantly at the blank sheet on top.

The imprints of the doodling he had done before lunch were still visible where his pencil had pressed through to mark the under sheet, but the paper with the writing on it was gone. He took a look in his wastebasket, then examined a larger one by Miss Shriver's desk.

What he had put down could mean nothing to anyone, but Harold Lawson was a stickler for office efficiency. Miss Shriver had strict orders never to throw away his notations. A few figures destroyed without his permission might mean the loss of an entire day.

He settled down to the Long Island appraisals only to find that he couldn't work at all. After a time, he took a battered pipe from a drawer, packed it full of shag and lit it. Puffing moodily, he walked to the door and looked out into the main office. The half nearer to him was lined with shiny desks. The farther half was crowded with a dozen rows of greenish files stacked head high. The entire place was vacant, with the positive emptiness peculiar to a Saturday afternoon.

Lawson crossed to the files, looked down one long aisle and returned to his cubicle. There he found himself distracted by a window washer leaning back calmly against his safety belt twenty stories above the street, on a building across Broadway. A man's life depended on so many little things—a piece of leather no thicker than a finger—two small hooks cemented into a wall—

Paper crackled in the main office, a sound no louder than the rustle of a mouse in a bureau drawer.

Harold Lawson put down his pipe and walked to the cubicle door. It was nearly time to turn on lights and the sixth floor of the Receivers' Building was fading into softness in the waning light of the gloomy winter afternoon.

Over the tops of the intervening files he could see the smooth bulk of the opened vault door. He half-closed his blue eyes and stared harder. He was a man of stable nerve, used to dealing in cold hard facts unmixed with fantasy and visionary concepts.

It annoyed him to feel the pump of blood pounding through his body to cloud the keenness of his brain. Yet the door was unquestionably moving—not very much, but moving. It had altered its position as he watched, swung farther closed, changing its angle with the wall.

Lawson left the cubicle, moving silently on the balls of his feet, every muscle of his powerful body under rigorous control. He took the long way around to the vault, keeping close to the wall. When he was near to the corner of the office with the entrance to the vault almost in sight, pattering footsteps sounded down one of the aisles between the metal files.

Lawson shouted, "Who's there?" and moved forward swiftly.

The pattering footsteps broke into a run. Lawson dashed into one of the metal-walled alleys and saw instantly that he was wrong. The footsteps were in the adjoining aisle. Before he could correct his mistake, a door had opened and closed. Immediately he heard a crash, a groan, and a fall.

He rushed for the door that led to the reception room and jerked it open, then checked himself within a foot of stumbling over a man lying face down close to the opposite door which led to the elevator hall.

Lawson knelt down and turned him over. It was Carl Bentley, and a trickle of blood was seeping down his temple from a crescent-shaped wound. Lawson picked him up, carried him back to the main office and laid him gently on a long mahogany table.

For a second he listened to Bentley's heavy breathing.

"Hell!" he said, and walked back to the vault. The crackling paper which had alarmed him was explained. The impounded checks of James Sprague and Company had been wrapped in brown paper and tied with heavy twine.

They were loose now, spread all over the big vault's floor.

Lawson gathered them together and tied them up. He picked up Bentley's bifocals from where they had fallen, put them in his pocket and went back into his cubicle to call Inspector Davis on the phone.

3

"He slugged me!" Carl Bentley squinted at the Inspector from under a gauze turban and squirmed unhappily on the hardness of an office chair. A doctor had come and gone.

"Who slugged you?" asked Davis.

"A man."

"What did he look like?"

"Well—" Bentley closed his eyes. "He was medium-sized and sort of medium-looking."

"And had pants on," Davis suggested.

"No—an overcoat."

"Oh, no pants!" Davis tasted his mustache and decided it wasn't fit to eat.

"I mean he had an overcoat on—sort of medium—"

"Like his hair?"

"I couldn't say." Mr. Bentley opened his eyes again and gazed at the Inspector with the terror of a frightened robin. "He had a hat on."

"On his head, I suppose."

"Yes. I was very much confused."

Davis said, "You and me! Where did this medium-sized exhibitionist slug you?"

"On my head."

"The location in the office, Mr. Bentley, please. Not the portion of your body."

"Right by the door to the hall."

"Do you mind if I ask Carl a couple of questions?" Harold Lawson consulted his wristwatch. "I have an appointment at five, uptown."

"It would devastate me," said Davis, sitting down.

"What?" asked Bentley.

"Did you ever see this fellow before, Carl?" Lawson asked him.

"Never in my life. All I know is—"

"He was middle class," Davis mumbled. "Sort of like a respectable whore."

"I tell you I couldn't see him very well. I didn't have my glasses on."

"That's true, Davis," said Lawson. "I found them on the vault floor. Tell me, Carl, what were you looking for in there?"

"I was checking on the amount of M. T. & T. certificates purchased by James Sprague." The Comptroller spoke more easily, as if he might be on firmer ground.

"Why didn't you come direct to me?"

"I didn't know you were here, Mr. Lawson. When I left you at lunch I thought you were going home."

"Did you think everyone had left without closing the vault door?"

"I didn't think anything about it. I've often worked up here when the office looked deserted."

"How did you happen to drop all those checks and your glasses on the floor?"

"I don't know," Bentley said after a short reflection. "Something startled me."

"Probably a hippogriff." The Inspector solaced himself with a toothpick.

"I think it was the man who hit me in the door."

"I think it was the door who hit you in the head," said Davis. "It's a medium-sized door with a hat on."

"I don't give a tinker's damn what either of you think!" Mr. Bentley burst out in a spasm that approached hysteria. "There was a man watching me while I was in that vault. He started to shut me in. I saw him move the door."

"Hold on," said Lawson. "Don't fly to pieces, Carl. You haven't mentioned that before."

"Mentioned what?" Bentley made an effort to get himself under control.

"About the door."

"I haven't had a chance. All you two have done is pick on me. It's hard to concentrate with my head in a whirl."

"Mine's about to sling its ears off, too," said Inspector Davis, with a moody chew on the piece of wood between his teeth. "What's about the door?"

"I saw it move myself," Lawson told him. "I could see the top of it over the files from my office here." He motioned the Inspector to the cubicle door and pointed. "See what I mean?"

"Now just what good would it do anyone to shut Bentley into that vault?" the Inspector demanded grimly.

"What good did it do to kill Blake Hadfield?" asked Lawson. "There's a time lock on that door, Davis. If I'd come out and found it closed—" Lawson shrugged uncomfortably. "I'm afraid we'd have found Carl in there on Monday."

"Hadfield had killed himself when I talked to you last night." The Inspector dropped his toothpick into a cuspidor. "What changed your mind?"

"You and Captain Maclain," said Lawson. "You're the one who recommended he be called in. I hope together you'll manage to do something soon. The newspapers are getting to be a bore."

"They could sue me for my impure thoughts." Davis swung on Carl Bentley. "Start from the time you saw this moving door, if you don't mind."

"I dropped the checks and ran."

"Discarding your glasses first, I suppose."

Bentley took out a handkerchief, wiped the bifocals in question, and put them on, guiding the frame cautiously by the bandage over one ear. "When the door started to move, I don't believe I had them on."

"Why?"

"I was cleaning them, I guess. I do it automatically when I'm nervous about something—like I did just now."

"What were you nervous about in the vault?" Davis cracked out.

"About somebody closing the door," said Bentley meekly.

"But you didn't see this man?"

"No, Inspector."

"How was that?"

"He must have been in back of the door."

"What made you suspicious of that? Did you hear him?"

"Not exactly. Somebody started—"

"Yeah," said Davis hastily. "Somebody started to close the door. Now that makes everything simply too, too, u-tray! You didn't see him. You didn't hear him. He was back of the door, pushing it closed. So with him—medium-sized, of course—in back of the door, you start to run. How fast can you run, Mr. Bentley?"

"Not very fast, I imagine."

"Not very fast, Mr. Bentley imagines." Davis turned to Lawson appealingly. "I know who was in back of the door!"

"Who?" asked Lawson, his forehead deep in furrows.

"Pavlo Nurmi, the fleeing Swede," said Davis. "He gives Mr. Bentley a head start and beats him out to the hall by running through another office, then slugs him as he tries to get out the door."

"You forgot something, Inspector," Bentley put in acidly.

"Yes," said Davis. "I forgot he had no pants on."

"You forgot I stopped," said Bentley and gingerly touched the lump on his brow.

"You stopped? What for?"

"I heard someone else coming after me."

"That increases my speed, Mr. Bentley. What the hell did you stop for?"

"I was in a panic. I'd dropped the checks and my glasses, and without my glasses I can't see very well. Without stopping to pick up anything, I ducked out of the door and started to run."

"For where?"

"The outside hall. I wanted to get downstairs. There are several aisles between the files. I took the first one I saw."

"Which was that?"

"He was in the second," said Lawson. "I heard him when he started to run."

"Go on, Mr. Bentley. You ran down the second aisle—"

"Until I heard someone else moving softly to cut me off. That must have been Mr. Lawson circling around the office. I stopped to listen."

"And what did you hear?"

"I heard someone yell, 'Who's there?'"

"Did you answer?"

"No."

"Why not?"

"I was scared, I tell you. I'd thought I was alone."

"Didn't you recognize Mr. Lawson's voice?"

"Certainly not. I'd have answered if I had."

"How long did you stop?"

"I can't say. It was until after Mr. Lawson yelled and started toward the files. Then I ran again."

"Did either of you hear anyone else run?"

"Certainly," Bentley assured him. "The man who was back of the door ran down another aisle."

"Did you hear that, Mr. Lawson?"

"Frankly," said Lawson, "I'm not sure. Maybe I thought the other man was Bentley. All I can swear to is that I heard footsteps in one of the aisles."

"And nothing else?"

"I heard the opening and closing of a door."

"What door?"

"I couldn't see," Lawson told him. "By that time I was in the first aisle."

Davis turned back to Bentley. "Then he must have heard you open and close the door."

"But he didn't," said Bentley with a satisfied smirk. "I heard the door myself. I took another way into the reception hall. You'll find the door is still open from the stenographers' room. Shall I show you?"

"No," said Davis. "Then what happened?"

"As near as I can remember, as I opened the door to the elevator hall I heard someone move behind me. I swung around and this man hit me. That's about all."

"He must have packed a wallop to cut your head open."

"I think," said Bentley, "he had brass knuckles on."

"You're sure you didn't dream this and knock yourself out by running into the open hall door in the reception room?"

"Why should I?" Bentley asked most logically. "To think up such a thing would be a lot of trouble, after all."

"Women cause a lot of trouble, too," said Davis. His heavy eyebrows arched in a scowl. "Have you found that out, Mr. Bentley?"

The Comptroller moistened lips gone suddenly dry. "I don't know quite what you're referring to."

"The dames," said Davis and slowly winked one eye. "The frills, the frails, the skirts, the moolies, some stuff, eh, Bentley, you old goat? We know about them, don't we, eh, you and I?"

"What are you getting at, Inspector Davis?"

"I'm getting at this, Mr. Bentley." Davis's mustache made a rectangle over a thin straight line. "My Department can't let many things slip by. Why didn't you inform us that you met Allen Doxenby last night in a bar?"

"I suppose you told him that, Mr. Lawson."

"Lawson has told me nothing," said Davis. "We happen to have had a man tailing you."

"You mean a detective was following me last night?" Bentley wet his lips again.

"Now you've got it," said Davis.

Mr. Bentley removed his glasses. "Then you'll have definite proof that I had nothing to do with the death of T. Allen Doxenby, Inspector. That's fine!"

There were footsteps outside. Sergeant Archer came in and said, "We picked up the Munson girl."

4

Dan O'Hare lived alone in a small room with an Irish family in the Bronx whose tastes were as simple as his own. His job as night guardian of the M. T. & T. paid him only eighty dollars a month, but his living costs were low and his amusements limited to an occasional movie in the afternoon.

Ten years of continuous employment had grooved his life with habit. His savings account was added to with a regularity that marked the tenth of each month to the receiving tellers in the huge marble Wall Street Savings Fund.

Now and again he voiced an insincere lament to Mrs. Shaw, his landlady, about his unnatural hours. Actually he had learned to sleep much better during the day, and almost regretted the week end off each month which relieved him from Saturday morning at seven until the same hour Sunday evening.

Dan feared nothing that lived. He had confidence in his own brawny frame and double confidence in his ability with a gun. But Dan was Irish, and sometimes in the smaller hours of the night, with sleep pressing close, his thoughts drifted back to tales of his long-dead mother who had told him of the Wee Ones under the bushes, and the haunting cry of the banshee.

Lower Broadway was lonely enough at night, but its depopulation impressed him even more when he relieved his once-a-month assistant on a Sunday evening. Then the lower part of the city seemed to Dan to have a different air, a feeling of waiting as though the streets, drained to isolation by hours of idleness, were holding their breath waiting for a million absent workers who might never return.

The rumbling underground trains ran farther apart and scurried away faster, glad to be gone. Passers on Broadway moved furtively, conscious that they were intruders. It was rare to hear the friendly sound of a taxi swishing past with a brush of air.

Hadfield's death hadn't helped. Dan had put in a few bad months after the Sprague affair six years before, months when he avoided the corner office, not on account of what he feared, but on account of things which were not there.

Now, what with Hadfield tumbling down out of the dome to leave a stain on the tile . . . ! Washed and washed, they had, and still Dan's probing eyes could tell the spot was there. He avoided it carefully when he returned to his cubbyhole at the back of the lobby after letting his relief man out of the little door.

He'd seen an ancient watchman in a movie once, a fellow in knee breeches who went about his work carrying a lantern and keeping everybody awake all night what with shouting out all the time.

"Sunday night, seven o'clock, twelve hours to go, and all is well!" Dan muttered aloud. His voice drifted up into the dome and came down again.

"The divil take it!" he said to no one, and sat down in his cubbyhole to look at the working of his gun.

He was on his rounds at quarter past eight when he heard the bell. Dan punched two more keys on the third floor and took the elevator down, glad of the interruption. It took a living, breathing finger to push a bell.

Sergeant Archer's great bulk thrust itself in through the little door.

"Indade, it's glad I am to see you," said Dan. "I thought it might be Calligan himself now. He sticks his ugly head in of a Sunday night to say hello now and again."

Archer grinned. "It wouldn't be to put a cup of coffee in his ugly stomach, would it now?" He brushed a few light flakes from his collar. "It's turned warmer, Dan, and started to snow. It'll probably turn to rain."

"Indade, it will that now." Dan hitched his clock forward. "And I'm the one could tell you. The calves of me legs has started to pain. I'm on me rounds. Will you be staying here till I'm back again?"

"I'll come along," said Archer. "Let's go."

They rode upstairs together. When O'Hare had finished his fourth-floor rounds, they walked back down to the third.

"I suppose you're wondering what brought me," said Archer as the elevator started up.

"I wonder about nothin', that, ain't me business."

Dan stopped the car and they both got out. "I see you've

moved the two men off the doors. They were doin' no mite of good that I could see, but we had some nice talks. For my part I'd wish them back again."

"It's our own way of doing things, Dan—no chances, see? Whoever shoved Hadfield was gone before we put those men on duty."

"Indade." Dan swung his time clock forward and inserted a key. "He was gone before he ever pushed him, Sergeant."

"What do you mean by that crack?"

"There are certain things, Sergeant, that's niver seen by the likes of you and me."

"Cut it, Dan," said Archer uncomfortably. "You'll get to believing that stuff. Will you answer a few questions for me?"

"An' what might they be?"

"Since last Monday night have you found anything lying around—money, say? Or a fountain pen? Or a paperweight where it shouldn't be?"

"Indade, and you'd have heard of it, Sergeant. After the instructions you and the Inspector left me, I'd not be lettin' you down. I told you about the drinkin' glass that was gone."

"That's okay, Dan. We heard about that from Captain Maclain."

"There's a queer one, now. Him and the little dog fair snoopin' around."

Archer laughed. "He has another dog that same size that I'd hate to have after me. Don't let the Captain fool you, Dan. He's blind, but there's nothing he doesn't see." The Sergeant paused while Dan used another key. "Did you ever find out how that front door came to be open, Dan?"

"No more than you," said Dan. "Unless the boy went downstairs while I'm on me rounds—went out and come back in."

"Well, I'll be an Orangeman's uncle!" said Archer. He took out his notebook and wrote something down. "Speaking of Maclain, Dan, his partner's in town and leaving tonight from the airport. The Captain asked me to tell you that after his partner left he might come down."

"Here?" asked Dan with a frown. "Him and the little dog?"

"Who else?"

"Should I let him in, Sergeant?"

"Of course."

"I have orders," said Dan, "to leave no one in here prowling around."

"You have our okay on Maclain, and two little dogs if he happens to bring them. Tell him anything he wants to know."

"That will be nothin'—for that's what I know, Sergeant."

Archer clapped him on the back. "Don't get to seeing things. I'll run on down the stairs. I have to report back in."

"You'll go down with me," said O'Hare. "I'm after lockin' the door."

Archer stopped at the elevators and pointed to the indicator of the other car still at the ninth floor. "Isn't that thing fixed yet?"

"That it is," said Dan.

"Why don't you bring it down?"

"Because 'tis better up and out of the way. Them accountants is always after riding it up themselves in the day, and leavin' it unexpected on some floor. That's what broke it before."

They got in the other car and rode down. Archer paused halfway out the little door. "Don't forget about Maclain. Try to let him in quickly, Dan. Remember he's blind."

"It's meself will run when I hear the bell."

"Good night, Dan."

"An' the same, Sergeant." Dan closed the little door and made sure the lock was on. For a while he stood staring at it, then he went into his little cubbyhole and dialed the phone.

Steam hissed gently in the basement as he started his nine-o'clock round. Dan looked at the gauge and saw that the proper pressure was on, scarcely enough to keep him warm. Mr. Bentley was forever kicking about the bills. Why couldn't Dan O'Hare wrap himself up warm? Mr. Bentley, indade! Let him stay one night in the building and he's the one would know 'twas colder than a tomb.

He took a look at the fire door. Queer now, that business of Mr. Hadfield. That fire door hadn't been opened in years before the police tried it. They had it well sealed now—little pieces of lead with twisted wires and strips across the bolts. Yet someone had slipped out somewhere, unless Hadfield had jumped or the lad had pushed him down.

Drunk the lad was. Aye, Dan knew! 'Twas himself, a good man in years long gone, that the fiery stuff had brought down. Praise Mary he was off of it now—a wee bit late withal, with his best days past.

The vacant desks on the lobby floor stared at him as he passed, another mute reminder of other days long gone. He shot his flashlight through the glass of the doors into the vacant bank. PAYING TELLER glinted in gold over the tarnished bars of a window. He didn't even have to go in there any more—nothing left to pay or steal.

He took the elevator up to the third floor, skirting the invisible spot on the lobby floor. Two and three were vacant, great vast lofts of space without so much as a carpet to cover the shameful nakedness of the floor.

Up to five and walk a floor back down. Files of old appraisals, all proved wrong. Files of old assessments, old ideas, make a lot of money quick, and the Devil take the hindmost! The Bond and Mortgage Department—twelve keys to punch, to Dan O'Hare. It didn't take long.

Seven and six—like the money in an old Irish song! Guaranteed First Mortgage Certificates, a gilt-edged, gold-embossed, brass-bound guarantee that the funds you had saved for a lifetime were lost forever. Two hundred million dollars. Twelve keys to Dan O'Hare.

Up to nine, and walk a floor back down. Desks and chairs and files, and the thought of a blind man crashing to death over a balcony railing. The thought of a blind man sitting in his office and watching a watchman make his endless rounds.

Light again, and the comforting feel of the crawling birdcage. Coffee on the electric ring in the snugness of his cubbyhole. Dan O'Hare at the lever.

Going down!

The coffee bubbled up, savory and warm. Dan switched off the electric ring, reached for his bread box, and cursed as a large gray shadow scurried across the floor.

Well, he'd get the spalpeen now! That was himself—the one who'd eaten his bread for weeks, who'd not let his dinner alone. He'd hung his gun on a peg while he ate, but he couldn't be shooting at rats with a gun. He took a heavy nightstick from a hook in the corner and stalked his quarry into the lobby.

He had it there, cowering in a corner by the elevator. Dan made a rush. The rat squeezed itself into the thinness of a mouse and vanished through an opening in the grill. Dan heard a startled squeal and scratching feet as the rodent tore around. It was trapped in the solid concrete well of the elevator shaft.

Dan clutched his club more firmly and opened the door to

the vacant shaft. The ancient elevators ran no lower than the lobby floor. He shone his light down into glittering red eyes, and shut it off again. Mr. Rat would bother him no more. On hands and knees he backed until his legs were hanging in the shaft, and lowered his frame into the pit.

Standing on the bottom of the shaft, he moved the beam of his flashlight about the oil-covered floor, and crossed himself quickly. It was a single eye glaring back at him now, a big eye winking at the torchlight with a million blazing streaks of color as though the end of a rainbow had been caught in a single crystal ball.

Rats were never the best of luck, and the Wee Ones had put things into his head. 'Twas not enough to be staring at the lost glass eye of a giant—he must be hearing things, too, in the quiet of the night: soft movements like, echoing down from the overhead darkness of the lobby's dome.

Close by him, a spark flashed blue with a startling electric sputter, and machinery began to whir its clanking song.

"Holy Mother, protect us!" whispered Dan. "'Tis the elevator above me coming down!"

The descending car stopped two feet above the lobby floor. Cursing, O'Hare stuck his head up through the opening nicely in position to meet the swung-down butt of a heavy gun. Five minutes later the elevator started upward bearing the unconscious O'Hare.

CHAPTER VII

1

SPUD SAVAGE came into Rena's bedroom early Sunday afternoon. The Captain had bought tickets for the symphony concert at Carnegie Hall, four tickets. Spud stretched himself out on the bed, lit a cigarette, and watched his wife arrange her dark wavy hair which was beginning to show the faintest streaks of gray.

He smoked his cigarette half down before he said, "Lovely gal!"

"Thanks, old dear," said Rena. She blew a kiss into the dressing table's triple mirror.

"Self-complacent dame, aren't you?" Spud returned her aerial caress and gave a derisive grin. "You know I'm not referring to you. You're just—well, skip it, before I slop over!"

"Sybella Ford, I suppose?" Rena half-turned her head and expertly patted her hair. "There's an ash tray on the table beside you. Quit putting them on the floor."

"What do you think, Rena? Is it serious? Dinner last night, concert this afternoon—he's even asked her to go to the airport to see me off tonight."

"She bullies him, darling. He was dancing last night, remember?"

"Nuts," said Spud. "You've bullied him for years—and me."

"And you married me," Rena reminded him.

"Well, I'll be damned," said Spud. "I never thought of that before."

"Not any more than you've thought of marriage in connection with Duncan Maclain. He's a man, Spud—strong, handsome, brilliant. Both of us have been so close to him we've begun to regard him as a machine."

"He's sensitive as the devil. If she hurts him—" Spud crushed his cigarette in the tray.

"So sensitive that it's an armor, darling, a shield against anything false or tawdry."

"You must like her."

"I think she's wonderful, and so do you." Rena came and sat beside him on the bed. "You're selfish in only one thing, Spud—your affection for Duncan Maclain."

"He's met plenty of women before."

"So had you before you married me."

"But that's different." Spud slipped an arm about her slender waist.

"Quite," she agreed. "He's blind, Spud. It would take him longer to make a selection. For twenty-four years he's been learning to move with greater swiftness, but at the same time, darling, he has learned to move with increasing care. If he has picked Sybella Ford to marry, he knows he's right. She's been chosen with the same unerring facility with which he strikes a key on his typewriter. Duncan Maclain can never erase an error, Spud. He's had to master perfection. He can't be wrong."

"Damn him!" Spud said fiercely. "I love him because he can't be wrong and can still carry on under such an inhuman strain. What's Sybella got, Rena, that other women have lacked? Why should she appeal to Dunc's emotions and fascinate his screwy brain?"

"She has a dead man to thank for that, Spud."

"Hadfield?"

"Yes. She was a friend of his for several years. It got her accustomed to being around a man who was blind. She lost all the nervous gawkiness most women have around them which Duncan is so quick to feel. He was equally at ease with her from the instant she stepped into his office last Tuesday. You watched her last night. No coddling, Spud. She treats him exactly as though he could see. Besides, she's smart and attractive, and likes you and me. Don't think he doesn't feel that, too!"

"He feels everything," Spud agreed soberly. "You're fairly smart yourself, Rena, old dear. You're lucky to be married to me."

"I'm lucky to have spent a few years as secretary to Duncan Maclain."

"You just wait," said Spud, tightening his hold on her waist. "I'll tell her you make passes at him. I'm the lad that can put a flea in the smart Sybella's ear."

Rena leaned over and kissed the tip of his nose. "You're a lamb, darling!" She was smiling, but one of her grave soft eyes was bright with an unshed tear.

The Captain was silent during most of the afternoon, but brightened up after the concert over cocktails in the penthouse living room.

Sergeant Archer telephoned shortly before six. Spud listened quietly as the Captain told Archer he intended to visit O'Hare that night, but made no remark when Maclain hung up the phone.

Spud's plane left at ten. Cappo drove them to La Guardia Field in the Packard. Rena and Sybella went inside to look over the Administration Building, leaving Maclain and his partner a few minutes to talk alone in the car.

"I don't like this Hadfield business, Dunc," Spud said abruptly. "Drop it, won't you?"

Maclain chuckled, but inflexible lines showed on his face as he took an electric lighter from the arm of the seat and applied a cigarette to its white-hot glow.

"Afraid I can't handle it alone?"

"Don't talk like a fool!"

"What, then?"

"Even the police have been forced into a suicide alley. There's nothing to go on, Dunc. You can't prove a man was killed by an absent person."

"No? What about time bombs and arsenic?"

"Both leave traces, Dunc. In the history of crime there's never been a machine that could push a man over a railing or out of a window—not even a blind man—and Doxenby could see."

"Davis and Archer think it's murder, Spud. So do you, or you wouldn't ask me to let go. Science progresses, Spud, even in murder. There's something so subtle afoot that it has to be uncovered. What would the underworld do to society if an undetectable or unprovable method of murder was placed in its hands?"

"How can you prove the unprovable crime, Dunc, or detect the undetectable?"

"By detecting and proving," said Duncan Maclain.

"That will eventually take guinea pigs," Spud told him with

BLIND MAN'S BLUFF · 165

intense earnestness. "This business is too damn simple, Dunc, too open-and-shut, too aboveboard. It stinks with a lot of nice people beaming respectability, answering all your questions correctly, gripping your hand and looking you straight in the eye."

"I haven't been able to see them," said Maclain. He leaned farther back in the corner and doused his cigarette in an ash tray set in the arm. "If I remember correctly, Spud, guinea pigs were used to very great advantage in a little job of spytrapping we worked on about a year ago, when I was chasing an elusive odor of violets."

"Yes," said Spud, "but none of the guinea pigs was named Duncan Maclain." He leaned closer and closed his powerful fingers on the Captain's knee. "I know you too well, Dunc. You can put things over on anybody but me. You're in a mess that ordinary police methods won't break."

"Maybe that's why I'm in it."

"Shut up a minute and listen to me. I'm not a fool. You're in love with a woman, Dunc, and God knows I'm so happy about it I could cheer, and Rena is, too. But be careful of it, Dunc. Now that you've found it, don't toss it away.

"For the first time in your life you're in danger. You live by your brain, and the brain of a man in love is never quite crystal-clear. You're playing with a killer who has stood the Police Department on its ear. I happen to know your methods. If you can't break this any other way, you'll dig up enough facts to make yourself a menace, and deliberately stick your neck out to let this murderer try his game on you."

"So what?" the Captain snapped.

"So be careful this isn't the time you get your neck broken, Captain Duncan Maclain. Promise me just one thing."

"I'm sticking until this killer is caught, or dead."

"I know that," said Spud. "But I want your promise on this. Otherwise I'll get leave from Washington and stay right here, if I have to kiss a congressman to do it. Keep Dreist with you, Dunc. Go back to the penthouse now and get him. That dog is your one chance if you want to stay alive and see this out. Don't go near that M. T. & T. without him. Don't go anywhere without him. Will you give me your word, Dunc? Day or night don't get any farther away from that devil than the end of his chain."

"Okay, scary pants, I'll promise," said Duncan Maclain.

Spud clasped his hand. The car door slammed. A moment later the Captain heard the roar of a warming plane.

Rena and Sybella got back in. Cappo slid open the window over the driver's seat and asked, "Is you goin' downtown now, Cap'n, suh?"

"Home first, Cappo," said Maclain.

The Sunday night traffic was heavy. It was nearly eleven by the time the Packard had let Sybella out at the Richelieu Shop on Madison, and crossed Central Park to Maclain's apartment again.

Once inside his office, the Captain made directly for the telephone. Rena sat down and lit a cigarette, watching the lightning strokes of his finger as he dialed O'Hare's night number at the M. T. & T. building. She puffed slowly, listening to the faint purr in the receiver caused by the steady alternate ringing of the bell.

"No answer?" Rena asked.

The Captain's hand reached for a row of buttons on the edge of his desk. From a loudspeaker behind the paneling a disembodied voice spoke over his direct connection with the Time Bureau.

"When you hear the signal, the time will be exactly ten fifty-one."

Maclain disconnected and dialed again. The unanswered phone bell purred on, endlessly it seemed to Rena. Maclain pressed his time-signal button a second time. Two minutes had passed, ten fifty-three.

The Captain left his desk and walked to the terrace door. Dreist lived outside in a steam-heated private kennel of his own.

"See if you can get Harold Lawson at the Hotel Mandeville," he said to Rena. "If he's in ask him if he has a key to the M. T. & T. building. Tell him I'll call by for him in fifteen minutes. I want him to go downtown with me. Then try the M. T. & T. yourself, and keep ringing."

The Captain stepped out onto the terrace, took six paces to the right and unfastened Dreist's chain. The police dog was heavier than Schnucke, with a broad full chest replete with power. His powerful fighting jaws were white with gleaming teeth that with one quick crunch could splinter a bone.

He was trained to work from the Captain's right, since Schnucke's post was on the left. The instant the chain was loosed, he took his place close to his master's knee, loyal to death, and afraid of nothing: a killer on the side of the law. Braver than the many men he had trapped, to bring them down in groveling terror, it was fun to Dreist to charge in the face of a blazing gun.

The Captain stepped back inside and closed the door. "Stand, Dreist!" he ordered, and turned to Rena.

"Mr. Lawson's waiting for you. The watchman still doesn't answer. Maybe he's on his rounds."

"I'm afraid he's punched his last time clock," said Duncan Maclain. "I'm afraid he knew what I badly wanted to know!"

2

The soft melting snow had mingled with rain, leaving a grayish layer of slush on the New York streets. The Captain's Packard sped down Park Avenue with clinking chains drawing a set of black parallel bands through the surface scum. In spite of the Captain's urging, Cappo at the wheel was forced for safety's sake to take it slowly.

Schnucke, drowsy with the comfortable warmth of the heated car, was crouched in comfort at Maclain's feet. Seated in front by Cappo, Dreist kept his watchful eyes on passing traffic, pulling now and again against the restraint of his heavy chain.

Lawson broke into the Captain's thoughts with a question. "What could possibly have happened to O'Hare?"

Maclain wound down a window for ventilation. "Anything's a guess. All I know is he didn't answer his phone. You brought your key?"

"Yes. Did you give him plenty of time to finish his rounds? He might have been upstairs."

"He starts his rounds on the hour, doesn't he?"

"I believe so. I'm not sure."

"I am," said Maclain. "I listened to him a few nights ago. It takes him about forty minutes to cover the building. Then he returns to the little room he uses on the ground floor. His phone's in there."

"Who could have anything against O'Hare, Maclain?"

"Who had anything against Sprague, Hadfield, Doxenby, or Bentley?" The Captain crossed his legs and nursed a knee.

"You heard what happened yesterday afternoon?"

"Yes. Part of it, at any rate."

Lawson was silent for the space of a traffic light. "Somebody took a piece of paper from my desk while I was out to lunch. I'd been scribbling on it what it seemed various people might get out of Hadfield's death. It was rather an alarming setup, Maclain."

"How would Bentley profit?" the Captain asked.

"He wouldn't have. What made you think that?"

"If he didn't take that paper from your desk, there must have been another person in your office yesterday afternoon."

"The police think his story isn't true."

"And you?"

"I'm not so sure." Lawson stared out at the darkened buildings on Fourth Avenue. "Davis has a theory that Bentley may have been dipping into the present funds of the M. T. & T. It's not a nice thing to think of, but I'm putting an auditor on his books first thing tomorrow."

"What gave Davis that idea?"

"Did he tell you Bentley was mixed up with a girl?"

"Bentley?" Maclain reached down and petted Schnucke's ear. "Women certainly break out in the damnedest places, Lawson. Who's the girl?"

"Her name is Sophie Munson. She has a reputation that even Lux won't clean. Archer picked her up yesterday for questioning."

"Did you hear any of the answers?"

"A few. Archer brought her to my office and confronted Bentley. Apparently they'd been tailing, or shadowing him, or whatever they call it." Lawson paused. "The girl was mixed up with T. Allen Doxenby. Bentley might have had plenty of reason to kill Doxenby, Captain Maclain."

The Captain whistled softly. On the front seat, Dreist turned his head and stared back through the glass.

"The old army game, I suppose—blackmail," said Maclain.

"That's what Davis and Archer think—except for one thing."

"He couldn't have killed him," said Duncan Maclain.

"How did you figure that out?"

"It's apparent, isn't it? Bentley was being shadowed. How could he kill a man with a detective on his trail?"

"That's what Bentley claims."

"Have you considered, Lawson, that everybody concerned is claiming almost the same thing?"

"No, I hadn't." Lawson sounded perplexed.

"Well, consider it. It's true," the Captain said. "You say you made out a list of those who might benefit by Hadfield's death. Did you also list where they were at the time?"

"No."

"Try it," said Maclain. "Try it with Doxenby's death, as well."

"How would the same people be involved there?"

"Make it singular instead of plural, Lawson. Ask me how the same person was involved. After all, that's what we want to know."

"Well, how?"

"A highball glass with Sprague's fingerprints on it, a glass that came from Blake Hadfield's set. That's one thing. Another is Doxenby's knowledge of Hadfield's business, his almost *intimate* knowledge of it, I might say."

"I hadn't thought of that."

"You'll have to take my word for it."

"Could he have learned that from Bentley through the Munson girl?"

"I don't know how much Carl Bentley knows about Hadfield's affairs. Do you?"

"After what happened yesterday I know he's plenty interested," Lawson stated with a positive slap of his hand on his knee. "When he was interrupted he had all of the Sprague Company's checks dug out of our files. He gave me a story of wanting to check on Sprague's investments in M. T. & T."

The Captain sat listening as the Packard crossed car tracks and turned south on Broadway. "Will that statement hold water, Lawson?"

"It might. After all, Bentley's the Comptroller. He might be called upon to check into anything any day."

"Or it might be duties coincident with interests," suggested Maclain.

"Frankly, Captain, it smacked of that to me. Nothing has come up in our department concerning the Sprague case in a long time. Why should Bentley start digging into its old files all of a sudden yesterday? Then, if he was really knocked out, his actions certainly interested somebody else, too. Who could that be?"

"A man," said Maclain. "If Bentley's tale is true."

"He claimed he'd never seen his assailant before," Lawson reminded him.

"There is one person who might give us the truth," said Duncan Maclain.

"Who?"

"Elise Sprague. She's smart, and as a secretary is very close to Bentley. I think she'd be bound to remember if anything had come up about her father's company during the past week—assuming it came up in an ordinary routine."

"I'll ask her tomorrow," Lawson promised. "I hope to God nothing more happens to get in our way."

"I'm holding my breath and my gun, Lawson," said Duncan Maclain.

Cappo swung the Packard in a quick U-turn, hopped out and opened the door.

The Captain said, "Mr. Lawson and I won't be long, Cappo. Stay parked right here." He reached in the front and unfastened Dreist's chain from a staple in the seat-back. With a double turn about his hand, he snapped an order to heel, and turned again to his chauffeur. "Keep your eyes open, Cappo," he told the giant Negro. "There may be trouble. Stop anybody who comes out the door we're going in."

"Yassuh, Cap'n." Cappo touched his hat. "I'll try."

"Don't break any arms, Cappo—just stop them." The Captain grinned. "I've seen your tries before." He turned to Lawson. "Don't ring. Just let us in quietly."

Harold Lawson slid his key in the lock. Maclain's two dogs stepped quickly through the opening, followed by the Captain and Lawson, who closed the door.

"Where's the elevator?" asked Maclain. He spoke quite low.

"They're both up," said Lawson with equal quiet. He crossed the lobby with the Captain by his side and stopped at the shaft. "The one that's running is on the third. The other one's still on the ninth floor."

"Let's go up the stairs." Maclain reached down and unsnapped the chain from Dreist's collar.

"What are you going to do?" asked Lawson.

The Captain walked quickly to the foot of the stairs. "Guard!" he ordered Dreist. "I'm going to make sure, Lawson, that nobody gets out that door. Dreist will stay right where he is until we come back downstairs, but you stay close to my side, and whatever you do while you're in sight of Dreist, don't pull a gun."

Lawson's voice was not entirely steady. "I haven't one. What do you think has happened to O'Hare?"

"I don't hear any footsteps," said Maclain. "I think we'd better hurry and find him."

They climbed the stairs hurriedly. Lawson whispered, "If the elevator's on the third—"

"Exactly," said Maclain. "He should be somewhere on the third or second floor."

They left the second-floor balcony for the old main office. The Captain said, "This is unfurnished. I can tell by the sound of our footsteps. You could see his flash, or I could hear him if he was here."

"And alive," Lawson reminded him.

"Where are the lights?" asked Maclain.

Lawson located a wall switch and turned it. "There aren't many bulbs left, Captain, but I can see he's not on this floor. Let's try the third."

They went on up and covered it from one side of the building to the other. It proved equally bare. Back out on the third-floor balcony the Captain checked Lawson suddenly with a hand on his arm.

"Listen! I'm certain I heard him upstairs. Hurry, Lawson!" He raised his voice and shouted, "O'Hare! O'Hare!" then ordered, "Forward, Schnucke, quick! Quick!" and started for the stairs.

He stopped as quickly as he had started. O'Hare's unmistakable Irish voice had answered. "Mother of God, save us!" His words and his scream went soaring into the dome.

The Captain and Schnucke were almost down to the lobby before the falling watchman struck the tiles to lie forever still as Hadfield had done a week before.

Lawson said in a scarcely distinguishable voice, "Now it's Dan O'Hare."

"Don't move from my side, Lawson!" Maclain's command was flat as the marble floor. "I'm putting the dog on the prowl. Search, Dreist! Search!" He pointed a hand up the stairs, and like a dark comet the dog was gone.

The Captain went forward and knelt by Dan O'Hare. For a moment his surgeon's fingers were busy. Then he said, "Call the police, Lawson, and come back immediately. Dreist will attack if you're not near me." His voice was low and steady like a prayer.

Side by side they stood together listening endlessly as Dreist's flying feet scurried over floor after floor like a bird dog on the run, and returned each time inexorably to speed once more up the marble stairs. Ten, fifteen, twenty minutes, and only once the Captain spoke.

"He can smell and hear, Lawson. Nobody can escape him."

The clattering doorbell rang as Dreist pushed one of the swinging doors open, came in from the back office into the lobby and trotted up to Maclain.

Davis, Archer, and three more men piled through the little door. The Captain pointed and said, "O'Hare, this time, Davis. Over there."

The Inspector snapped out orders and men ran up the stairs. Maclain said stonily: "Dreist covered the building from roof to basement, Davis. He just got back. We were here when O'Hare fell. This time I *know* there was nobody there."

"I can't take more of this, Maclain." The Inspector's voice was tired and old.

"You won't have to," said Maclain. "This time the killer slipped, as they always do. Get me O'Hare's time clock and I'll give you his murderer's name."

"And where is it?" asked Davis grimly. "It isn't by him where he fell."

"It's at the bottom of the elevator shaft where the car's on the ninth floor. You'll find oil on the bottom of O'Hare's shoes, Davis. The only place he could have walked in it was down there."

Davis pushed back his hat.

"You mean he dropped his clock there?"

"How else would it get there?" asked Duncan Maclain.

3

The big clock on the wall of Inspector Davis' office ticked off another lugubrious minute and pointed to a quarter past one. Footsteps sounded along the corridor. A man in uniform opened the door and said, "Here they are."

Davis made a silent motion of assent. In a chair in one corner, flanked by his two dogs, Captain Maclain closed his eyes as though he might be dozing, and lowered his chin.

The patrolman on the door opened it wider and said, "Come in."

"Sit down, please." The Inspector's face was as noncommittal as a doorknob with a gray mustache, but the drawn tightness of his voice nullified part of his exterior calm.

"What's happened now, Davis?" Phil Courtney removed his overcoat, and the Captain judged the lawyer's injury was better. At any rate, he had finally managed to get a sleeve over his left arm.

"I asked Lieutenant Hadfield to drop down and talk with me," said Davis. "It's very late, I know. It really wasn't necessary for the rest of you to come along."

Julia Hadfield said, "It's my fault, Inspector. I insisted that

Phil and Elise come, too. They were still at our apartment when you phoned."

"They've been there all evening, I suppose?"

"Almost," Seth told him shortly. He removed his service cap, but kept his greatcoat on as he sat down. Elise drew a chair up close and took Seth's hand.

"Oh, you were out for a while?"

"Yes," said Seth. "With Elise."

"Rotten night, isn't it?" Davis took a toothpick from a small jar on his desk and thrust it in one corner of his mouth. "Maybe you went to a picture show?"

"I understood you had dropped all charges against Seth," Courtney intervened smoothly.

"Charges?" Davis lifted his heavy brows. "We kept Lieutenant Hadfield here one night for his own protection about a week ago. He was—" The Inspector raised one hand and wobbled it back and forth. "What shall I say?"

"Stinko," said Seth. "Look, Inspector. If you have anything on your chest, get it off, will you? It's late and all of us have been upset. I'm not a fool. You've had me trailed, and Elise trailed. We even bought one of your little fellows a drink the other night. If you're interested in anything we've done, surely Oscar, the faithful shadow, can let you know."

Davis combed his mustache with his lower teeth. "You and Miss Sprague pulled a neat one in the subway tonight. The way you popped in and out of doors indicates you must be mystery fans."

"Good lord, Davis!" Phil Courtney exclaimed. "The boy's home on leave. Can't he have a little fun?"

"Sure," said Davis grimly. "We're chasing a playful creature right now—some chap who is simply brimful of bubbling humor—pushing folks off of balconies and out of windows. It has us in stitches, Counselor. Ha-ha! Some fun!"

"The Department has announced that Mr. Hadfield and Doxenby committed suicide." Courtney's lips set. "Has anything happened to change your mind?"

"What mind?" asked Davis. "I've had a clean one on every day for a week like a suit of underwear." The toothpick broke between his teeth and he spit it out on the floor. "After you shook our shadow in the subway, Lieutenant, where did you go?"

"Downtown," said Elise, tightening her fingers on Seth's. "Tell him, Seth. Sooner or later they're bound to know."

"Yes," said Davis. "Sooner or later. You went downtown. Then where did you go?"

"We took a taxi."

"Wait, Seth," Julia broke in. "There's some reason back of this questioning. Before my son is required to answer anything, I think we're entitled to know. Don't you, Phil?"

Courtney answered with caution. "That's probably so. As Seth's adviser, I feel he shouldn't tell you anything until we know."

There was a slight stir in the corner. "Dan O'Hare, the watchman, is dead," said Duncan Maclain.

"God above!" Seth exclaimed aloud.

"I'm frightfully sleepy," the Captain declared. "Tell us the truth, Seth. It will be the best thing by far."

"Maclain's right," said Davis. "You certainly pick bad nights, young man, to visit the M. T. & T."

"What happened to O'Hare?" Seth gently disengaged Elise's hand.

"I'm sure you'd better wait, Seth," Courtney advised with sudden decision.

"Damn it to hell!" flashed Davis. "I'll slap that boy in jail right now if he doesn't come clean, and you can put your creaking legal machinery in motion to get him out. I'm sick of petting people. Blake Hadfield was killed while he was there. He was supposed to be home Friday night when Doxenby was killed. How do we know he didn't dodge our shadow then? Now, to-night—" He calmed down like a rocket at the top of its flight. "You'd better answer my questions, Seth."

"Why not?" Seth's young face was tragic. "Ask them, and I will."

"Why did you duck our shadow?"

"I didn't want him to know where I was going, naturally. It might have looked suspicious."

Davis mumbled. "How do you think it looks now? You got a taxi when you left the subway downtown?"

"Yes."

"Where?"

"Chambers Street."

"Why? The M. T. & T. isn't far."

"It's sleeting like blazes. Elise waited in the taxi for me."

The Inspector said politely, "Would you mind stepping outside, Miss Sprague? If we can get an independent check on this, it will save a lot of time."

"Not at all." She left the office and the patrolman closed the door.

"When you reached the M. T. & T. building," Davis went on, "do you recollect the time?"

"It was somewhere around ten thirty, I believe." Seth was speaking more steadily, his eyes watching the dogs by Maclain.

"You didn't check it?"

"No. But it couldn't have been much more. We left Phil and Mother at the apartment just before ten."

"Did they know where you were going?"

Seth hesitated.

"It was I," said Julia, "who advised him to go downtown."

Davis said, "Do you mind telling why?"

"Yes." Julia's chin set in a stubborn line.

"It's unimportant, of course," said Davis. "We're only trying to find what caused three men to die."

"Four," said Captain Maclain.

"Yes," said Davis. "Four."

"This can have nothing to do with it." Julia gave a determined sigh.

The Inspector shrugged and turned to Seth again. "Half past ten, eh?"

"Yes, about that."

"Did you ring?"

"Yes."

"And Dan O'Hare answered?"

"No."

"Oh, then you didn't go in?" The Inspector rumpled his mustache between forefinger and thumb.

"Yes. I rang a few times, and finally decided O'Hare was on his rounds. It was sleeting, as I said before, so I unlocked the door and went in."

"Where did you get the key?"

"I used Elise's key."

Davis said *"Hmm!"* and smoothed his mustache into place again. "It was a bad night to take a young lady on such a trip downtown. Couldn't you have left her at home?"

"She insisted on coming."

"Why?"

"She thought I might get down there and O'Hare would refuse to let me in."

"Tell me, Seth," said Duncan Maclain. "Did Elise mention particularly that O'Hare had orders to admit no one?"

"Yes, Captain Maclain. She said I couldn't get in unless I was with someone who worked there."

"Thank you." The Captain settled down once more.

"So you didn't see O'Hare until after you got in?" Davis started his gentle battering again.

"I didn't see him then."

"Do you expect that to be believed?" Davis' question was stern.

"You can believe what you like," said Seth. "I'm telling you the truth. I talked to him, though."

"But didn't see him?"

"That's what I'm trying to tell you, Inspector. He called down from one of the balconies and asked, 'Who's there?' I told him that I wanted to go up to my father's office for a minute."

"Did he ask you what for?"

"No." Seth shook his head emphatically. "I said Miss Sprague was waiting outside in a taxi."

"And then?"

"He said I'd have to wait until he finished his rounds or walk up, so I walked. Neither of the elevators was on the lobby floor."

The Captain straightened up. "Could you swear it was O'Hare?"

Seth said doubtfully, "Why, no. I couldn't see very well when I looked up. There's a single powerful bulb hanging in the middle of the lobby. It blinds you badly."

"How many times have you heard O'Hare's voice?"

"Only once, I believe, Captain. Last Monday when he let my father in."

"Do you happen to remember what he asked you then? I mean the very first thing when he came to the door."

Seth thought a moment. "I don't think he asked anything. I was a bit on the offside, you know."

"Didn't your father have to explain anything before O'Hare would let him in?"

Seth was thoughtfully silent a second time. "Yes, since you mention it, I believe so. O'Hare said something about having to get authority to let my father in."

"Where did he get it?" asked Maclain.

Seth said, "I'm sure I don't know. If he got it any place, it must have been after we were in." Dreist moved restlessly, and Maclain said soothingly, "Down! Could you judge what floor O'Hare was on when he called down to you?"

"The sixth, at a guess. On my way upstairs, the elevator was there. It was still there, if I'm not mistaken, when I walked back down."

"That's funny, Davis, isn't it?" remarked Maclain. "For the first time in ten long years, Dan O'Hare, while making his rounds, stopped an elevator on an even floor."

"Meaning what?" asked Davis.

"That the voice that spoke to Seth tonight didn't belong to O'Hare."

The office was quiet. The Inspector leaned back and asked very softly: "What did you take from your father's safe tonight?"

"Nothing," said Seth defiantly. "There was nothing there."

"What were you looking for?"

Courtney put in, "Seth went down on my advice, Inspector, to see if his father had some papers of personal import only. They can have no bearing – "

Duncan Maclain stood up and stretched. "Cut it, Davis, and let's go home."

He turned to face Courtney. "The police know all about it, Mr. Courtney, the data—the name of the home. They know Seth is telling the truth. He only shook *his* shadow in the subway. Miss Sprague's stayed on."

"Damn it," said Davis heatedly. "I'm not finished!"

"Well, I am for tonight. You're wasting good energy, Davis, and you'll need it. I promised you a killer's name, but you'll need more than that. You'll need proof to burn him. Now, give Seth his adoption papers out of your desk, and let's go home. That's what Blake Hadfield started to write about in the note he left. That's what he took Seth down there for. You've gained nothing by keeping your mouth closed about them until today."

4

By Monday morning, Sunday night's sleet had finally made up its mind and turned into a cold, penetrating rain instead of snow.

The Captain slept late, and Cappo brought his breakfast to the office about noon. Although he couldn't see them, the vagaries of the weather strongly affected Duncan Maclain. Over his breakfast, he huddled closely into the warmth of his heavy silk dressing gown and concentrated on coffee, almost neglecting the other dishes on his tastefully arranged tray.

After his third cup he felt some better. He touched a button starting a record on the Capehart, lit a cigarette, and rang for Cappo to remove the tray.

The music didn't suit him. He changed to another record, and still it sounded wrong, inharmonious, and a shade off key.

Perhaps it was Duncan Maclain and not the music that was off key. With a gesture of impatience, he disconnected the Capehart and took his jigsaw puzzle from the drawer. Schnucke trotted up after a time and nuzzled at his knee. Maclain scratched a place just behind the tip of her nose and said, "Now, I'd play hell getting married, wouldn't I?" She gave him no help so he ordered her to lie down.

Twenty-four years in a colorless land of angles, smell and sound—the warmth of Spud's voice, the feel of a dog's head as it rested on his knee, the smell of roses, coffee, perfume, and the pleasant bite of a good cigar, the quiet of New York at midnight in the spring, a quiet still broken by its ceaseless roar.

And danger. Peril. Battling with wits against men with functioning eyes. Winning! That was champagne to a man who could not see; that was proof that Duncan Maclain was as good as, and better than, most men who had sight . . . .

"You're married to your dog." Sybella speaking.

"I don't mean any offense, but Hadfield had been shot and blinded, and many blind men arouse a lot of sympathy." Lawson speaking.

"You're blind, but you pick up one hell of a lot that others miss." Archer speaking.

And Spud. You could trust Spud: "For the first time in your life you're in danger. You live by your brain, and the brain of a man in love is never quite crystal-clear. You're playing with a killer who has stood the Police Department on its ear." . . .

"Damn them all!" said Duncan Maclain, and crashed his clenched fist down in the midst of his puzzle. As suddenly as the lightning streak of temper had come it was gone, and his face had set in a dangerous mask.

Schnucke stood up trembling at his outburst. "Lie down, old gal," the Captain told her gently. "I'm about to demonstrate the impossible—that a man can be in love and still have a brain that's more than crystal-clear."

They had all been wrong, as the music was wrong—just a shade off key. Davis and Archer and Duncan Maclain had all been trying to build a series of murders around the M. T. & T.

The cornerstone was wrong.

Duncan Maclain released a piece of the puzzle he was holding, found another, and placed it. Working swiftly he formed a foundation of other pieces around it.

Sprague, Hadfield, and Dan O'Hare. Chance had brought them death in a single building, but T. Allen Doxenby had died in his own apartment. And T. Allen Doxenby was decidedly a vital link in the murder chain. What had Doxenby to do with the M. T. & T.?

"Nothing at all," whispered Duncan Maclain, and laid his cornerstone.

Sprague was the cause of the murders. James Sprague, the first one dead, head of the Sprague Investment Company— James Sprague and Company, Investment Brokers. He had killed four men including himself, quite unwittingly.

Why?

Because he was under indictment at the time he died and about to go to jail.

The Captain found another piece that fitted, and thoughtfully patted it down. James Sprague was about to prove to his friend Blake Hadfield that he, James Sprague, was not guilty as charged.

How could he prove it?

Just one way. By exposing the guilty one. That would never, never do! Before he could prove such a thing, James Sprague must be put out of the picture.

"Holy Moses!" said Duncan Maclain, and relinquished a piece of the puzzle. Suppose Sprague's killer had himself attempted suicide and failed? Sometimes, building puzzles without eyes to see, you built the picture upside down!

Seth Hadfield wasn't Hadfield's son at all, but Seth certainly hadn't killed James Sprague and blinded his foster father. At that time Seth was only fourteen or fifteen at the most.

The Captain leaned back in his chair and clasped his hands behind his neck. Just a year or so before he had made a statement to a state policeman in Hartford, Connecticut. The statement was: "The worst murders in the history of crime were committed by a twelve-year-old boy."

He sat up with a jerk and returned to his puzzle. He was getting away from fundamentals, sidetracked by a few sleight-of-hand tricks. Disappearing change. A vanishing fountain pen. A dropping bottle in an airshaft.

Well, they'd found the watchman's clock where he had said they would, in the bottom of the elevator shaft.

The Captain pressed the heels of his palms tight against his sightless eyes. He had, in the past, worked out the exact location of a stolen fortune concealed in the subways under New York City. He had solved the method of murder used to hang a man on the balcony of Doncaster House hotel. Now, somebody was plunging people to their deaths. With what? A fountain pen? A crystal paperweight? A bottle of Scotch? A ball of wrapping twine?

Or was there something deeper? Something far more complicated than such boyish weapons? The answer was as elusive as a schoolboy's puzzle—take the rings apart and put them together again. It's right in your hands and still you can't work it.

In the name of everything that added up to common sense, what horrible contrivance could cause a man to scream in terror and leap from his kitchen window? What device dug up from the lowest level of hell could wring such a cry from the throat of a man as strong as Dan O'Hare and cause him to jump to his death to the lobby below?

Search and try. Try and search. Duncan Maclain felt as though he were falling himself. The missing answer was certainly laying him low.

He was glad when the telephone rang to announce Inspector Davis, even though the Inspector bustled in and said without preamble, "You promised me the name of the killer if I found you O'Hare's clock. I found it. Now, let's go."

Maclain said, "Sit down," and opened a drawer beside him. He took out a small paper disc with a hole in the center and handed it to Davis. The paper was divided into spaces by straight black lines like tiny slices of pie. Punched between the lines were several minute raised figures. The combination of lines and numbers indicated on the disc, taken from O'Hare's time clock, the keys he had punched and the time.

"Well?" The Inspector's brows made a line.

"He didn't cover anything after his nine o'clock rounds.

Rounds take him forty minutes. That means we don't know what happened to him after twenty minutes to ten."

"That," said Davis, "we already know. What was he doing upstairs when he answered Seth Hadfield at ten minutes past ten?"

"At half past ten," said Duncan Maclain.

Davis set his mouth tighter and said, "So? Young Hadfield lied. We have a pretty good check on taxis, Maclain. The taxi dropped him at the M. T. & T. at five past ten. The clock showed a fifteen-minute wait before he came out again."

"Let's get down to brass tacks, Davis," the Captain said with a pleasant smile. "I'm breaking my neck to help you, but I can't do it if you hold things back. I didn't know about that adoption until you told me last night. You didn't get me the card from the time clock until two hours ago."

"I had to get the key to the clock from Bentley. It's locked so the watchman can't tamper with it." Davis left his chair and began to pace the floor. "Maclain, this killing of Dan O'Hare has got us sore."

"I was afraid of that," said Maclain. "Bank presidents under a cloud and cheap blackmailers aren't so bad. But a decent old fellow like O'Hare—well, I know how you feel. You've built a case against young Seth. Tell me more."

"Him and the girl." Davis perched sideways on the edge of the desk and watched Maclain run fingers through his crisp dark hair.

"Motive?"

"Several," said Davis, "including dough. Will you admit there's a chance that Blake Hadfield killed Sprague and then tried to commit suicide, and only blinded himself?"

The Captain interlocked his fingers. "After which, he walked to Sprague's body and carefully planted the gun. Then he went back to his desk and collapsed, blinded, into his chair."

"Nuts!" said Davis. "I know what won't and what will hold air. The Hadfield kid was there and saw it, and it just happens his mother, so-called, can't prove he wasn't. On that particular night six years ago, he went to a picture show."

"You interest me, Davis. So he was there. Why?"

"He happened to go and see Hadfield just like he did last Monday night and didn't want his mother to know. Blake Hadfield had this meeting with Sprague at the M. T. & T. and took the kid down there. The kid saw the shooting and switched the gun."

"And Doxenby?" Maclain asked slowly.

"Was also there. He was a lawyer, Maclain. I'm going to prove he was retained by Sprague to get him out of the hole. Doxenby saw the kid change the gun. Doxenby took a glass. He's held that glass over the kid's head, claiming the kid left fingerprints on it. There's also a chance that Doxenby switched the gun instead of Seth. The result's the same."

"Possible, thus far," said Maclain.

"Do I need to go on?"

"I'd like to hear the rest. Monday night for instance."

"The kid pushed his old man over in a drunken brawl. You've had to admit he was the only one there. Money for him and his girl—and killing the man who ruined and murdered his sweetheart's father."

Maclain was silent, but a muscle throbbed along his lean jaw.

"Let's take Doxenby's killing," said Davis.

Maclain broke in. "I thought you were trailing this pair."

Davis said, "They went to a show the night Doxenby was

killed. They could have slipped out and returned, or Seth could, and have left her in the theater."

"Why?"

"Blackmail again."

"And why did Seth kill O'Hare?"

"Because," said Davis with quiet triumph, "O'Hare was the only one left who knew that six years ago young Seth Hadfield was there."

The Captain drew a long deep breath and let it out like a sigh. "Even your Commissioner has labeled Doxenby a suicide, Davis. How did Seth get out of that apartment? I'm throwing your question back at you. Is he Superman?"

"I'm arresting him for his foster father's murder." The Inspector's voice was cold as a chill. "I can prove damn well he was there."

Maclain reached out and touched the Inspector's knee. "Who's at the M. T. & T. today?"

"Nobody. I closed it up for the day to make another search."

"Will you get your emergency squad to do a job for me?"

"What?" asked Davis suspiciously.

"Turn out all the lights except those on the eighth floor among other things," said Captain Maclain. "The only way to break this case is bluff, Davis. I'm riding for a fall! "

CHAPTER VIII

1

BRIGHT DAYS or gray, starry nights or dull—inside or out, it was never dark to Duncan Maclain. Darkness was absence of light, and consequent inability to see, but Maclain's whole world was blackness. He saw with his fingers, his nose, his ears, his taste, and his memory of figures—steps counted in the past.

In such a world, the breaking of day or the falling of night meant little. In such a world, the time, by clocks, was only the number of an hour, and there was no such thing as gloom.

He was equally efficient by day or night, or with lights off or on. Several men and one woman had misjudged that efficiency and died. It was difficult for the normal person to grasp that a man without eyes, subjected by his own strong will to years of training, might become a greater fighting machine than one who could see.

Maclain was subject to no distractions that afflict the normal person in a world of light. His power of concentration, uninterrupted by the greenness of trees, clouds in the sky, a fly on the wall, was close to perfect. Many normal people intent on concentration have to close their eyes. Maclain's were always closed.

Schnucke had eyes, but she was as helpless in blackness as the normal person. There, Maclain came into his own. While the man with eyes was groping, Duncan Maclain could see.

Out of a welter of innocuous objects he had formed a mental picture. It had a lot of parts—Hadfield's missing fountain pen and change, a lowered Venetian blind, an onyx-based paper-weight surmounted by a crystal ball, a broken bottle of Scotch, Julia Hadfield's hallucination that her husband had fallen down the elevator shaft, the heavy round watchman's clock carried on his rounds by Dan O'Hare.

Maclain had pieced them together with meticulous caution, turning them back and forth, this way and that, and the answer was not pretty. The answer was death, unprovable death by a noiseless time bomb, a bomb that went off unexpectedly accompanied by a single sound, the shriek of its victim being dashed to destruction. The answer was an infernal machine, a machine that destroyed not only its victim, but every trace of its mechanism as soon as its work was done.

There was something more to be done than to catch the machine's inventor; a bigger job, the job of proving in detail the working of the machine. This was no mad scientist pitting his crazy brain against the world. This was a man who had watched the ponderous working of the law courts, a man who had thought up, or stumbled on, a method of killing so simple and yet so complete that it furnished an impassable barrier to the electric chair.

There was only one perfect method of murder—a murder that left no trace of murder and at the same time furnished the perpetrator with an ironclad, unbreakable alibi.

This was it, if the Captain's picture had no flaws. To break it was the task of Duncan Maclain, and he had just one chance, a chance that he would be underestimated because he was blind.

If his chance misfired, well, he was leaving a resumé of what he believed, a record dictated to the Ediphone, but that was far from proof. In the event he was wrong, it wouldn't be much help to Duncan Maclain.

He pressed the time-signal button on his desk.

"When you hear the signal the time will be exactly ten forty-five."

He had checked all afternoon; rechecked all evening. It was getting late, and time to check again. He reached for the telephone.

"Davis?"

"Yes."

"Is everything set?"

"Yes." A pause. "Maclain, you're a blithering fool."

"Listen, Larry. I have only one thing to say. I'm going down there with Dreist within a half an hour. You'll cost me my life if you put a man on watch at that door. I'm hot, Davis. If you've followed my instructions I won't be hurt, and you'll have your killer caught redhanded in the middle of a kill. If you try to get funny and protect me—well, we'll have no proof of anything and I'll be killed another way."

"I hope to God you know what you're doing, Maclain."

"Thanks, Davis, I hope so, too. By the way, I rang up Julia Hadfield this afternoon and asked the time by the clock on her living-room table. It's twenty minutes fast, Davis. Sometimes, it's more. It gains. I don't like to say I told you so."

"Neither do I," said Davis speaking close to the mouthpiece, "but Courtney went home right after Seth Hadfield started downtown with the girl last night, or that's what he says."

"In two hours, Davis," said Duncan Maclain, "we'll know."

As he hung up the phone he took a small cylindrical tube

from his drawer, put it to his lips and blew. It made no sound, but Dreist heard it and leaped up from where he had been lying close to the office door. He stopped beside the Captain's chair and stood looking up at Maclain, his pointed ears raised questioningly.

The Captain touched Dreist's wedge-shaped head. "They trained you well with your soundless whistle, didn't they?" he said softly. "I hope you'll answer as quickly, old boy, when I blow it downtown."

Rena came in, and Dreist growled. The Captain sternly ordered him down.

"Captain," Rena said directly, "I wish you wouldn't go. Why can't you wait until next week end when Spud's back in town?"

"If I happened to be alive by then, it still wouldn't do. I'll be okay, Rena, if I'm not interfered with. I'm taking Dreist, and this." He held up the whistle.

"It still puzzles me," said Rena with a frown. "How does he hear it if it makes no sound?"

"Don't worry," the Captain told her. "Its vibration is too high for human ears, but any dog can hear it. I checked Dreist with it all over the M. T. & T. building this afternoon when I had him downtown. He'll answer it from the ninth floor to the lobby, either up or down. Phone downstairs and have the doorman get me a taxi, Rena, and give me my hat and overcoat."

"Gun?"

"I have it." He patted his shoulder holster.

"Schnucke?"

"No. The building's been darkened except for the eighth floor. Tonight I'll have to find my own way around. She couldn't see and would be in the road."

"Come back," said Rena as she held his coat.

"I always have," said Duncan Maclain.

Inside or out, it was never dark to Duncan Maclain.

His hand was as steady as the hand of a taxi starter as he opened the door with a key supplied by Elise Sprague, and bent his tall form to get through the tiny door.

"Guard, Dreist!"

The click of a lock as the small door closed. The building was cold, not even O'Hare's small oil-stove on tonight, the stove that he used when the steam was off to warm his little room.

Eleven steps up and make a turn, then take eleven more. That put you on the second floor, and again you made a turn. Fifteen paces on the balcony and you found the stairway once more. It was easy going after that—twenty-two steps to every flight, fifteen paces on each balcony, never less or more.

On the eighth, it was slightly different. You turned left there, instead of right, and put a hand on the railing to guide you. Nineteen paces brought the spot where you left the rail and turning left found a swinging door.

But before you left the rail, you stopped and listened. If you were right, there was someone else in the building; a noiseless someone waiting to see what a blind man was doing there so late at night alone, someone cursing the lights that were out, some-one who would be surprised and happy and maybe a little suspicious when you turned them on in Hadfield's office.

Perhaps you were standing in the ray of a torch right now. You couldn't see it or feel it. It might be passing over your face, probing and judging, moving from your body to the rail. But no, there had been no click of a flashlight turning on, no tiny sound like a dropping pin, no breathing. The host was some-where back of the swinging door, the host who had come ahead to wait knowing that Dreist, once on guard, would let nobody in.

Three steps across the balcony and through the swinging door, a swinging door hooked open. Why was a door hooked open? Because things could be moved more easily—heavy things—when you moved them out from the hall.

Your own breathing was louder now, pushing in closer about you. The dome above the balcony was outside and a ceiling was over your head. That made your breathing louder, but anyone else's breathing would be louder, too, if they were standing near you in a hall.

Six more steps and through an office door thoughtfully hooked open, too. Very thoughtful. The soundless whistle would reach Dreist's sensitive ears just that much quicker—Dreist waiting in the downstairs hall.

And now you had to remember. There were desks in here and files, and no Schnucke here to guide you—patterns you needed now. Three and two and turn and touch. Then on again, and eleven steps, and you've found the office wall.

Lights!

Turn the switch and touch the bulb to see that it gets warm. It's never dark to Duncan Maclain. Lights, professor! Lights for the host who's waiting. Lights for the killer who thinks he's creeping noiselessly along the hall.

Put the gun on the desk edge.

Start with the small buffet. It's not in the drawer. It's not in the cupboard. Take the drawers out and search behind them. Reach and feel. It's not in there at all.

Try the directors' table. Two drawers there. The blind man hunts well. Let him find it, and we'll know what he's looking for.

Now, the globe in the corner. Surely nothing there. Under the cushions of the divan. Lift the seats of every chair.

Hadfield's desk. Try the righthand drawers, then the middle. What's that rustling back of the middle drawer? Papers rustling. Pull them out and lay them down where all can see:—

The Statement of Blake Hadfield of
What James Sprague Confided to Me.

See if there are any others there, and blow your whistle!

It's time right now to reach for the gun, the gun that was on the desk edge, the gun that's gone—the gun that's in the killer's hand with Dreist's feet pattering up the stairs.

A flash of stars in a working brain as the butt of the gun cracks down on the Captain's head. Duncan Maclain is out of the way, but the dog has Bentley as he steps through the curtains behind the desk and vainly tries to fire at the snarling dodging attacker leaping for his arm.

Down on the floor, Mr. Bentley, or Dreist will tear you to pieces. Down on the floor, Mr. Bentley! You can't show a gun around Dreist. Stay right still, Mr. Bentley.

It's dark for Duncan Maclain!

2

In a universe devoid of light, the only darkness is darkness of the brain. The blind awake to thinking, not to blinking sleep-heavy eyes against the dazzling light of a morning sun. Awakening was a period of bodily repose, not of motion, to Duncan Maclain.

First it was necessary to remember where you were. Lying

inert and unmoving, you worked the restored receptivity of the mind. If you were in your own bed, the texture of the sheets and covers was familiar; the smoothness of the pillow against your cheek was as comforting as the clasp of an old friend's hand.

Then you listened. If it was not yet morning, the lack of sound would warn you to settle down and sleep a little longer. Morning brought sounds and smell—the increased murmur of traffic filtering up through an open window, the muted ring of a frying pan as Sarah Marsh went about her duties in the kitchen, the cheering aroma of eggs and coffee. You were in your home and day had come again.

As the use of his blotted-out faculties returned to the Captain, his first sensation was excruciating pain. The agony was centered in his head, an all-enveloping throbbing that for a moment clouded his memory. Automatically he moved to press one hand against his skull and found that restraining bonds of some kind were fettering his arm. Where most men would have struggled, a bright red signal light began to blink a mental warning in the Captain's clearing consciousness.

He was awakening to unfamiliar surroundings, and his body was in an unfamiliar position. To move in such a situation was perilous. The only immediate safety for the moment lay in careful analysis, and the much more difficult task of remaining absolutely still.

Some hard, inflexible object was pressing painfully into his wastline, gouging his silver belt-buckle forcefully into the pit of his stomach. Nausea seized him, and for a second or two life itself was obscured by a hazy film. One lone idea persisted, dominating everything.

He had to be still.

The idea seemed too strongly ingrained to be the outcome

of a passing whim. He couldn't move his arms, anyhow. If he couldn't move, then why was it so vital not to try to move?

A creeping wave of dancing red dots engulfed him. He fought it off by exerting every atom of a powerful will. With the retreat of the dancing dots, he found that thought was starting to function—not very much, at first, but enough to remind him that something had gone wrong somewhere.

Somewhere, some well-laid plan had slipped, and now it was necessary to be still.

More thoughts, growing more vivid now, like a dancer shedding her seven veils. A man in an office, and a dog downstairs. There wasn't any question any longer. This body with the pinioned arms, the aching midriff, and the pounding, splitting head, was his own. He even knew his identity now, and where he was. This man, hanging across a railing where two men had hung before him, was unquestionably himself, Captain Duncan Maclain.

Poetry now:—

> The brain of a man in love is never clear!
> He's stood the whole Department on its ear!

There was something wrong with the meter, as there had been with the plan. To a man who lived by numbers, only perfection would do. He straightened it out by substituting "He has" for the contraction "he's" in the second line.

Well, the Police Department wasn't the only one. Duncan Maclain was standing on his ear, slung over a balcony railing with his arms bound and his thrumming head hanging down.

How long could a man hang like that, keeping very still? And listening. Listening for what?

For somebody who was breathing.

Certainly. It had been going on for a long time now, the regular inhale and exhale, louder than it should be. Or was it? Maybe sounds were deceiving when anyone felt so ill.

And what was the use of keeping still? Movement was the answer after you knew where you were.

The Captain tried it with one leg, testing it with circumspection. When he discovered that it moved without restraint, he tried the other. It, too, was free.

The answer was simple. If he was hanging head down over a railing in the M. T. & T., then by stretching out one foot he was bound to find the floor. Once his feet were on the floor he could try to unloosen his arms, and stand.

He stretched one leg to its full extent and discreetly pointed his toe, moving it around in a vacant circle. He was cold when he drew it back, attacked by an encroaching chill. His foot had touched no floor and the picture of how Blake Hadfield and Dan O'Hare had crashed to death was sickeningly lucid.

The Captain groped with fingers, moving them without disturbing the set of his rigid arms. His fingers found the metal at the base of a post which supported the balcony railing, they closed about the smooth steel bar in a death grip, and held on. Without releasing his vise-like grip, the Captain flexed his elbows back and forth.

The bonds began to slip. He moved his elbows again and the bonds uncoiled from about his arms with the silky speed of a slithering reptile and were gone. An instant later, the clammy stillness of the M. T. & T. was shattered by the report of a discharged gun.

Duncan Maclain pulled himself up and over the railing. Seconds ticked as he stood erect on the balcony floor. Then with one hand resting on the railing, he began to move along. A few steps farther, and he touched the other man, the man whose breathing had been beating so steadily against his sensitive ears.

The Captain's hands moved down until he felt the heavy twine which bound the unconscious man's arms securely to a post of the railing. He put a foot on the twine where it ran along the balcony floor. Seizing the man by the collar, the Captain pulled him farther up. Then, reaching down, he unloosed the impeding twine. He dragged the man on over the railing and stretched him out on the floor.

It was easy to follow the twine he had held in place with his foot. He wound it up as he went along fifteen paces to where it disappeared through a crack in the elevator door. There was a weight on the end. Maclain hauled it in as a fisherman might land a prize from a well. Undoing the end of the twine from the trigger guard, he pocketed the weight, a heavy gun which he recognized as his own.

Knock your victim on the head. Hang him feet outward over a railing and keep him there by binding his arms around a post with twine. Tuck one loose end in, not too tight, for the friction will hold him until he moves—he's almost on balance, anyhow. On the other end of your twine you hang a weight. Any sort of a weight will do—a paperweight, a bottle of Scotch, a watchman's clock, or a gun. The weight goes down a shaft or out another window, any good place where the twine it takes with it won't be found too easily.

Your victim does the rest. He recovers consciousness after a while and struggles to get free. That's easy, for the cord that holds him is only tucked in. You've seen to that. When he tries to stand—well, down he goes and you're way off uptown some place at the time his watch is smashed in the fall. And they'll never prove that you hit him on the head—it's just as if you covered a little cut by making a bigger one. Who could ever find it, huh? Who could find a little bump covered by the big ones made in a fall?

Have you got it, boys?

A time bomb made of string and a scream. An infernal machine that the victim sets off himself when you are far away. A death trap loaded with gravity, doubly loaded this time—Duncan Maclain and another.

As Davis says, "Some fun!"

The Captain headed back for Hadfield's office. There was water there to revive the unconscious man. Making his way through the files, he heard a whimper, and terrible lines of hatred made his strong face momentarily ugly. He tightened his fingers around the butt of his gun.

"Dreist!" he called as he opened the office door.

The whimper sounded again, and paws scratched feebly on the carpet. The Captain knelt down and felt the warm tongue on his hand, and something warmer staining the office floor.

He stood up slowly and went to Hadfield's phone. It was disconnected, and suddenly the unconscious man on the balcony was forgotten, angles were forgotten, and counting his steps.

Blundering out of the office, he crashed into a chair, shoved it aside, and struck a desk. The shock of pain brought calmness. Feeling his way, step by step, he crossed the building and located the switchboard. He made three tries at plugging in before he reached Central and heard Police Headquarters answer.

Davis and Archer were out.

"What's the time?" Maclain demanded.

"It's twenty past one."

"Get a veterinary over to the M. T. & T. building on the double," the Captain ordered.

"But Captain Maclain!" The man at Headquarters sounded doubtful. "Inspector Davis' orders were—"

"The hell with his orders!" said Duncan Maclain. "My dog's been shot." He pulled the plug from the board and left the phone.

Out on the balcony, the man began to groan.

The Captain made his way slowly back to the washroom in the foyer of Hadfield's office. He soaked a face towel and went outside again to kneel by the man and apply the icy wet of the towel to his forehead.

"Quiet!" the Captain warned. "We're still in danger. Stay right where you are."

The man on the floor said nothing, but ceased to moan.

Duncan Maclain went downstairs slowly. His muscles ached and his head was still spinning wildly. He was on the bottom landing, eleven steps from the lobby, when he heard the sound of voices and the scrape of a key in the little door.

The door swung open and a man stepped in. A torchlight clicked, and suddenly the little door slammed shut again. Fists beat on it, and Davis' strong voice shouted:—

"What do you think you're trying to pull? Let us in!"

The man standing down on the lobby floor said just one word, "Maclain!"

"You weren't satisfied with murdering four people and trying to kill two more tonight. You had to shoot my dog," said Duncan Maclain. "Well, this is journey's end. You're in here now, back to see if the victims fell as per order, or maybe you thought you'd be in time to see them fall. I am quite alive, and you'll never get out again."

The Captain dropped like a man struck with a sledge. A bullet whined above his head and threw up talcum from the plaster wall. He fired four times, shooting in an arc at the sound of the gun which had fired first, then walked on down and opened the door.

"Lawson shot my dog, so I killed him, Davis. Bentley's up on the balcony. If Dreist dies, I'll kill you, too," said Duncan Maclain.

3

Seth and Elise had departed for some unknown destination after a noon wedding followed by an informal reception in Duncan Maclain's penthouse. The elated young officer had received a wedding present of seven days' additional leave, procured for him by some of the Captain's legerdemain.

Phil Courtney, Julia Hadfield, radiant in a tailored suit of light gray, Rena Savage and the Captain had adjourned to Sybella's apartment for cocktails later in the afternoon.

The crackling fire was comfortable. A wintry sun had appeared after Monday's rain, but had only succeeded in adding glisten and sparkle to an otherwise bitter day.

Maclain was restless. He circled the living room with Schnucke, touching the heavy draperies at the windows, appraising the furniture with fluttering fingertips, and even locating the clock on the mantel and a couple of pictures on the wall.

"That's a Van Gogh," Sybella told him as his light touch moved from the second picture. "Here's your cocktail. The chair right beside you is vacant."

"He had a passion for yellow, didn't he?" The Captain sat down and took his drink.

"The one up there is—" Courtney began.

"Please don't tell him," Sybella interrupted.

"Thank you, Sybella." Maclain sipped his cocktail and put it down. "Very few people understand, Mr. Courtney, that I touch a frame on the wall and fill it with a picture of my own. It only garbles things in my imagination when an attempt is made to describe it to me. It's as though an author overdescribes a character. The result is never quite convincing or the character very real."

"I can understand that easily," said Julia. "There have been times when I wished that characters in the talkies would relapse into silence again so that I could supply dialogue to suit me."

Rena said, "I agree. It was rather nice."

"I've been living in a movie of my own for the past week," Courtney put in with a laugh. "I have to get down to work on settling Blake's estate. Dare I ask a few questions, Captain, or will you run me out?"

"You may fire when ready," said Rena. "What do you think the Captain risks his neck for? I can assure you that explaining things is the only part that's fun."

Maclain grinned. "What chance has any man against his secretary? What do you want to know, Mr. Courtney?"

"Don't be modest, Duncan," Sybella told him. "We want to know everything that's happened since this murderous interlude was begun."

"I don't believe I need to tell you about Lawson's method of murder, do I?" the Captain asked thoughtfully. "The papers were full of diagrams this morning, I understand."

"What I'd like to know," said Courtney, "is what gave you an inkling of how it was done."

The Captain drank more of his cocktail and said, "Missing

change and a fountain pen. Hadfield had them with him and they were gone. Seth didn't have them, neither did you, Mrs. Hadfield, or Dan O'Hare. Where had they gone? The same question applied to a paperweight from Hadfield's desk and a length of sash cord cut from the Venetian blind."

Sybella said, "I'll stooge for you if it makes you happy. Where had they gone?"

"The police combed the building and they *had* gone, but they overlooked the bottom of the elevator shaft. They really had no reason on earth for looking there. If they had, they'd have found the cord from the Venetian blind attached to a length of twine, and the twine in turn attached to the base of the crystal ball."

"That was clever as hell," declared Courtney. "There wasn't a trace of string or anything left on the balcony after Hadfield's fall."

"He improved on it with Doxenby and O'Hare. He found he didn't need the sash cord. The heavy twine wrapped a few times around the arms would hold his victim in place as well as heavier rope."

"What did he tie Doxenby to?"

"The radiator," said Maclain. "Only he hung him out the window head first instead of feet first, the method he'd perfected in the M. T. & T. There were no windows opposite, and the areaway was dark so the chance of his being noticed on the eleventh floor was nothing. Doxenby recovered from his knock on the head, kicked his feet loose, and there you are. Mr. Lawson was up here by then, sitting in the chair you're in right now."

"And what in the name of goodness has that to do with Blake's change and fountain pen?" asked Julia.

"He must have tried hanging Blake over the railing head down, the first time," the Captain explained. "Then he decided feet first was more certain. The railing is three feet eight inches in height. Well, you'll see what I mean if you care to give it a try. I understood it better after last night."

The Captain finished his drink and held out his glass. "And the change?" Sybella asked as she poured him another.

"Fell out of Blake's vest pocket together with his pen and tumbled down to the lobby floor. Lawson had to collect it on his way out and at the same time dodge O'Hare. He was more careful after that."

Sybella said, "I still don't get why he left that highball glass in Doxenby's place, and overlooked a note on Doxenby's calendar bearing an appointment and his name."

"Suicide," said Maclain. "He played everything to make it look like suicide all the way. That was his game, from the murder of James Sprague on. He even brought you to consult me, hoping I'd clinch the suicide idea by saying that Blake Hadfield couldn't accidentally fall.

"Then the idea began to leak out that Sprague might have been murdered. So Mr. Lawson decided to hang it on Doxenby. If Doxenby had that glass marked with Sprague's prints, Doxenby must have been there. Then Doxenby was guilty and committed suicide. After all, how could anyone have killed him?"

"But how did he know only Sprague's prints were on the glass, Captain?" asked Rena.

The Captain smiled and said, "He was there watching most carefully everything that went on, and listening, standing in the little foyer."

"You've missed something," Courtney said after a second's delay. "How did he know Hadfield was to meet Sprague? How did he know Hadfield and Seth were downtown?"

"The same way he knew that I was going to put that question

to Dan O'Hare," said Duncan Maclain. "That's why he murdered Dan—because he couldn't stand the answer. Night before
last, Mr. Courtney, Dan O'Hare called his own murderer on
the telephone and passed on the word, given him by Sergeant
Archer, that I was coming there."

"You mean that every time anybody came into that building
at night O'Hare called Lawson on the phone?"

"You've hit it, Mr. Courtney. Those were O'Hare's orders
from the State Insurance Department. Consequently, there
could only be one murderer and that must be someone connected with the Department, a man who knew every time his victims were there, a man who knew the hours of the watchman's
rounds, a man who knew Mr. Bentley kept twine in his drawer."

"But Bentley fits all that."

"He certainly does." The Captain sighed. "Except that Bentley wasn't working there when Sprague was killed. That's what I
wanted to ask O'Hare: whom did he call?"

"It seems such a trifle over which to kill a man," said Julia.

"O'Hare's life or his," Maclain said grimly. "Murder builds
you a paper house and you must keep adding to its founda-
tions. There was another item, Mrs. Hadfield, an item of a
crystal ball. Something took Dan O'Hare into the elevator
shaft. I don't know what, but the soles of his shoes showed
traces of oil. Lawson must have seen him go down, and seen
him find that crystal ball. Lawson had not had a chance to recover it, for there had been a policeman posted on the door until last Sunday."

He paused and turned his head toward Julia. "That was
the hallucination you had, Mrs. Hadfield, when you got that
strange impression that your husband might have been in the
shaft. At the same time he fell, you heard something striking

against the walls of the shaft close by you, the fall of the crystal paperweight ball."

"And O'Hare's clock?" asked Rena.

"Helped to clinch things as Lawson was afraid it might. It gave absolute proof that O'Hare had been out of commission for over an hour before he fell. That was dangerous, for it might give a strong clue to the method of murder. Consequently, Lawson used it as he had used the bottle of Scotch and the paperweight, hoping it would lie undiscovered and unexplained at the bottom of the shaft, like the crystal ball."

Courtney looked at his watch. "There are forty-nine other things, Captain Maclain. Who attacked Bentley in the State Insurance office? What was he doing mixed up with that blackmailing little so-and-so, and what was your plan last night that brought this mess to a close?"

"Some of the answers to that would be guesswork, as I haven't had a chance to talk to Carl Bentley," Maclain explained. "As to last night—"

"He nearly fluffed." Rena smiled. "The only thing that saved him is the fact that he never fluffs. It's like his typing. It drives me crazy because he never makes an error."

"I can't erase," said Duncan Maclain. "I was sick of murder and not a little frightened at the method. If my theory was right, that it was a delayed trap, and I was almost convinced from the testimony of O'Hare's clock, the best thing was to try it. Then I'd be sure to know."

He leaned back in his chair. "I set a trap. I talked things over with Lawson yesterday afternoon, and Sybella helped me. I told him I had information that Hadfield had left a paper containing certain statements confided to him by Sprague while Sprague was under arrest awaiting bail.

"I said I thought that Bentley was guilty and I hinted that almost everything was clear except how Hadfield, Doxenby and O'Hare were killed. I pointed out that O'Hare must have called Bentley every time a victim entered the M. T. & T. Then last night, Sybella told Lawson that I was going to go down to make a search for that paper alone.

"A fake paper stating that Lawson had looted Sprague and Company and hung the blame on Sprague six years ago was typed by Rena, and placed in Hadfield's desk by me in the afternoon. Lawson would have to kill me to get that paper. All of you know what happened."

"But what was supposed to happen?" Courtney demanded.

"I knew Lawson would pick up my gun off the desk," said Maclain. "I was going to blow my supersonic whistle for Dreist. But after I had Lawson trapped, I was going to give him a chance to read that paper, and also a chance to shut Dreist in Hadfield's office and work on me outside. I didn't know how that murder stunt worked and I intended to find out. Everything went perfectly until Carl Bentley, playing hero, stepped through the door. He'd been trailing Lawson and thought he was saving me."

"And what if your plan had worked?" asked Julia.

"Lawson would have hung me up and Dreist would have stayed in the office where I intended to order him to stay. The police were to contact Lawson when he got home and ask him for a key, saying they were searching for me. He'd have gone with them to be in at the fall, just as he went down with me to find O'Hare."

The Captain sipped his drink. "You can see how close he'd figured his method. If I had already fallen, my smashed Braille watch would show that I fell while he was uptown. If I hadn't—

well, the building was dark and he'd have a good chance to reach in the elevator shaft on his way upstairs, pull a string with the gun tied on the end, and help me to fall while he was nowhere near me."

Courtney drew a deep breath and bit the end from a cigar. "You take frightful chances, Captain Maclain. It seems a little foolhardy to me."

"My hat was padded to somewhat dull the blow—and the police emergency squad had strung a net across half the lobby on the sixth floor. That's why all the lights were out. I can't erase," said Duncan Maclain.

The Captain was reclining in the depths of an easy chair with a Braille book open on his lap when Rena came into his office to say good night. She watched the journey of his moving fingers over the raised dots, took a look at his enrapt expression, and quietly went out again, deciding that he was lost in some world of his own.

As usual, she was right, for Duncan Maclain was reading mechanically with little regard to the text. Out of a week's welter just one thought had stayed with him. That was Spud's statement: "You live by your brain, and the brain of a man in love is never quite crystal-clear."

Well, whose brain was it, anyhow? Did it belong to Davis and Archer, to Spud and Rena, to a public too simple-minded to keep itself out of one mess after another, or to Duncan Maclain?

Suppose it wasn't quite crystal-clear? Surely he had a right to cloud his own mind up once in a while with a few extraneous matters.

He closed the book on his knees, pursed his lips and suddenly smiled with the realization that he was mentally cursing out

Spud for nothing but solicitude and at the same time reveling in the unusual pleasure of being thoroughly unfair.

For nearly twenty-five years he had lived in a fortress of his own construction, building it around him with careful craftsmanship. Its secret towers and dungeons had risen wall by wall, cemented by a determination to let no outsider in.

He liked it. The other occupants were a man and his wife and two dogs who never disturbed or distracted him. What matter if the huge chambers were periodically swept by chilly winds or if the clammy moss of loneliness grew in scattered spots on the turreted walls?

Fortresses were built for fighting. Yet it might be ironical to find he had left no exit, and that after every invader was repelled he couldn't get out himself to hold a woman in his arms and dance in victory on the village green.

Captain Duncan Maclain, the warrior, who had beaten life and who was trying now to dance in a suit of impregnable clanking armor, a suit his own determined hands had skillfully riveted on.

A telephone rang somewhere in the penthouse.

Rena came in and said, "Carl Bentley's downstairs."

The Captain touched his Braille watch. "It's half past ten."

"He says he wants to talk to you. He's leaving town."

"Tell him to come up." Maclain restored the book to the shelves, went to his desk and sat down.

Carl Bentley stopped hesitantly inside the office door.

"I hear you're leaving the M. T. & T.," said Duncan Maclain. "Come in and sit down. Have you another position?"

"Comptroller of a munitions plant." Mr. Bentley took a chair and deposited his spectacles on the edge of the Captain's desk.

Maclain said, "Fine."

"I wanted to apologize, Captain, before I left town."

"If there's any fault, Mr. Bentley, it's mine."

"I stuck my neck out and got your dog shot. Lawson shot him deliberately over the top of the office partition while Dreist was guarding me on the floor."

"Dreist's going to live, but Lawson's dead," said Duncan Maclain. "It's difficult to kill a fighter with a heart as courageous as Dreist's. He's crippled in two legs, but the vet claims he'll recover entirely. He's been shot once before."

"I feel you should have some explanation of my conduct," Carl Bentley said with a touch of indecision.

"Just as you like, Mr. Bentley."

"It won't take me long. I've been over it with the police once before. You can understand my close contact with the M. T. & T. led me indirectly into the affairs of James Sprague and Company. That in turn caused me to become suspicious of Mr. Lawson. I started to prove that Lawson had looted Sprague's company when he worked there as bookkeeper and accountant."

"You'd have helped things by saying something earlier."

"I had no proof of anything, Captain, until Saturday afternoon, when I found what I wanted in Sprague's impounded checks in the vault of the State Insurance office."

Maclain said, "Oh?"

"I had to make the acquaintance of a girl, Captain." Mr. Bentley put on his glasses. "It was distasteful, but not difficult. She'd been—what shall I say?—running around with Lawson for some time. She started, at his suggestion I believe, to put the arm on me." Mr. Bentley gave a nervous cackle. "I mean to say, she was trying very hard to get some information out of me.

"You'll be interested to know that Sophie Munson—her present name, I believe—once worked for the late T. Allen Doxenby." Bentley wiped his brow. "At his suggestion also, Miss Munson was, er, also putting the arm on me."

"You seem to have been in a pair of arms," said the Captain with a grin.

"Well," said Bentley, "it wasn't that exactly. Actually this young lady passed on quite a lot of useful information to me. We formed a tentative partnership, as it were, to put the arm on Mr. Lawson—a little blackmailing based on information this delightful young lady handed me.

"It all dates back many years ago when Lawson embezzled over a quarter of a million dollars from James Sprague. Mr. Lawson became uneasy when Sprague and Company failed, and consulted a lawyer."

"My mind certainly wasn't clear," muttered Duncan Maclain. "Go on, Mr. Bentley. Lawson consulted T. Allen Doxenby."

"Mr. Doxenby suggested that Lawson might throw the blame onto Sprague, which Lawson did, I believe, quite successfully. But Mr. Doxenby, Captain, never played straight with anyone. Mr. Doxenby went to Sprague with the statement that he could clear him, not stating how. Sprague made an appointment with his friend Blake Hadfield to meet Doxenby at night at the M. T. & T., and Mr. Doxenby arrived just in time to witness the murder of Sprague and the blinding of Hadfield by Lawson."

"Merciful heavens," said Maclain. "And Lawson's been under that shyster's thumb ever since! He cleaned the city of one louse when he dropped him out the window."

"Yes," Mr. Bentley agreed. "Frankly, I was a bit worried that he had the same idea in store for me as soon as he learned I was, er, talking with the naïve Sophie. That's why I was so upset last Saturday afternoon."

"What did happen there?"

"I went up after lunch, Captain, thinking Mr. Lawson had gone home. He'd eaten part of his noon meal with Sophie and me. I found a paper on his desk, an excellent specimen of his handwriting. Not only writing, but figures. I happen to be something of an expert on handwriting as well as accountancy. I've made a study of Albert Osborn, Hans Schneickert, Locard, and many others."

"Sometime I'd like you to make a study of me," said Maclain.

"A difficult problem, Captain," Bentley told him soberly. "I was comparing Lawson's writing with checks signed by James Sprague and with various other documents when I dropped some of the checks. I had to move the vault door to pick them up, and I heard someone else in the office. Immediately after, Lawson called out." Carl Bentley removed his glasses and wiped his brow. "I'm a small man, Captain Maclain, and I wasn't happy about being in an office with just Harold Lawson. I dropped my glasses and ran, but I had a chance to stop and hit myself on the forehead with a heavy seal."

"Rub it in," the Captain said. "Why?"

"It would be most helpful if Lawson thought that somebody else, maybe a policeman, was trailing me, or possibly after me; and particularly I didn't want him to know I was afraid of him, or checking on him. He was a violent man, Captain Maclain."

Maclain stretched out his hand. "I want to shake hands with a brave one, Mr. Bentley. Following Lawson into that building last night, knowing what you did about him, was tops in bravery."

Carl Bentley shook hands and stood by the desk a trifle flustered. "It really wasn't all my fault that I interfered and spoiled your plans, Captain. Before Major Savage went away he placed your safety in my keeping, so to speak. It was sort of up to me. He told me—"

"I haven't any desire to hear what Spud Savage told you," said Duncan Maclain. "He's already told it to me. I would like to inquire what the devil your position has been in the M. T. & T."

"Well," said Mr. Bentley doubtfully, "there was some question about the statements furnished during the past several years by Mr. Hadfield and certain of his associates. I was sort of checking up."

"What statements?" asked Maclain.

"It's going to take a hell of a lot of money to win this war." Mr. Bentley sounded rueful. "Collecting it is up to the other members of our department and me."

"Good Lord!" said Maclain weakly. "You're a 'T.'"

Mr. Bentley polished his glasses. "I've heard the term 'T-man' used before to apply to my work. I prefer to be known as a Tax Investigator of the Income Tax Department of the United States F. B. I."

"Anything you want to call yourself, Mr. Bentley," said Duncan Maclain, "is aces with me."

He sat down still more weakly as Carl Bentley eased out of the door, to return in a second or two.

"Your glasses are right here," said Maclain.

"I forgot to offer my congratulations, Captain. I heard that Mr. Courtney and Mrs. Hadfield intended to marry this year, and that you were considering it, too."

"Where you fellows get your information beats me," said Duncan Maclain.

The office door clicked shut and the Captain reached for his

Ediphone. For minutes he held the mouthpiece in his hand before he pressed the button and started a halting dictation into the phone. When the record was nearly full, he hooked it up with the Capehart and played it back.

The sound of his own voice filled the quiet room.

Halfway through, he pulled the record from the machine and smashed it on the edge of the desk.

"I've never been afraid in my life," he muttered angrily. "I'm not going to start it now. I'll bluff if I can't do anything else— bluff the way I did with Lawson—blind man's bluff. No woman on earth is going to intimidate me!"

He reached for the telephone, dialed it, and steadied his elbow on the desk. His hand was shaking, but his voice was clear and firm.

"Sybella?"

"Yes, Duncan."

"I just thought of something. Why the hell don't you marry me?"

THE END

DISCUSSION QUESTIONS

- What kind of sleuth is Duncan Maclain? Are there any traits that make him particularly effective?

- Were you able to predict any part of the solution to the case?

- After learning the solution, were there any clues you realized you had missed?

- Would the story be different if it were set in the present day? If so, how?

- Did the social context of the time play a role in the narrative? If so, how?

- What role did the geographical setting play in the narrative? Would the story have been different if it were set someplace else?

- If you were one of the main characters, would you have acted differently at any point in the story?

- Did you identify with any of the characters? If so, which?

- Did this story remind you of any other books you've read?

Read on for the first chapter of

Baynard Kendrick's
THE ODOR OF VIOLETS

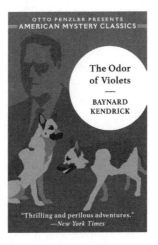

also available from

CHAPTER I

THE CRAGS was built high up on an eminence above the little town of Tredwill Village, west of Hartford, in the Connecticut hills. Ordinarily, the tall buildings of the city could be seen from the Tredwill home. Now, even the few scattered houses in the village below were hidden from view.

Norma Tredwill (Mrs. Thaddeus Tredwill, number four) sat down at the top of the stairs on a broad window seat and looked out through the mullioned panes. Her warm red lips, always ready to part in humor or sympathy, were pensively set. She stared through the frost-marked glass at the swirling snow, oblivious of the storm.

She was thinking of Paul Gerente. Ten years before, she had put him out of her life completely, determined to forget a year of marriage to him which had been nothing more than a short, unhappy episode in her career.

A step sounded down the hall. Norma stood up just as her stepdaughter, Barbara, came out of her room. Babs was wearing a trim tailor-made suit and carrying a mink coat over her arm. She was the only one of the Tredwill family who had never quite accepted Norma into the Tredwill home. For three years, Norma had vainly tried to break down the barrier between them, a barrier which was never apparent on the surface, but which Babs, in a thousand small ways, managed to make smartingly real.

"You're up early, darling," Babs said with a smile.

The politeness was always there, deference even, but it came through too readily to be genuine. Babs's tenderness was as apt as some adroit line of an author's spotted in a play.

Norma said: —

"You're up early yourself, Babs."

"The weather, probably. Are you coming down? It's a filthy day."

"I certainly agree." Norma looked at the coat on Babs's arm. "Don't tell me you're planning on going out! The wind will blow you away."

"New York," said Babs. "It's Stacy's idea. Christmas is on Monday. If we don't get in today, there'll be no presents for our darling father and you."

Norma refused to be piqued by Babs's tone. "Why not Hartford, if you simply must? It's not so far away."

"Stacy has something special picked out for Thad—and Cheli Scott too, I suppose. Leave it to my fifteen-year-old brother." Babs spoke with all the languid disparagement of an eighteen-year-old for one three years her junior. "It's New York, I'm afraid." She started down the stairs.

Inwardly, Norma sighed. Another conversation with Babs was ending in the usual way, bright and friendly up to a point. Beyond that they never seemed to go.

"Run along if you've a train to catch," said Norma. "Are you taking the coupé?"

Babs turned on the stairs and nodded absently. "Stacy's driving us into Hartford. We'll leave it at a garage near the station.

We're going to spend the night in New York with the Ritters and be back tomorrow. I don't think this snow can last another day."

Norma watched Babs descend the stairs. The girl's youthful beauty was almost too perfect, like a picture done in tints too bright,—gold and white, rose and blue,—which time might fade. Such coloring needed vivacity behind it, but Babs smoldered almost sulkily.

"The Tredwill men have all the temperament," Norma thought. Thad's two sons, Gilbert, twenty-eight, and Stacy, fifteen, though separated widely in years, were much alike. They were quick to laugh, constantly enthusiastic about something, although their cause might change in a day. Thaddeus himself had all the ingrained egoism of a genius. He ruled his house and his family capriciously, and sometimes noisily, but back of his heated displays of temper he looked at life with a humorous glint in his eye.

Norma heard Cheli Scott greet Babs downstairs. Cheli was a playwright, and Thad's protégée. She was working on a new play which Thad wanted to try out in his own small theater, an integral part of The Crags. The house always seemed more pleasant and alive when Cheli was a visitor. Norma liked gaiety and laughter, and Cheli was friendly and amusing—a delightful, considerate girl.

For a moment Norma listened, then she left her post at the head of the stairs and started slowly toward her own apartment at the end of the hall. In front of Babs's open door, she paused and stood indecisively looking in upon the disordered scene.

Babs depended on servants to keep the material articles of living in their proper places. Fastidious about her own appearance, she left behind her a limp trail of dresses, underwear, and stockings. The three-mirror dressing table was a jumble of make-up jars and glittering crystal bottles. Norma stepped inside and closed the door with a feeling of guilty intrusion.

At the back of the dressing table was a crystal bottle of unusual design. It was larger than the rest, and obviously new. The stopper of black, cunningly wrought glass was so skillfully made that it gave an illusion of an exotic black flower, slightly evil, thrust into the bottle by its stem. Colored cellophane had been rolled down to encircle the base of the bottle. The slim *flacon* rose out of it with an appearance of naked beauty, as though it were some tiny woman of glass who had dropped her dress to the floor.

Norma felt a slight touch of faintness, and sat down on the rose-cushioned bench in front of the dressing table. The triple mirror showed her piquant face pale above the blue satin of her house coat. The tiny freckle over the dimple in her left cheek glowed brightly, as it always did when she was perturbed.

Automatically she took her vanity case from the pocket of her house coat and touched her cheeks with rouge. She snapped the jeweled case shut and returned it to her pocket. The perfume bottle was possessed with magnetism of memories. Twice she reached out to touch it, but forced herself to keep her hands away.

She suddenly knew what had brought Paul Gerente back to mind. Ten minutes earlier, on her interrupted trip to breakfast, she had glimpsed that seventy-five-dollar bottle of Black Orchid through Babs's partly opened door.

That single glimpse had swept ten years away. The gift of a similar bottle had begun Paul's courtship. Norma smiled a trifle bitterly. A bottle of the same Black Orchid had ended her marriage to Paul. She had seen it in the bedroom of another woman, and there had been others, too. Paul Gerente had distributed his Black Orchid tokens of affection as liberally as his charm.

Norma made a slight *moue* of distaste at her reflection in the mirror, then stood up and left the room. She did not intend to allow a fantastically incredible idea to run away with her natural good judgment. Paul Gerente, once a famous stage name, had dropped out of sight after she divorced him. There had been various unsubstantiated rumors that he had lost his money in the market and taken to drink. Past association was flimsy evidence on which to base an assumption; just because Babs had an unusual bottle of expensive perfume was no indication that she was seeing Paul.

The house was very silent. Norma stopped again at the top of the stairway. From below she heard Cheli Scott say goodbye. Cheli's words were followed by the opening and closing of the front door and the whine of the starter as Stacy started the coupé. Norma waited until the clank of chains in gravel and snow told her that the car was gone before she went downstairs.

Cheli, brilliant in a suit of red velvet pajamas, was curled up in the depths of a great armchair in front of the blazing log fire in the living room. She looked up from the pages of a manuscript, brushed back thick brown curls to disclose a smile in her blue-gray eyes, and said, "Cheerio, sleepy-head! How do you like the snow?"

"I think it makes me hungry," Norma told her. "Have you and the rest raided the larder completely, or is there anything left for me?"

"Sausage and scrambled eggs in the hot plate," said Cheli. "Coffee in the Silex, and cornbread and rolls in the warmer."

"It's probably far too much." Norma walked in toward the silver-laden sideboard visible through the open folding doors and added from the adjoining room, "At my age, I have to keep a checkrein on my waistline. Thad has a producer's eye for bulges in the wrong place. I want to keep that 'You ought to be on the stage, my dear!' expression on his face when he looks at me."

"At your age!" Cheli laughed softly and rustled a page of her manuscript. "The sight of that skin of yours and your figure simply infuriates me. You're the irritating type that makes aging debutantes sore. You'll never look more than twenty-two."

Norma served herself, poured a cup of coffee, and carried her breakfast into the living room, where she settled herself at Cheli's feet on a bearskin rug. "Christmas compliments!" she told Cheli. "They always crop up around the theater about the twentieth of December, but they're still good, I suppose. You make me feel ready to buy you a new fur coat or a Buick sedan."

She sipped her coffee. "Have you seen Gil this morning?"

The blazing fire touched spots of color on the cheeks of the girl in the chair. "He had to go into New York," said Cheli, reading intently. "He took an early train. Helena and Thaddeus went with him. How come they didn't take you?"

Norma placed her cup and saucer and plate on the hearth. "Maybe my ears are deceiving me," she exclaimed lightly. "I knew Gil and Helena were going—but Thad! Big things must be brewing when my late-sleeping husband hauls himself out into the early morning snow." She tried the sausage and eggs and found them good. "I'm glad he didn't want me to go. He's a bear before eleven. I'm afraid the combination of an early train trip with Thad and Helena—" She ended on a vague note, feeling that she might have said too much already.

Pierce, the butler, gray in Thaddeus's service, came in and said apologetically, "Good morning, madam. I didn't know you had come down. Mr. Tredwill left a note for you."

He stepped soft-footed into the hall and returned with the note on a silver tray. Norma smiled. Under Thaddeus's training, Pierce could have fitted unchanged into any butler's role in movie or play.

"I'm a bad hostess, Pierce." She opened the note and read it as the butler cleared her breakfast things away.

"Late sleeping is to be excused on such a day," said Pierce with his slow, half-quizzical smile. "More coffee, madam?"

Norma shook her head. Thad's typical note had left her with a glow. "*I love you, my dear! You are life to me and all its possessions—yet today I must go! Forgive me if I do not return until tomorrow. You can reach me at the Waldorf-Astoria. Thad.*"

Cheli resumed the conversation as Pierce went into the dining room. Sometimes her frankness was disconcerting. "You don't like Gilbert's wife, do you?"

"Helena?" Norma gave an embarrassed laugh. "Perhaps it would be nearer the truth if you said she doesn't like me."

"I wonder if she likes anyone except herself." Cheli spread the manuscript over the arm of her chair. "That includes Gil. What nationality is she, Norma? She's a mystery to me."

"French, I believe. It's hard to say. She speaks so many languages fluently. The only thing I know is that Gil met her in Washington at the French Embassy."

Norma left her place on the rug and picked up a morning paper from the settee. The conversation was becoming difficult. She disliked discussing the members of Thad's family. Quick to take a hint, Cheli turned to her manuscript again.

The paper was opened to the theatrical page, telling her that Thad had read it over his early morning coffee. She glanced idly at a syndicated column headed, "Rialto Rumors." For a brief instant the room became unbearably warm. She sat down on the settee and smoothed the paper out over her knees.

"A familiar figure, too long absent from Broadway, was seen at Ronni's 41 Club," the column stated. "He was accompanied by an exquisite creature whom your correspondent identified as the daughter of a grand old master of productions. It would be interesting if Paul Gerente resumed his interrupted stage career by marrying into his ex-wife's family."

Norma sat quietly for a long time staring into the flames. Finally she said, "I hate to leave you alone here today, but I think I'll go into Hartford, Cheli."

"Don't mind me. I'm up to my ears in work."

Norma stood up. There was a train to New York from Hartford at three-thirty. She could catch another one back during the evening. It would give her a few hours in New York—all she needed.

"I may have dinner with friends in Hartford," she said. A cold lump was pressing her throat inside, making it difficult to speak or breathe. If Thad had seen that item—! "He can't have seen it," she assured herself silently. "He'd have spoken about it to me." She dismissed as foolish a quick idea that she might talk with Babs. The girl was too young, too self-centered, to see anything but Paul's charm—to know what such gossip would do to Thad. There was only one course open. It was dangerous to a point where it might wreck her marriage, but she had to take it. She must talk with Paul Gerente.

Erle Stanley Gardner, *The Case of the Baited Hook*
Erle Stanley Gardner, *The Case of the Careless Kitten*
Erle Stanley Gardner, *The Case of the Borrowed Brunette*
Erle Stanley Gardner, *The Case of the Shoplifter's Shoe*
Erle Stanley Gardner, *The Bigger They Come*

Frances Noyes Hart, *The Bellamy Trial*
Introduced by Hank Phillippi Ryan

H.F. Heard, *A Taste for Honey*

Dolores Hitchens, *The Cat Saw Murder*
Introduced by Joyce Carol Oates

Dorothy B. Hughes, *Dread Journey*
Introduced by Sarah Weinman
Dorothy B. Hughes, *Ride the Pink Horse*
Introduced by Sara Paretsky
Dorothy B. Hughes, *The So Blue Marble*

W. Bolingbroke Johnson, *The Widening Stain*
Introduced by Nicholas A. Basbanes

Baynard Kendrick, *The Odor of Violets*

Frances and Richard Lockridge, *Death on the Aisle*

John P. Marquand, *Your Turn, Mr. Moto*
Introduced by Lawrence Block

Stuart Palmer, *The Pengiun Pool Murder*
Stuart Palmer, *The Puzzle of the Happy Hooligan*

Otto Penzler, ed., *Golden Age Detective Stories*
Otto Penzler, ed., *Golden Age Locked Room Mysteries*

Ellery Queen, *The American Gun Mystery*
Ellery Queen, *The Chinese Orange Mystery*
Ellery Queen, *The Dutch Shoe Mystery*
Ellery Queen, *The Egyptian Cross Mystery*
Ellery Queen, *The Siamese Twin Mystery*
Ellery Queen, *The Spanish Cape Mystery*

Patrick Quentin, *A Puzzle for Fools*
Clayton Rawson, *Death from a Top Hat*

Craig Rice, *Eight Faces at Three*
Introduced by Lisa Lutz
Craig Rice, *Home Sweet Homicide*

Mary Roberts Rinehart, *The Album*
Mary Roberts Rinehart, *The Haunted Lady*
Mary Roberts Rinehart, *Miss Pinkerton*
Introduced by Carolyn Hart
Mary Roberts Rinehart, *The Red Lamp*
Mary Roberts Rinehart, *The Wall*

Joel Townsley Rogers, *The Red Right Hand*
Introduced by Joe R. Lansdale

Vincent Starrett, *Dead Man Inside*
Vincent Starrett, *The Great Hotel Murder*
Introduced by Lyndsay Faye
Vincent Starrett, *Murder on "B" Deck*
Introduced by Ray Betzner

Cornell Woolrich, *The Bride Wore Black*
Introduced by Eddie Muller
Cornell Woolrich, *Deadline at Dawn*
Introduced by David Gordon
Cornell Woolrich, *Waltz into Darkness*
Introduced by Wallace Stroby